A HORSE OF A DIFFERENT COLOR . . .

"My name is Pericles. I come from Quaestor."

Quaestor! Magic, distant, Imperial capital!

Her anger at this mal's insolence was subsumed by excitement. "You mean you've actually traveled all the way from the capital to meet me?"

"It took a great deal of time and searching to find someone like you," the horse murmured. "I needed someone young . . . you are that. Only a young human would be responsive to what I have to offer."

"And what, pray tell, do you need me for?"

The horse dropped its head and seemed to consider how best to continue. It looked oddly at her.

"Laugh if you will," it said, "I have a dream that needs fulfilling."

By Alan Dean Foster
Published by Ballantine Books:

THE ADVENTURES OF FLINX OF THE
COMMONWEALTH
   For Love of Mother-Not
   The Tar-Aiym Krang
   Orphan Star
   The End of the Matter
   Bloodhype

NOR CRYSTAL TEARS

CACHALOT

ICERIGGER

MISSION TO MOULOKIN

SPLINTER OF THE MIND'S EYE

WITH FRIENDS LIKE THESE . . .

THE BLACK HOLE

MIDWORLD

With Friends Like These...

Alan Dean Foster

A Del Rey Book

BALLANTINE BOOKS • NEW YORK

A Del Rey Book
Published by Ballantine Books

Copyright © 1977 by Alan Dean Foster

Library of Congress Catalog Card Number: 77-6132

ISBN 0-345-32390-4

Printed in Canada

First Edition: December 1977
Sixth Printing: October 1984

Cover art by Michael Whelan

ACKNOWLEDGMENTS

"With Friends Like These," copyright © 1971 by The Condé Nast Publications, Inc., for *Analog Science Fiction*, June 1971.

"Some Notes Concerning a Green Box," copyright © 1971 by August Derleth for *The Arkham Collector*, Summer 1971.

"Why Johnny Can't Speed," copyright © 1971 by UPD Publishing Corp. for *Galaxy Science Fiction*, September–October 1971.

"The Emoman," copyright © 1972 by UPD Publishing Corp. for *Worlds of IF*, October 1972.

"Space Opera," copyright © 1973 by Knight Publishing Corporation for *ADAM Magazine*, February 1973.

"The Empire of T'ang Lang," copyright © 1973 by Ballantine Books, Inc., for *The Alien Condition*.

"A Miracle of Small Fishes," copyright © 1974 by Random House, Inc., for *Stellar #1*.

"Dream Done Green," copyright © 1974 by Terry Carr for *Fellowship of the Stars*.

"He," copyright © 1976 by Mercury Press for *The Magazine of Fantasy and Science Fiction*, June 1976.

"Polonaise," copyright © 1975 for *Beyond Time*, by Alan Dean Foster.

"Wolfstroker," copyright © 1977 by Alan Dean Foster. A substantially different version appeared in *Coq*, March 1974.

"Ye Who Would Sing," copyright © 1976 by Avenue Victor Hugo for *Galileo Magazine*, Number 2.

For JoAnn, who has my future,
I give now a little of my past, with love

Contents

Introduction

When I was very young, which was not so very long ago, my friends and I wanted to grow up to be firemen, policemen, airline pilots, and presidents. I suspect it says something for my generation when you consider that as youngsters our aspirations were to be successful civil servants. Certainly no one ever came up to me after a hard afternoon of sockball or kick-the-can and said, "Alan, when I grow up, I'm going to be a science-fiction writer."

Even more certainly, I never said it to anyone. But it happened. Where, as my mother was once wont to ask, did I go wrong?

Probably by giving me all those comic books. Comic books *are* dangerous to the American way of life, you see. I've always agreed with that theory. A child raised on comics can't help but grow up with a questing mind, an expanded imagination, a sense of wonder, a desire to know what make things tick—machines, people, governments.

No wonder our gilded conservatives are afraid of them.

I don't remember when I first started drawing spaceships. I know I blossomed in the fifth grade. They weren't very good spaceships, but in my soul I knew they were astrophysically sound. Someday I'd design real ones. I might have become an engineer, save for one inimical colossus who always loomed up to block my dream-way: mathematics.

I wasn't helpless, but neither did I display a precocious aptitude for differential calculus. My feelings were akin to those I experienced when I discovered that it took more than six piano lessons to play Rachmaninoff's Third Concerto—or even his First Concerto. Mentally, I drifted, my chosen profession blocked off to me at the tender age of eleven.

If it hadn't been for that damn book, *The Spaceship Under the Apple Tree* . . .

I persevered with my school work, finding in myself certain talents for the biological sciences. Math always cropped up somehow, somewhere, stopping me. What to do? I was good at English and history, but I wanted to design spaceships, dammit!

I kept on drawing them, knowing it was futile, but unable to resist the smooth lines, the sensuous curves of propulsive exhausts, the sharp stab of some irresistible power-beam. When I started fiddling around with writing, I stayed away from science fiction. Impossibly complex, intricate, challenging . . . I wrote love stories, mysteries, even fantasy. How could I consider writing science fiction when *The World of Null-A* read like Chinese? I didn't even read that much sf, turning instead to natural history, politics, science, literature—I immersed myself throughout high school in tons of such nonscience fiction.

Little did I know.

It started in college, at UCLA. The more arcane philosophy I was forced to read, the more I looked forward to relaxing with the directions of the good doctor Asimov. Thomas Hobbs drove me to relax in the humor and humanity of Eric Frank Russell. The painful details of political science were less hurtful when salved with judicious doses of Robert Sheckley, or buried beneath the smooth logic of Murray Leinster. I read enormous amounts of science fiction.

I discovered E. E. Smith and John Taine, whose space–time concepts made those of the lectures I attended shrink into laughability.

But I was that second-most-crippled college bastard, a political science major (the worst, he who majors in

English). No where to go save law school. So I girded myself for the challenge. At least I would someday make money.

And in my senior year, with required courses laboriously shoveled away, I discovered the motion-picture department at UCLA. And screenwriting. I found they would give me credit for—oh glory of glories!—watching movies! And for writing, for writing any old yarn that came into my head.

School changed from drudgery to pleasure. I told stories and watched them, and that was all that was required of me. And I learned the joy of those whose lives were concerned primarily with artistic creation, saw the naked exuberance of a young guest-instructor displayed while he taught a seminar in the films of director Howard Hawks. Peter Bogdanovich wasn't an especially fine instructor, but he was enthusiastic. His enthusiasm has done him right well since he taught that class.

He gave me a *B*, but wrote on my final exam, "You have good instincts . . . you should continue."

But law school still beckoned. Until a miracle happened. Despite unspectacular grades, perhaps because of a good Graduate Entrance Exam score, possibly due to the odd letter I wrote in which I explained I wished first of all to be the world's greatest gigolo and, second, to write, I was accepted into the graduate writing program.

My parents wailed silently, stoically, and finally reconciled themselves to the idea of their young Perry Mason blowing a fat raspberry at the whole legal profession. I turned down USC Law School and entered the wacky world of graduate film at UCLA. I started at the unprodigal age of twenty-two to write, seriously, for the first time.

I wrote a love story set in Japan, a western, a sexy comedy. I wrote a science-fiction detective film. I wrote an epic. And I started, to amuse myself, to write science-fiction stories. I would become a combination Ellison/Stapeldon/Clarke/Heinlein. I would smear brilliance like the high-priced spread across reams of virgin twenty-pound rag.

. My first attempt was about an aluminum Christmas tree that took root and started to grow. It was rejected. Often.

Crushed? I was wrecked, ruined, psychologically destroyed. I should have gone to law school, vet school, learned a trade. I would starve, miserably, begging for chocolate-chip danish in the streets . . .

I sold a story. My twelfth. And it wasn't even written as a story. But the next one was, and it sold too. I kept getting rejection slips, but some of them weren't mimeographed, they were actually written to me. I joined the Science-Fiction Writers of America and met my gods—and was crushed when they turned out to be human. Sometimes more than human, sometimes less. But I was *one of them*.

I began to understand how a leper feels.

Harlan Ellison expressed an interest in a story of mine. Would I care to come over to his place to talk about it? Did Washington free the slaves? Did Lincoln cut down cherry trees?

I met *the* Harlan Ellison. I'll never forget his first words to me, the first words from a Writer to a writer.

"First of all, Foster, you know that ninety percent of this story is shit."

But basically, he liked the ending. Would I try again?

Did Washington free the slaves? Did Lincoln . . . ?

In two days I buried Ellison under three or four complete rewrites. Becase I was excited. Because I was anxious. And because the next week I had to report to the Army. Yup. And I also wanted to finish the novel I was working on, my first.

I never satisfied Harlan, but I finished the novel. It was rejected. And then it sold. And I—I was lost. I was one of the happy lepers, come what may. I might be a starving leper, I might be a wealthy one, but I had chosen my disease.

I got out of the Army, went to work writing press

releases for a tiny local public relations outfit. I also ran the duplicating machine and cleaned out the fish tank. I made $400 a month, to start. A year and some months later, I began to feel like those fish.

If I could only find something I liked, something to put seafood in my mouth while I resumed writing. I knew nobody made a living writing science fiction, except people like Heinlein and Anderson and Asimov and what the hell, they were immortal anyway, so what difference did it make?

A part-time teaching position opened at Los Angeles City College. I applied and was accepted. Furthermore, I enjoyed it. A course in film history and one in writing. I've also taught writing at UCLA, and even a seminar on the works of H. P. Lovecraft.

I kept writing. Things Started To Happen. Books sold, stories sold. Other people would pay to share with me yarns I wrote for my own enjoyment. I was happy, content. Who wouldn't be? I've never known a storyteller who was unhappy when telling stories.

Now I'm a writer, but I feel guilty. This is too much fun. It's sinful to enjoy life so much. I haven't suffered enough to be a writer. I like other human beings, I like this sad, smoggy world. I like my agents and my publishers and editors. I even like critics. I love my wife, who is much too beautiful for me.

Clearly, there is something drastically wrong with me.

Or maybe it's all a dream—yeah, tomorrow I'll wake up and have to go read law books; put on a suit and tie; smile at people I'd like to be honest with. But for now, today, this minute, I'm going to enjoy every second of that dream.

I can't give it to you. But I can share a little of it. It's in this book.

With Friends Like These

With Friends Like These...

My favorite writer of science fiction was, and still is, the inimitable Eric Frank Russell. When I was turning in short stories to the magazines instead of papers to my college professors and collecting rejection slips instead of credits and grades, I often wondered why Russell had stopped writing. I miss him.

At the 1968 World Science-Fiction Convention in Oakland, John Campbell told me that Russell was his favorite writer, and that he too sorely bemoaned the lack of yarns Russellian. So I decided to try a Russell-flavored *Terra über alles* story. Campbell liked it. He never sent acceptance letters—just checks.

And man and boy, *that* was a change from rejection slips.

As she commenced her first approach to the Go-type sun, the light cruiser *Tpin*'s velocity began to decrease from the impossible to the merely incredible. Her multidrive engines put forth the barely audible whine that signified slowdown, and she once more assumed a real mass that the normal universe could and would notice.

Visual observation at the organic level became possible as the great ship cut the orbit of the last gas giant. Those of the vessel's complement took the never dull opportunity to rush the ports for a glimpse of a new solar system; those whose functions did not include the actual maneuvering of the craft. Curiosity was a fairly universal characteristic among space-going races. The crew of the *Tpin*, although a grim lot, were no exception.

Within the protected confines of the fore control room of the half-kilometer-long bubble of metal and plastic, Communicator First Phrnnx shifted his vestigial wings and asked Commander First Rappan for the millionth time what-the-hell-equivalent they hoped to find.

"Phrnnx," Rappan sighed, "if you haven't been sufficiently enlightened as to the content of the legends by now, I fail to see how I can aid you. Instead of repeating yourself for the sake of hearing yourself oralize, I suggest you bend a membrane to your detection apparatus and see if you can pick up any traces of that *murfled* Yop battleship!"

Phrnnx riffled his eyelids in a manner indicative of mild denial, with two degrees of respectful impatience. "We lost those inept yipdips five parsecs ago, sir. I am fully capable of performing my duties without any well-intentioned suggestions from the bureaucracy. Do I tell you how to fly the ship?"

"A task," began Rappan heatedly, "so far beyond your level of comprehension that . . . !"

"Gentlebeings, gentlebeings, please!" said the Professor. Subordinate and commander alike quieted.

The "Professor"—his real title was unpronounceable to most of the crew—was both the guiding force and the real reason behind the whole insane expedition. It was he who rediscovered the secret of breaking the Terran Shield. He came from a modest three-system cluster nearly halfway to the Rim—far removed from their own worlds. Due to the distance from things and to their own quiet, retiring nature, his folk took little part in the perpetual cataclysm of the Federation-Yop wars. What small—if important—role they did deign to play in the conflict was not determined by choice. Rather, it was engendered by the Yop policy of regarding all those peoples, who were not allies of the Yop, as mortal enemies of the Yop. There was room in neither Yop culture, nor Yop language, for the concept of a "neutral." Yop temperament was such that their total complement of allies came to a grand total of zero. The members of the Federation had matured beyond prejudice, but it was admitted in most quarters that the Yops were not nice people. Possibly some of this attitude stemmed from the Yop habit of eating everything organic that moved, without regard for such minor inconveniences as, say, the intelligence of the diner, or his desire to be not-eaten.

Against them was allied the total remaining strength of the organized galaxy; some two hundred and twelve federated races.

However—due to diet, perhaps—there were a lot of Yops.

The avowed purpose of the expedition was to make that latter total two hundred and thirteen.

The Professor continued in a less stern tone. "If you *must* fight among yourselves, kindly do so at a civilized level. At least out of deference to me. I am an old being, and I possess a perhaps unreasonable allergy to loud and raucous noises."

The others in the room immediately lowered their voices in respect. In the Federation age was a revered commodity, to be conserved as such. And there was the Professor's age. His antennae drooped noticeably, his chiton was growing more and more translucent, losing its healthy purple iridescence, and his back plates were exfoliating in thin, shallow flakes. That he had held up as well as he had on this trip, with its sometimes strenuous dodging of Yop warships, was in itself remarkable. He seemed to grow stronger as they neared their objective, and now his eyes, at least, glowed with a semblance of vitality.

All eyes were trained on the great mottled sphere turning slowly and majestically below them.

"Planet Three," intoned Navigator First. "Primary colors blue, white, brown, green. Atmosphere . . ." and he dropped off to a low mumbling. At last, "It checks, sir."

"And the gold overlay?" asked Communicator Phrnnx, for being among the youngest of the crew, his curiosity quotient was naturally among the highest.

"That, gentlebeings, means that the Shield is still up. After all these years I'd thought perhaps . . ." The Professor made what passed for a shrug among his people. He turned from the port to the others.

"As you all recall, I hope, the phenomenon below us, the Shield, is the direct result of the Old Empire–Terran Wars of ages ago. At that time, the inhabitants of this planet first broke free of their own system and started to come out to the stars.

"They found there a multiracial empire nominally ruled by a race known to us as the Veen. The Terrans were invited to join the empire, accruing the same rights and privileges as had historically been granted to all new space-going races for thousands and thousands of years."

"And they refused," put in Rappan.

"Yes, they refused. It became quickly apparent to the Veen that the Terrans intended to carve out a little pocket empire of their own in another sector of space. Since Terra was so far away from the center of things, so to speak, the Veen decided that for the sake of peace—and the Veen—this could not be allowed to take place. Accordingly, there was a war, or rather, a series of wars. These lasted for centuries, despite the overwhelming numerical superiority of the Veen. Gradually, the Terrans were pushed back to their own home world. A standoff ensued, as the Veen and their

4

allies were unable to break the ultimate defenses of the Terrans.

"Then a great scientist of one of the allied races of the Veen discovered, quite by accident, the quasi-mathematical principle behind the Shield. The nature of the Shield forbade its use on anything smaller than a good-sized moon. It was thus useless for such obvious military applications as, for example, a ship defensive screen. Then someone got the bright idea of enveloping the entire planet of Terra in one huge Shield, making it into an impenetrable cage. At worst, it would provide the Empire with a breathing spell in which to marshal its sorely battered forces. At best it would restrict the Terrans to their own fortress until such time as the Veen saw fit to let them out. The chances of the Terrans accidentally stumbling onto the same principle was considered to be slight. As you can now see, this indeed has been the case." The Professor sighed again, a high, whistling sound.

"However, the wars with Terra had also depleted the resources of the Veen tremendously. Those races which had been allied to them only by virtue of the Veen's superior knowledge and strength saw an irresistible opportunity to supplant the Veen in the hierarchy of Empire. The result? The Time of Conflicts, which resulted in the breakdown of the Empire, the final elimination of the once-proud Veen, and after considerable bickering and fighting, the formation of our present Federation—in a much more primitive form, of course."

He returned his gaze once again to the blue-white planet circling below, its land areas blurred in the shifting golden haze which was the by-product of the Shield. They had already locked in to the Shield station on the planet's only satellite. "Unfortunately, the Ban still remains."

Rappan broke away from his console for a moment. "Look, we've been through all that. The supposed rule states that the penalty for breaking the Shield either

5

partially, or completely, is death, for all those concerned. But that *murfled* law is millennia old!"

"And still on the books," retorted old Alo, the Commander Second.

"I know, I know!" said Rappan, adjusting a meter. "Which is one reason why every being on this ship is a volunteer. And if I thought we had a choice I'd never have commandeered the *Tpin* for this trip. But you know as well as I, Alo, we *have* no choice! We've been fighting the Yops now for nearly three hundred *sestes*, and been losing ever since we started. Oh, I know how it looks, but the signs are all there. One of these days we'll turn around for the customary reinforcements and *piff!*, they won't be there! That's why it's imperative we find new allies ... even if we have to try Terra. When I was a cub, my den parents would scare us away from the *Grininl*-fruit groves by saying: 'The Terrans will get you if you don't watch out!'"

" 'Ginst the Edict," murmured Alo, not to be put off.

Navigator First Zinin broke in, in the deep bass-rumbling of this heavy-planet civilization. "There will be no Edicts, old one, if the Yops crush the Federation. We must take *some* risks. If the Terrans are willing to aid us—and are still capable of it—I do believe that GalCen will agree to some slight modification of the rules. And, if these creatures have fallen back to the point where they can be of no help to us, then they will not be a threat to us either. GalCen will not be concerned."

"And if by chance mebbe they should be a bit angry at us and decide to renew an ancient grudge?" put in the ever-pessimistic Alo.

"Then the inevitable," put in Zinin, "will only be hastened."

Philosophizing was of needs broken off. The *Tpin* was entering the Shield.

Green, thought Phrnnx. *It is the greenest nontropical planet I have ever seen.*

6

He was standing by the end of the ramp which led out from the belly of the cruiser. The rest of the First Contact party was nearby. They had landed near a great mountain range, in a lush section of foothills and gently rolling green. Tall growths of brown and emerald dominated two sides of their view. In front of them stretched low hillocks covered with what was obviously cultivated vegetation. Behind the ship, great silver-gray mountains thrust white-haloed crowns into the sky. Had the *Tpin* been an air vessel, the updrafts sweeping up the sides of those crags would have given them trouble. As it was, they merely added another touch to the records the meteorologists were assembling.

Somewhere in the tall growths—which they later learned were called *trees*—a brook of liquid H_2O made gurgling sounds. Overhead, orinthorphs circled lazily in the not unpleasant heat of morning. Phrnnx was meditating on how drastically the Shield might have affected the climate of this world when he became aware of Alo and Zinin strolling up behind him.

"A peaceful world, certainly," said Zinin. "Rather light on the oxygen and argon, and all that nitrogen gives it a bit of odor, but on the whole a most pleasant ball of dirt."

"Humph! From one who burns almost as much fuel as the ship I wouldn't have expected compliments," grumbled Alo. "Still, I'll grant you, 'tis a quiet locale we've chosen to search out allies. I wonder if such a world did indeed spawn such a warlike race, or were they perhaps immigrants from elsewhere?"

"They weren't, and it didn't," interposed the Professor. He had relinquished the high place to the commander and his military advisers, as their conversation had bored him.

"Mind explaining that a mite, Professor?" asked Alo.

The Professor bent suddenly and dug gently in the soft earth with a claw. He came up with a small wiggling thing. This he proceeded to pop into his mouth and chew with vigor.

"Hmmm. A bit bitter, but intriguing. I believe there is at least one basis for trade here."

"Be intriguing if it poisons you," said Phrnnx with some relish.

The Professor moved his antennae in a gesture indicative of negativity, with one degree of mild reproach. "Nope. Sorry to disappoint you, youngster, but Bio has already pronounced most of the organics on this planet nontoxic. Watch out for the vegetation, though. Full of acids and things. As to your question, Alo. When the Terrans . . ."

"Speaking of Terrans," put in Zinin, "I'd like to see one of these mythical creatures. I don't recall seeing any cities on our descent."

"Neither did Survey. Oh, don't look so smug. Navigator. Survey reports their presence—Terrans, not cities—but they estimate no more than a hundred million of them on the planet. The only signs of any really large clusterings are vague outlines that could be the sites of ancient ruins. Might have expected something of the sort. People change in a few *Ipas*, you know."

"*My* question," prompted Alo once more.

"Well, when the Terrans went out into extrasolar space and began setting up their own empire, the Veen decided at first to leave them alone. Not only was there no precedent for a space-faring race not accepting citizenship in the empire, but the Terrans weren't bothering anyone. They were also willing to sign all kinds of trade agreements and such. Anything of a nonrestrictive and nonmilitary nature."

"Why'd the Veen change their minds, then?" asked the now interested Phrnnx.

"Some bright lad in the Veen government made a few computer readings, extrapolating from what was known of Terran scientific developments, rate of expansion, galactic acclimatization, and so on."

"And the result?"

"According to the machines—and the Veen had

ood ones—in only one hundred *Ipas* the Veen would have to start becoming acclimatized to Terra."

Zinin was the only one of the three listeners who expressed his reaction audibly. Surprisingly, it was by means of a long, drawn-out whistle.

"Yes, that's about how the Veen took it. So they decided to cut the Terrans down to where they would no longer be even an indirect threat."

"Seems they did," said Alo, gazing up at the gold-flecked Shield sky.

The Professor spared a glance the same way. "Yes, it would seem so." He stared off in the direction of the commander's post where a force-lift was depositing a ground car. "But it's enlightening to keep one other little thing in mind."

"Which is?" said Alo belligerently.

"There *are* no more Veen."

Survey had detected what appeared to be a small blip between the foothills. It was, therefore, decided that a party consisting of Commander Rappan, Navigator Zinin, Communicator Phrnnx, a philologist, a xenologist, and, of course, the Professor would take a ground car down to the structure and attempt a First Contact. Despite vigorous protests, Commander Second Alo was restricted to acting captain.

"Give the crew land leave," instructed Rappan. "Shifts of the usual six. Maintain a semialert guard at all times until further notice. I know this place looks about as dangerous as a *mufti*-bug after stuffing, but I intend to take no chances. At first sign of hostilities, raise ship and get out. That is a first-degree order. You have others on board who can operate the remote Shield equipment. In the event that all is not what it seems, I don't want to leave these creatures a way out."

"Noted and integrated, sir," replied Alo stiffly. And then in a lower voice, "Watch yourself, sir. This place smells funny to me, and I am not referring to the nitro in the atmosphere, either!"

Rappan essayed a third-level smile, with two degrees of mild affection, nonsexual. "You've said that now on . . . let's see, thirty-nine planet-falls to date. But rest assured I will take no chances. We know too little of this place, the Professor included."

"Anyway, legends are notoriously nonfactual."

The little car hummed softly to itself as it buzzed over the dark soil. A cleared path is unmistakable on any planet, and this one ran straight as an *Opsith* through the fields of low, irrigated plants. Phrnnx had wondered idly what they were, and if they would appeal to his palate. The Professor had replied by reminding him of Bio's warning about plant acids and added that stealing the native's food would be a poor way to open friendly negotiations. Phrnnx discarded the notion. Besides, the vegetation of this area appeared to be disgustingly heavy in cellulose content—doubtless bland in flavor, if any. And there had been no sign of domesticated food animals. Was it possible these people existed solely on wood fibers? It was a discouraging thought.

He had no chance to elaborate on it, for as the car rounded the turn they had come to, they were confronted by the sight of their first native. The car slowed and settled to the earth with a faint sigh.

In the nearby field a shortish biped was walking smoothly behind a large brown quadruped. Together they were engaged in driving a wedge of some bright metal through the soft soil, turning it over on itself in big loamy chunks. The name of this particular biped happened to be Jones, Alexis. The name of the quadruped was Dobbin, period.

The two natives apparently caught sight of the visitors. Both paused in their work to stare solemnly at the outlandish collection of aliens in the groundcar. The aliens, pop-eyed, stared back. The biped wore some kind of animal-skin shirt. This was partly hidden by some form of artificial fabric coveralls and boots. Seeing this, it occurred to Phrnnx that they must have

ome kind of manufacturing facilities somewhere. The
quadruped wore only a harness, again artificial, which
was attached to the metal wedge. It soon grew bored
in its survey of the aliens and dropped its head to crop
patiently at the few sparse bits of grass that had so far
managed to avoid the plow.

Commander Rappan's instinctive reaction to this
first move was to reach for his pistol. He was momentarily abashed to find it missing from its customary
place in his shell. The Professor had insisted that
contact was to be open and trusting from the first.
Consequently, all weapons had been left back on the
ship. The Professor had also looked longingly at the
bristling gunports of the *Tpin,* but the commander and
his advisers had adamantly refused to leave the ship
unprotected. The Professor had patiently explained
that if the Terrans were going to be any real help
against the Yops, then the guns of the *Tpin* would
hardly be effective against them. And if they
weren't going to be, then the guns weren't needed. As
might be expected, this argument went far over the
heads of the soldiers.

But Rappan still felt naked, somehow.

The native made no threatening gestures. In fact,
he made no gestures at all, but instead continued to
stare placidly at the petrified load of explorers. After
several minutes of this, Rappan decided it was time
things got moving. Besides, the native's unbroken stare
was beginning to make him feel a bit fidgety, not to
mention silly.

"You, philologist! Can you talk to that thing?"
Commander Rappan asked.

The philologist, a meter-tall being from a Ko star
near Cen-Cluster, essayed a nervous reply. "It remains
to be seen, sir. We have no records of their speech
patterns, and there were few broadcasts to monitor the
computers to as we descended." His voice was faintly
disapproving. "I am not even sure which of the two
creatures is the dominant form."

11

"The large one in the lead, certainly," said the xenologist.

"I believe the Terrans are described in the legends, when not as hundred-*foomp*-high fire-breathing monsters, as bipeds," said the Professor quietly. "Although it also has four limbs, two are obviously manipulative. I suggest that one."

"I shall have to work from next to nothing," protested the philologist.

"I don't care if you do it holding your breath, but get out there and do *something!* I feel like an idiot sitting here."

"Yes, sir,"

"Yes, sir—*what?*"

The philologist decided that this would be an auspicious time to essay a First Contact. He hurried out the door. At least, he thought, the native couldn't be much more difficult to communicate with than the commander. He wished fervently that he was back in the community nest.

Trailing the philologist, the party made its way to the two natives.

"Uh," began the philologist, straining over the guttural syllables, "we come in peace, Terran. Friends. Buddies. Comrades. Blut-bruderhood. We good-guys. You comprende?"

"Me, Tarzan; you Jane," said the Terran.

The philologist turned worriedly to Rappan. "I'm afraid I can't place his answer, sir. The reference is obscure. Shall I try again?"

"Skip it," said the Terran, in fluent, if archaic Galactico. "Ancient humorism. Surprising how old jokes stand time better than most monuments." He seemed to sigh a little.

"You speak!" blurted the xenologist.

"An unfortunate malady of which I seem incapable of breaking myself. Sic transit gloryoski. Up the Veen. But come on down to the house. Maria's making some ice cream—I hope you like chocolate—you're welcome to try it, although I don't think we'd have enough for King Kong, here."

Zinin decided to regard this unfamiliar aphorism as a neutral compliment. There wasn't much else he could do. He tried to hunch his three-meter bulk lower, gave it up when he realized that he didn't know whether the promised ice cream was a food, a paint, or a mild corrosive for cleaning out reluctant teeth.

"We appreciate your hospitality, sir. We've come to discuss a very urgent matter with your superiors. It involves perhaps more than you can comprehend." Here the Professor peered hard at the native, who looked back at him with placid assurance. "Although I have a hunch you might have some idea what I mean."

If the Terran noticed a change in the Professor's glance he gave no sign, but instead smiled apologetically.

"Ice cream first."

The Terran's residence, when seen from close up, was a utilitarian yet not unbeautiful structure. It appeared to be made mostly from native woods with a hint of metal only here and there. A small quadruped was lying on its entrance step. It raised its head to gaze mournfully at the arrivals, with wise eyes, before returning it to its former position on its forepaws. Had the Professor known anything about the history of Terran canines, this quiet greeting would have been interesting indeed.

The building proved to admit more light and air than had seemed probable from the outside. Furniture appeared to be mostly of the handmade variety, with here and there an occasional hint of something machine-turned. Bright colors predominated but did not clash, not that the Terran color scheme meant anything to the visitors anyway. At least the place was big enough to hold all.

The Jones's mate was a sprightly little dark woman

13

of indeterminate age, much like her husband. A single male sibling by the name of Flip stared solemnly from a window seat at the grouping of guests assembled in his parents' den. He had a twig, or stick, which he would sometimes tap on the floor.

"Now, Alex . . ." said the woman, fussing with a large wooden ice-cream maker, "you didn't tell me we were having visitors. How am I supposed to prepare for these things if you don't tell me about them in advance?"

The native smiled. "Sorry, hon, but these, um, gentlemen, just sort of dropped in on us. I promised them some ice cream."

"I hope they like chocolate," she said.

When they had been seated around the room, each being curling up according to the style fitting to its own physiognomy, Commander Rappan decided to break into the cheerful dialogue and get down to business. Fraternizing with the natives was all very well and good. No doubt the Xeno Department would approve. However, he was not so sure that his colleagues, hard-pressed to hold off the Yop waves, would see things in the same way.

Unfortunately, this thing called *ice cream* got quite a grip on one's attention.

Zinin was one of the few present to whom the concoction had proved unappealing. He leaned over and whispered to Phrnnx, "These are the deadly fighters we are supposed to enlist? Conquerors of the Veen fleets? Stuff of horror tales? Why, they look positively soft! I could crush that male under one paw. He hardly comes up to my eyes!"

"Few of us do, oh hulking one," replied Phrnnx, adding a gesture indicative of second-degree ironic humor. "But that is hardly an indication one way or the other. Although I admit they *do* seem a bit on the pastoral side."

Zinin snorted.

14

"What star system are you folks from? Not all from the same, surely!"

"Indeed," said the Professor. It occurred to him what had troubled his thoughts ever since they had met these natives. For a race that had not had extra-planetary contact for umpti-thousand *Ipas* they were treating the crew of the *Tpin* like next-door neighbors who popped over for a visit every time-period. Even the sibling—where had *he* disappeared to?—had been fully self-possessed when confronted by what must be to him utterly strange beings. It was just a touch unnerving. "You might be interested to know that the Veen have been extinct for some 450,000 of your time-revolutions."

The biped nodded understandingly. "We guessed as much. When so much time passed and nothing happened, one way or the other, friendly or hostile . . . we assumed that we'd been forgotten and filed away somewhere."

"Not forgotten," said the Professor. "Legends persist longer than their creators, sometimes. There was a period of . . . confusion . . . at the end of the Veen-Terran wars." Was that a twitch of reaction in the native's face? Yes? No? "When the bureaucracy set up by the Veen was submerged by a wave of would-be empire-builders, interstellar government pretty well collapsed. It took a while for things to straighten themselves out. Which is why we have not contacted you till now." Could he read the lie? "Another problem has arisen."

The biped sighed again. "I was afraid this mightn't be a social call. What is your problem, Professor?"

Backed at certain intervals by succinct comments from Rappan, he began to outline the present desperate situation with respect to the Yops, ending with a plea to forget any past differences and come to the aid of the Federation.

The Terran had listened quietly to their arguments, unmoving. Now he sat in an attitude of intense concentration, seeming to listen to voices and thoughts outside their ken. When he at last raised his face to them again he wore a serious smile.

"I must, of course, consult with and deliver your message to my . . . 'superiors.' Such a decision would be difficult for us to make. As you can see for yourselves"—he made an all-encompassing gesture—"we have changed our mode of existence somewhat since we fought the Veen. We are no longer geared to the production of war matériel. Incidentally, we hold no grudge against any of you. I have no idea if my ancestors and yours ever met, let alone battled with one another. We never even really held animosity toward the Veen. In fact, I'd give a lot to know exactly *why* they went to war with us in the first place."

Phrnnx had heard the Professor's explanation and looked expectantly in his direction, but that worthy remained silent.

"Of course," continued the Terran after a while, "as a gesture of your goodwill we would naturally expect you to lower the Shield. Despite a hell of a lot of scribbling and figuring, that's one thing we could never quite do."

"Of course," said Rappan determinedly.

The biped stood. "It will take me a while to convey your message to my superiors. In the meantime, do feel free to enjoy the countryside and my poor home." He turned and walked into another room.

The female eyed them speculatively.

"I don't suppose any of you gentlemen play bridge?"

Phrnnx was wandering through the nearby forest, following the path made by a cheerful stream. He had quickly grown bored with studying the simple native household, and, unlike the Professor or Commander Rappan, the intricacies of Terran "bridge" were a touch more intellectual a pastime than he wished for. The two scientists had found plenty to keep them occupied profitably, but after reporting to the ship their accumulated data and the word that things seemed to be progressing satisfactorily, there had remained little for a communicator to do.

The dense undergrowth led away from the house at a right angle. With the sense of direction his kind possessed he was not afraid of getting lost, and the damp coolness of the place was the closest thing he'd found to the rain forests of home. It was full of interesting sounds and new smells. The native female had assured him that no dangerous creatures lurked within its inviting shadows. He was thoroughly enjoying himself. Orinthorphs and small invertebrates—"insects," they were called—flitted rapidly from growth to growth. He could have snatched them easily in midair with his long suckers, but was mindful of strange foods despite the Professor's assurance that the native organics were edible. Besides, he was not hungry. He strode on in high spirits.

The hike was about to come to an unpleasant end.

The trees appeared to cease abruptly off to one side. Espying what seemed to be a glint of sunlight on water, he turned in that direction. His supposition was correct. In front of him was a large clearing which bordered on a good-sized lake. In the foreground stood the diminutive figure of Flip, the native's offspring. He was gazing at a pair of massive, glowering figures in space armor. These did not fit into the picture.

Yops!

Phrnnx stood paralyzed with shock. The Yop battleship that he thought they had lost near that red dwarf sat half-in, half-out of the blue-green lake. He assumed it was the same one. Its gunports were wide open. Troops were clustering around a landing portal on one side of the kilometer-and-a-half-long monster. Dirt had been gouged out on all sides by the sheer mass of the huge vessel. These two figures in the foreground were doubtlessly scouts.

How in the central chaos had they slipped in past the cruiser's screens? Unless they, too, had found a way to negate the Shield—and this seemed unlikely—

then they must have entered by way of the temporary hole made by the *Tpin*. A quick glance at the sky showed the now familiar gold tinge still strong. So they hadn't destroyed the generating equipment on the planet's satellite, then. Yop invisibility screens were known to be good, but this good? . . . His speculations were interrupted by what happened next.

The nearest Yop reached down and lifted the Flip in one massive, knobby claw. It held it like that, steady, while it examined the youngster along with its partner. The boy, in turn, appeared to be examining them with its wide, deep-gray eyes. Both were making the motions and gestures which Phrnnx knew indicated Yop laughter.

What followed occurred so rapidly that Phrnnx, afterward, had difficulty in reconstructing the incident.

The Yop raised the youngster over its horned head and swung it toward the ground with every intention of smashing the child's brains out. But the boy abruptly slowed in midair, turned, and landed gently on its feet. The Yop was staring at its now empty hand in surprise. The expression of placid innocence, which had heretofore been the child's sole visage, shifted all at once into a strong frown that was somehow more terrifying than any contortion of rage could have been. It said, in a very unchildlike tone of voice, two words:

"Bad mans!"

And gestured with the twig.

The two Yops glowed briefly an intolerable silver-white, shading to blue. It was the color of nova—a chrome nova. The two scouts "popped" loudly, once, and disappeared. In their places two clouds of fine gray ash sifted slowly to the ground. The boy pointed his stick at the multiton Yop warship. "More bad mans," he said. The ship abruptly glowed with the same intolerable radiance. It "popped" with a considerably louder and much more satisfying bang. The boy then turned and went over to the brook. He began slowly stirring the water with his stick.

Phrnnx found he could breathe again. The feathers on his back, however, did not lie down. All that remained of the invincible Yop battlewagon was the faint smell of ozone and a very large pile of fine multicolored ash. This was patiently being removed by a small breeze.

The boy suddenly looked up, turned, and stared straight at where Phrnnx was crouching behind the bole of a large pine. He started to stroll over.

Phrnnx ran. He ran hard, fast, and unthinkingly. He was not sure what a "bad mans" was, but he had no wish to be included in that category—none whatsoever. No sirree. He ran in a blind panic with all four legs and a great sorrow that his ancestors had traded their wings for intelligence. Ahead, a dark, cavelike depression appeared in the ground. Without breaking stride, he instinctively threw himself into the protective opening.

And into the closet of the world.

Phrnnx awoke with the equivalent of a throbbing headache. He almost panicked again when he remembered that last moment before blacking out. A touch of the hard, unresisting metal underneath reassured and calmed him. He had thrown himself in a cave— only it hadn't been a cave. It had been a hole. A hole filled with machinery. Yes, that's right! He remembered falling past machinery—levels and levels and levels of it. He did not know it, but he had fallen only a mile before the first of the automatic safety devices had analyzed his alien body chemistry, pronounced him organic, alive, and reasonably worth saving, and brought him to a comfortable resting place at the fifty-third level.

He staggered to his feet, becoming aware of a faint susurration around him. Warm air, and the faint sounds of the almost silent machines. A slow look around confirmed the evidence of his other senses . . . and he almost wished it hadn't. Machines. Machine upon machine. Massive and unnoticing, they throbbed with life and power all around him. He could not see the end of the broad aisle he stood on. He turned and staggered over to the edge of the shaft he had obviously fallen into, following the current of fresh air.

A quick look over the side made him draw back involuntarily. His race was not subject to vertigo, but there are situations and occasions where the reality transcends the experience. There is too much relativity in a cavern, even an artificial one.

Above stretched over a mile of levels, seemingly much like this one. Very faintly and far away he could just make out the tiny circle of light that marked the surface and his entranceway to this frighteningly silent metal world.

He could not see the bottom.

He found himself giggling. Oh yes, pastoral indeed! Quite. Not prepared to turn out war matériel. Certainly not. No capability whatsoever. No cities, remember? Handmade furniture. Quaint way to live. Didn't say by what kind of hands, though. Poor, degenerated natives! Cannon fodder, he'd seen it in Commander Rappan's eyes.

But the commander hadn't peeked in the basement.

When the hysteria had worked itself out, he took several deep gulps of the fresh air. There had to be a manual way out. Stairs, a lift, something! He had to get back and warn the others. He tried his pocket communicator, suspecting that it wouldn't work. It didn't. A communicator who couldn't communicate. He almost started giggling again, but caught himself this time. He began to search for a way out. He did not know it, and probably would not have cared anyway, but his situation was remarkably analogous to that of a very ancient and very imaginary Terran female named Alice.

"I am pleased to say," began the native known as Alexis Jones, "that the committee . . . government . . .

ruling body? I forget the relevant term. Anyway, we have agreed to do what we can to aid your Federation. These Yops . . ." and he paused momentarily, "do not sound like very nice people—"

"They're not!" interrupted Zinin fervently.

"And even if we only add a bit of manpower to your gallant effort, we will be happy to be of assistance. We are a bit," he added apologetically, "out of practice."

"That's all right," beamed the commander. At first he had regarded these disgustingly peaceful and soft-seeming bipeds more of a liability than an asset. Then it occurred to him that the Yops, too, were familiar with the Terran legends. Could be the materialization of a real legend might disconcert them a bit. Of course these peaceful mammals would have to be thoroughly instructed, or their appearance would merely make the Yops go into fits of laughter, but . . . "We appreciate your desire to aid in this great crusade. I am certain this historic arrangement will go down in history as one of exceptional benefit to all the races concerned. As a prelude to further discussion, I have ordered . . ."

He paused, open-mouthed, concentration broken. The Terran was staring upward. His face had . . . changed. It was brightening, expanding, opening hitherto unsuspecting vistas to their startled gaze, like a night-blooming flower. Within those two small oculars, previously so gray and limpid, there now glowed a deep-down fire that seemed to pierce upward and spread over all present like a nerve-deadening drug. It made the commander draw back and Zinin hiss involuntarily.

"The Shield Is Down!" shouted the native, flinging its arms wide.

"The Shield Is Down!" answered his wife.

And all over the planet, among all the members, large and small, of the Brotherhood of Warmblood; the dogs, the mice, the cats and orcas, birds and

21

shrews; ungulates, carnivores, herbivores, and omnivores, the great telepathic shout went up:

"THE SHIELD IS DOWN!"

And in the field Dobbin and the small brown dog began to discuss the ramifications at length.

The man turned to face his visitors, who were silent.

"You have done us a very large favor, gentlebeings, and we are oh, so grateful! How many years we labored to find the answer to the Shield, how many years, only to discover that it could only be applied, or retracted, *from an outside source*. Now that it is down, we will *not* make the error of allowing it to be put up again. Once again, gentlebeings, we are in your debt. Our agreement still holds. If you will return to your ship we will . . . commence preparations to follow in ours." The native smiled, and it was at once a lovely and terrible thing to see. (Among the known creatures of the universe, only the Terran human bares its fangs to express friendship.)

"It has been *so* long," the Jones sighed wistfully, "since we have had a decent war!"

Back on the *Tpin* it was a thoughtful yet jubilant Rappan who confronted a very bedraggled Communicator First.

"Commander," panted Phrnnx, "listen! You mustn't drop the Shield! This whole world . . . it's a sham, sir! A fake. We've been fooled, and badly. These natives aren't as primitive as they'd like us to think. I *saw*, sir! Machines, automatic factories, synthetic food-processing plants—the *whole planet*, Commander—it's filled with their machines! I fell into it—accident—the machines down there are programmed to answer questions . . . I asked . . ." He paused for breath, became aware then that no one in the happy control cabin was paying any attention to him. Most of the crew were telling jokes, patting each other contently on their back-equivalents, and preparing for a lift-off. Only the Professor seemed unaffected by the otherwise universal giddiness. Phrnnx turned to the elder.

"Professor, I'm telling the truth! Tell them, make them listen, we've got to . . . !"

The Professor turned a spare eye on him. "Oh, I believe you. If those *muftils* could control their glee long enough to listen to you, they'd no doubt believe you, too." He paused. "Have you looked at the sky recently?"

Phrnnx ran to a port and stared wildly upward.

"The Shield's gone!"

The Professor favored his announcement with a first-degree nod, indicating positive acknowledgment. "Indeed it is. Commander Rappan had left orders with Commander Second Alo to drop it as a sign of good faith the moment the Terrans agreed to sign the mutual-defense-pact edicts with us." He looked thoughtfully at the port. "The Jones and his mate seemed to know exactly when the generating machinery on the satellite cut off. Even the animals were acting in a most peculiar fashion as we returned to the ship." He shivered slightly.

"I, for one, shall be less unhappy than I first thought at the prospect of leaving this place."

"What makes you think that, now with the Shield off, they'll hold to their agreement to help us?"

"Two reasons, youngster. First of all, the Jones said that they would, and I have a hunch that they are the kind of folk who put much store by their word. And also, I kind of think they could have turned it off anytime they wanted to, after our initial penetration."

Phrnnx did not answer. He was watching the sky grow darker outside the port as the ship rose beyond the atmosphere, watching the stars come out, remembering a picture . . . a little boy, two Yop scouts, and a battleship. Then a little boy and a battleship. Then just a little boy. And the machine that had soothed his traumas, deep under the crust of the planet.

"Sir," began Zinin to the commander, and his great

23

voice was strangely muffled, "they're coming . . . in their ship, like they said they would."

Phrnnx yanked himself back to reality—if such it still could be called—and joined the others who were now occupied at the fore port.

Below, great masses of puffy white clouds. Brown and green land masses, unchanged. Blue oceans, unchanged.

Except one.

In the middle of the planet's second ocean, great, impossible masses of thick columnar crystals began to leap upward from the waters. Translucent at first, the chalcedony towers began to pulse with deep inner fires: blue, purple, gold, carmine, and finally a strange, yet familiar silver-gray. The ionosphere, tickled, began to surround the flashing needles with auroras, clothing them in blankets of coruscating radiance.

Following, the planet began to move after the *Tpin.*

On board the cruiser it was very quiet.

"I see," whispered Rappan idly, "that they are bringing their moon along also."

"You get accustomed to something like that," breathed an engineer. "A moon, I mean."

Old Alo was making mystic signs with his tentacles. "Egg of the Code, I almost feel sorry for the Yops!"

The crew picked up this thread of awed enthusiasm as they began to relate the impossible sight to their own personal views of the war. In no time the mood of jubilation was back again, stronger than ever. Stimulants were broken out and passed among those who indulged in them. The communicators—excepting one Phrnnx—began to ply the spacewaves with brazen, challenging messages, daring the Yops to locate them.

"Poor old Yops," whispered Phrnnx. "I can almost see Alo's point."

"Yes," replied the Professor. "There is only one thing that is worrying me."

"*What* is worrying you?" asked Phrnnx.

The Professor turned old eyes on him. They held irony, and they held musing.

"What," he said, "are we going to do with them when there are no more Yops?"

Some Notes Concerning a Green Box

"With Friends Like These . . ." was my first published story, but my first professional sale wasn't even conceived as a story.

In 1970 I discovered H. P. Lovecraft, Cthulhu, Yog-Sothoth, Wilber Whateley, and the rest of the Necronomical world of HPL. I was so taken I sat down and composed a long pseudoletter to August Derleth, hoping he'd get a laugh (well, a smile, anyway) out of it.

Instead, back came a letter from the Wisconsin Prometheus declaring that if I'd cut about forty percent from my story (story . . . what story? What's going on here?), he'd publish it in the next semiannual issue of *The Arkham Collector*.

Total payment was forty dollars. I never saw a finer work of art, a more impressive piece of draftsmanship, than that first check.

Sirs: I did not know what to do with these notes until a friend of mine suggested that I send them along to you, assuming, I suppose, that you might find them of some interest. They form an exceedingly odd story, one with which I am now not so sure I wish to be connected. I report them here as they occurred.

I do not as a rule frequent the facilities of the anthropology department, but an occasion made it necessary. Being a graduate student, I was able to obtain access to files which are kept from the eyes of careless undergraduates and casual visitors. It was in a far corner of the old manuscript-storage room that I first came across the box.

It caught my eye because it was clearly the only new thing in the ancient place. Curious, I made a seat for myself on a stack of old papers and examined the thing more closely. It was quite an ordinary-looking green box, except for the rather formidable-seeming lock on its cover and what I imagined (falsely, of course) to be some faint lingering phosphorescence around the edges. I tried the lid idly and discovered that the lock had not been fastened. More out of boredom than anything else, I then reached in and brought out the enclosed sheaf of papers. Most of these seemed quite new, but there were also a few scraps of some thick, coarse vellum which gave some indication of having been burnt at the sides. I imagined that they had been treated with some chemical preservative, for when I first opened the box, an odor issued forth which was noxious in the extreme. It dissipated very rapidly, however, and I thought no more on it.

The contents of the box included typed letters on which were inscribed in longhand various notes, charts, and a sketch, in addition to the yellowed bits of vellum. As the letters seemed to bear somewhat on my area of study, I carried the box and its contents to the main room and began to Xerox the material for later, more leisurely study.

Presently an elderly librarian chanced to pass. Espying the box, she became unaccountably agitated, and quite vigorously insisted that I make a halt to what I was doing. The poor woman was in such a state that I agreed to pause while she went to fetch the librarian-in-charge. At the sight of the box and its revealed contents, that portly gentleman became quite as incensed as the old lady, and the very first thing he did was to return every scrap of paper to the container in question and lock it securely. Containing his obvious anger, he took the old woman off to one side, carefully keeping the box tucked tightly under one arm. Puzzled, I strained to hear their conversation, but I could make out only a few disjointed phrases, for they were careful to speak very softly. The man said, ". . . who is he? . . . not permitted . . . should have been *locked* . . . delicate situation."

And the woman, ". . . didn't see! . . . no reason to suspect . . . ask him . . . safe . . ."

At this point they halted and the man returned to stare down at me intently. "Did you copy *any* of the material in this box, son?" I replied that I had not, at which words he seemed unaccountably relieved. When I ventured to inquire as to why I could not copy them, he replied that the manuscripts were as yet unpublished, and therefore not covered by copyright. He smiled for the first time since I had laid eyes on him and said, "No harm done, then!" and shook my hand. Continuing to play out the role, I replied that the material did not seem to offer me such aid anyway, so I was perfectly willing to forget the entire incident.

By a fortuitous coincidence, I had stopped earlier at the post office, having need to refresh my stock of envelopes and stamps. Now it so happens I have a friend who is also desirous of obtaining a position on our departmental expedition, and so I had placed my first copies in an envelope and sent them off to him by way of the library mail chute. As things turned out, it was unnecessary for me to write him and request the return of these copies, as the original envelope was returned to my apartment the next day, unopened, stamped "insufficient postage." Despite all my efforts to relocate that mysterious green box, I could find not a trace of it in its former cubbyhole, and deemed it injudicious to make inquiries.

The few copies I *had* succeeded in making consisted of the hand-marked letters and the scraps of yellowed paper. A quick survey of the materials convinced me that I was fortunate to obtain what little I had, as there was apparently a considerable defect in the copying machine. The old scraps, which had been printed in a dark black ink and covered with faded red stains, had failed entirely to be reproduced. It is most curious, as the stains themselves had been re-printed with perfect clarity. I have written to complain to the company, and in typically evasive manner, they replied that they never heard of such a thing.

The letters were apparently the work of two UCLA professors, and I was able to obtain some little information concerning them, which I here include:

"Jonathan Turner, Professor of Anthropology and Linguistics. Born, Providence, R.I., 1910. B.A., University of Maine, 1931. Worked way through college at height of Depression performing heavy manual labor. M.A., Yale, 1932, Ph.D., Yale, 1935, doctoral dissertation, *Some Inquiries into the Nature of the Minor Religions of Southern Louisiana and Alabama, with emphasis on the Cajun Peoples.* (This work, I found, is still available to the interested scholar from the Yale University Research Library, upon presentation of the proper credentials.) Member of American Anthropological Society, Academie Française, etc., etc. . . . Married Emaline Henry of Boston, 1937. Following her tragic death in 1960, moved to California and accepted full professorship with UCLA . . . Author of numerous books on a wide range of subjects, including a famous essay on the Atlantis-Lemurian myths.

"Robert Nolan, Assistant Professor of Archeology. Born, Beverly Hills, Calif., 1944. B.A., M.A., University of California, Berkeley. Ph.D. thesis in preparation. Winner of numerous prizes for originality of theory in the archeology of the Pacific area. Son of a wealthy Los Angeles lawyer."

As to more personal details regarding the two

scholars, I was able to gain some insight from certain of their former students. This line of research was made necessary because the erudite colleagues of the two men displayed a marked hostility toward any questions. Turner was a tall, leonine individual equipped with a full spade beard and an unkempt shock of equally white hair. In contrast, the much younger Nolan was squat and almost entirely bald. Built from the innocuous base of a common interest in skindiving, the friendship of the two men grew rapidly despite the difference in their respective ages.

In 1966, both men took their sabbatical leaves together. With the money Turner had saved and Nolan's not inconsiderable resources of prize monies and family accounts, they purchased and outfitted a small, powered schooner and announced their intention to sail to Easter Island and the South American coasts. Turner had always wanted to visit the area, and Nolan was desirous of carrying out some field work of an unspecified nature.

At this juncture information on the professors begins to grow sketchy and unreliable. It is known that they returned to Los Angeles in September 1966, in excellent health and high good spirits. Surprisingly, both men proceeded to resign their positions with the University. This, to the great consternation of their respective department heads, who were understandably depressed at the prospect of losing two such brilliant members of their faculties, one old and venerable, the other a youngster of exceptional promise. But neither man could be dissuaded, and following the setting in order of certain personal affairs, they announced their intention to return once again to the area of their former travels. It is also known that they brought back a number of well-preserved and extremely eccentric specimens of carved hieroglyphs and statuettes. These, Nolan maintained, had been found not on Isla de Pascua (Easter), but on its smaller and little-visited neighbor to the west, Sala-y-Gomez. It is also reported that they consulted with a number of supposed specialists in matters occult, among them a rather notorious and disreputable old bookseller in the downtown section of San Diego. The man's shop is no longer there, the structure it was located in having since been torn down and replaced by a multilevel parking lot, one section of which I am able to report sags at the oddest angle, despite repeated attempts to correct it.

Due to the obvious sincerity with which his department deplored his resignation, Professor Nolan agreed to keep in touch with his old friends by means of occasional letters which he would forward whenever the opportunity presented itself. These are the missives which I was able to copy so hurriedly at the anthropology library. On some, the postmark was stamped into the envelope with sufficient force to leave an impression on the letter within, and by judicious use of fingerprinting materials, I have been able to bring them to a legible state. These dates vary from February 3 to May 18, 1967. All are postmarked from Valparaiso, Chile, and one of them confides that the expedition was forced to remain there for such an extended period of time so as to permit the repair of storm damage to their craft.

A letter to the man mentioned in that missive as the repairman, a Señor Juan María y Florez, brought as a reply a note scrawled in an awkward hand, as though the wielder of the pen were unfamiliar with its use. Of the professors it had little to say, except that he, Florez, had always thought of professors as being very composed individuals, and that these two Americans seemed both nervous and jumpy. Instead he dwelt on the damage to their schooner, which was totally alien to him, a man who had worked on ships for over forty years. For example, he mentions that he did not feel Professor Turner's explanation of an "unexpected heavy swell" entirely accounted for the odd twisting of the four-inch steel bar of the schooner's left drive shaft, nor for how three of the four blades came to be broken off the screw. A local shipman in Long Beach assures me that Mr. Florez, despite his forty years, is here doubtless indulging a natural penchant for native exaggeration.

The first of these letters, dated February 11, includes in longhand the note "40 degrees, 9′ S, still on 110. Nothing visible on horiz. but Bob still conf."

This seemingly innocuous bit of information reveals on inspection a number of oddities. It would seem to indicate that although the letters to home were mailed from February to the middle of May, they were written *not* in Valparaiso, but while the professors were still at sea! Why the two men should do this and then wait to mail the letters *at staggered intervals* extending over three and a half months from the date of their arrival in Chile is beyond me. And the latitude given is *40* degrees *S.* It is quite clear. The "110" can only be the longitude. Thus, it must be inferred from this information that the ship was proceeding almost due south from Easter Island. But the most peculiar part of the phrase is the section which states "nothing visible on the horiz.," since this would seem to imply that perhaps the two men expected that there might *be* something on the horizon. This is blatant nonsense, since a quick glance at any map of the Pacific will suffice to show even the casual observer that there is nothing present in that section of ocean for hundreds of miles in *any* direction, let alone due south! It is interesting to note, though, that this course was taking them almost directly down the center of the subsurface mountain mass known as the Easter Island Cordillera.

The next letter carries in its margin the words, "Turned east, following Cook instruc." Once again consulting the Research Library files, I found that Captain James Cook had indeed passed this same section of sea in 1773 on his return voyage to England. What is *more* interesting is the fact that the following year the captain, usually a dead-accurate navigator, spent some considerable time wandering about in the area between 40 and 50 degrees latitude, and 120 and 130 degrees longitude. Certainly he could not have been there searching for something, as the area is as desolate a stretch of ocean as exists on this world.

The next legible note reads, "129 W, Bob discouraged, turning back w. current." This can only mean that Professor Nolan did indeed expect to find *something* in this empty piece of sea and, as one would anticipate, he had not. Also, the reverse side of the letter contains the admonition, "coord wrong? check Sydney Bulletin." At the time, this reference held no meaning for me.

There remained only one last notation of any consequence, and I have come to regard that one as the key to the entire baffling matter. It is at once the clearest and most mystifying of them all, and consists of three parts. The words, "check Lvcrft ref," some cryptic symbols in Professor Turner's hand, and one word, written underneath:

"CTHULHU"

The reference to a "Lvcrft" puzzled me utterly, until I chanced to mention it to a fellow student. He informed me that my "Lvcrft" was possibly H. P. Lovecraft, a writer of the 20's and 30's who wrote weird-fantastic stories. Searching out an index of the man's work, I was both surprised and pleased to encounter a tale containing mention of the odd word "Cthulhu," entitled *The Call of Cthulhu*. Procuring a book containing the indicated story, I read it with what was at first avid interest. My interest quickly flagged. I was disappointed! Here I had thought I had unearthed some potentially great scientific discovery which for some unknown reason certain parties were trying to suppress, when in actuality all I was doing was wasting my time with the childish fantasies of two grown scholars who presumably should know better!

Still . . .

Further along in the story I found references not only to that same *Sydney Bulletin,* but also to a certain mythical island or coastline that supposedly was found at "latitude 47 d, 9′, and longitude 126 d, 43′ "! If only as a source of some little humor, these coincidences piqued my lagging interest considerably. I subsequently wrote to a newspaper friend of mine in Melbourne, who promised to locate for me a copy of the *Bulletin* for the date indicated in the story (April 18, 1925). Several weeks later I received a letter from my friend apologizing, in which he informed me that the only known complete file of the *Sydney Bulletin* had perished in the Sydney University fire of 1929. I found this an especial curiosity since Lovecraft's story had been written in 1928.

Additional research turned up more disturbing facts. I must add that I continued to pursue these tiresome researches because I have to date been unable to uncover any information whatsoever regarding the whereabouts of Professor Turner or Professor Nolan, who apparently dropped out of sight after departing Valparaiso on May 21 of '67. I would greatly appreciate any information concerning same. As a last resort I attempted to get in contact with the only surviving relative of either man, but Professor Nolan's father retired from his law practice last year and moved to Europe.

A recent chat with the Chilean consul in Los Angeles produced as a by-product a kind and gracious letter from one Carlos Malpelo, the Valparaiso Chief of Police. He writes that after the date mentioned, 21 May '67, there is no additional information on the two American professors, but that there are two items of related interest which he thought I might find interesting. The first is that the professors spent much time at the Santiago University, and in particular with an old friend of Professor Turner's, the renowned Chilean linguist P. C. Fernandez. It is also noted that the professor was much pleased upon receiving from the two Americans a gift consisting of a sealed box containing a peculiarly formed statuette of unusually repugnant design.

Unfortunately there appears to be no way to confirm any of this, because Professor Fernandez was one of the many casualties of the recent great Chilean earthquake. The few Indian porters in his party who survived the quake were too shaken to do more than report the death of the professor and of their fellows. These men were found in the mountains the night after the quake, shivering and frightened. They were given food and clothing by the government rescue team and permitted to return to their families, except for one oldster who adamantly maintained in spite of the most determined expostulations that the professor was responsible for the quake. According to this patriarch, the professor had been performing some incomprehensible ritual with burning herbs and an odd little idol when the tremors had begun. At this point the old man's testimony lapses into insane drivel, as when he claims that the mountain across the valley from them got upon gigantic stone feet and stepped on the professor, killing most of the party with him. The poor man was placed in the public sanitarium for the poor at Rancagua, but apparently escaped last year from that well-known institution.

The other "items of interest" which the good Señor Malpelo forwarded to me was much shorter, but of no less import. It was a bit from a small Valparaiso newspaper stating that one Juan María y Gomez, given occupation, shipwright, was missing and presumed lost at sea during the night of a storm on June 6, 1967. A trawling fishing boat came upon the shattered wreckage of Señor Gomez's boat the next day. It is mentioned that the ship must have passed through an exceptionally violent part of the storm, because what pieces of the ship's fittings were found were battered beyond all recognition, even to the shaft of one of the ship's screws, which was twisted quite completely out of shape.

Lately, I have been showing the cryptic symbols which appeared in Professor Turner's hand above the word *Cthulhu* around the University. The reaction I get is peculiar in the extreme. Most professors who see it take it in good humor as an unusual student prank. Those few who do not find it funny exhibit an odd trembling of the hands when they first set eyes upon it, but cover up very quickly thereafter and pronounce the symbol an insulting hoax. They are quite forceful about this, and wish to have no more to do with it. I am much puzzled, as this seems to occur almost always with the older professors.

The first of the charts I copied shows the general area of the South Pacific. It has drawn in Easter Island, a rough duplication of Cook's courses for his voyages of 1773–75, and a number of other notations and markings, most of which are unintelligible. Most peculiar of these is an "X" at approximately 167 degrees *east* longitude, and 77 degrees south latitude. Under these coordinates are the notes "Halley's, '86," which doubtless refers to the next reappearance of the famous Halley comet, due back in our solar vicinity in 1986. A check of a *National Geographic* map of this area reveals that the above coordinates intersect on or very near Mt. Erebus, the 15,000-foot-high active volcano on McMurdo Sound in Anartica. What this has to do with the next appearance of Halley's comet is no doubt known only to Professors Turner and Nolan.

The second sketch is simply a crude map of the world with two lines drawn in on it. Although laughable in its simplicity, I was rather intrigued by this, as the two lines ran thusly: one went in a straight line from that "X" (Mt. Erebus?) to Easter Island. The other line runs from Easter, through the center of its neighbor, Sala-y-Gomez, to a spot in the Andes of Northern Chile. This, again coincidentally, happens to be the area Professor Fernandez was exploring when he was killed by the earthquake. Straight as an arrow, it continues onward with three other "X's" marked along its length. One is somewhere in the jungle of the Matto Grosso (memo: write the Brazilian Land Survey), another in the Brazilian Basin, the deepest part of the Atlantic Ocean, to end finally near Addis Ababa, in Ethiopia.

The last item was neither note nor chart, but rather a sketch-drawing of what seemed to be some enormous pyramidlike structure of ridiculous shape, with accompanying notes in Turner's hand. This was the sole item I managed to smuggle from the library intact. I regret that soon afterward I was offered a really ridiculous sum of money for it, no questions asked, from a wealthy professor I was consulting, and so sold it to him. He has since moved.

That completes what I have found to be an exceedingly odd collection of facts, and until Professors Turner and Nolan return (from wherever they are) I am afraid much of this material must remain as puzzling as ever. I hope you find it of some little interest. Besides, I have come to think it wise to have the facts in the hands of an unadvertised party. Lately I have had the feeling of being followed, especially at night. I was also forced to move from my former apartment after experiencing a spell of severe nightmares unique in their prismatic horror. The doctor at the University assured me that these are the natural results of overwork at school. This may be, but the series of twelve grooves, six to a side, that I found *etched into the glass* of my one window one morning after a particularly vivid phantasm of terror have made me cautious. One thing I *know*, and that is that they were not the result of overwork at school.

That is all I have to say about my work with the green box and its odd contents. I am quite happy in my new lodgings, and I am no longer troubled by nightmares. Also, I have been selected to go on the University expedition to the South Seas! My associate and companion will be a brilliant and eccentric cinematographer named Pickman. Only one last thing bothers me unreasonably. My new landlord has the most *peculiarly* colored yellow eyes.

Why Johnny Can't Speed

When I was a smaller kid than I am now, I used to play war on the highway. You know, sit in the back seat with a ruler or broomstick or just my hands, and annihilate the lady in the station wagon behind you, mow down the unknowing pedestrians on the sidewalks, blast that low-flying bomber (usually an innocent Piper Cub) out of the sky.

But the best fantasy was to turn the headlights into ray guns, the side-view mirror into a blaster, the tail fins into rocket launchers.

I've been in traffic tie-ups where I wished I still had that magical adolescent armory. So have drivers around me.

You can see it in their faces.

DEAR MR. AND MRS. MERWIN:

IT IS MY PAINFUL DUTY TO HAVE TO INFORM YOU THAT YOUR SON, ROBERT L. MERWIN, WAS KILLED IN COMMUTER ACTION ON THE SOUTHBOUND SAN

DIEGO FREEWAY IN THE VICINITY OF THE SECOND IRVINE RANCH TURNOFF, ORANGE COUNTY.

FROM WHAT OUR EVALUATORS HAVE BEEN ABLE TO RECONSTRUCT, YOUNG ROBERT APPARENTLY DISPUTED A LANE CHANGE WITH A BLACK GM CADDY MARAUDER. NO VIOLATION OF THE NORTH AMERICAN TRAFFIC CODE HAS COME TO MY NOTICE, BUT I WILL KEEP YOU INFORMED SHOULD ANY SUCH COME TO LIGHT. NORMAL INVESTIGATIONS ARE PROCEEDING. THE OTHER VEHICLE INVOLVED IS KNOWN TO ORANGE COUNTY POLICE. ITS OWNER WAS QUESTIONED BUT NOT DETAINED. DETAILS AND PARTICULARS ARE ENCLOSED. PLEASE ACCEPT MY PERSONAL CONDOLENCES.

YOURS SINCERELY,
GEORGE WILSON ANGEL
CHIEF, SOUTHERN CALIFORNIA DIVISION
CALIFORNIA DISTRICT HIGHWAY PATROL

ENCL: 1 RPT. ACCID.
       1 RPT. CORONER

Frank Merwin refolded the letter, replaced it in its envelope, and laid it on the flange of the lamp stand, near the radio. He held his wife a little more tightly. Her sobbing had become less than hysterical, now that the terrible initial shock had somewhat worn. He managed to keep his own emotions pretty well in check, but then he had driven the Los Angeles area for some twenty years and was correspondingly toughened. When he finally spoke again there was as much bitterness in his voice as sorrow.

"Geez, Myrt, oh, geez."

He eased her down onto the big white couch, walked to the center of the room and paused there, hands clenching and unclenching, clasped behind his back. The woven patterns in the floor absorbed his attention.

"Goddamn it, Myrtle, I told him! I *told* him! 'Look, son, if you insist on driving all the way to Diego by yourself, at least take the Pontiac! Have some sense,' I told him! I don't know what's with the kids these

39

days, hon. You'd think he'd listen to me just this once, wouldn't you? Me, who once drove all the way from Indianapolis to L.A. and was challenged only twice on the way—only *twice,* Myrt, but no, he hadda be a big shot! 'Listen Dad. This is something I've got to work out for myself. With my own car,' he tells me! I knew he'd have trouble in that VW. And I often told him so, too.

"But no, all he could think of to say was, 'Pops, the worst that can happen is I've gotta outmaneuver some other car, right? You've seen the way that bug corners, haven't you, huh? And if I get into a tough scrape, any other VW on the road is bound by oath to support me —in most actions anyway.'

"Whatta you tell a kid like that, Myrt? How do you get through to him?" His face registered utter bafflement. His wife's crying had slowed to a trickle. She was dabbing at her eyes with one of his old handkerchiefs.

"I don't know either, dear. I still don't understand why he had to drive down there. Why couldn't he have taken the Trans, Frank? Why?"

"Oh, you know why. What would his *friends* have said? 'Here's Bobby Merwin, too scared to drive his own rod,' and that sort of crud." His sarcasm was getting edgier. "Still felt he had to prove himself a man, the idiot! He'd already soloed on the freeways—why did he feel the need to try a cross-county expedition? But damn it, if he had to display his guts, why couldn't he have done so in the big car? Not even a professionally customized VW can mount much stuff.

"And on top of everything else, you'd think he'd have had the sense to shy off that kind of an argument? He had Driver's Training! Who ever heard of a VW disputing position with a Cad—a Marauder, no less! Where were his 'friends,' huh? I warned him about the light stretches between here and Diego, where flow is light, help is more than a hornblast away and some psycho can surprise you from behind an on-ramp!"

He paused to catch his breath, walked back to the

'amp stand, and picked up the letter. Familiar with the contents, he glanced at it only briefly this time. He offered it to his wife but she declined, so he returned it to the stand.

"You know what I have to do now, I suppose?"

She nodded, sniffling.

"Bob was taking that gift to a friend in Diego. I'm bound to see that it's delivered."

She looked up at him without much hope. She knew Frank.

"I don't suppose—"

He shook his head. His expression was gentle but firm.

"No, hon. I'm taking it down myself. I refuse to ship it and I certainly won't ride the Trans. Not after all these years. No, I'm going down the same way Bob went, by the same route. I'll have the J.J. tuned first, though."

She looked around dully, plucking fitfully at the delicate covering of the couch.

"I suppose you'll at least take it in to—"

"Hector? Certainly. In spite of what he charges he's damn well worth the money. Best mechanic around. I enjoy doing business with him. Know I'm getting my credit's worth, at least. We couldn't have me going somewhere else—now could we? Wouldn't want him to get the idea we're prejudiced or something. I've been going to him for, oh, five years. Almost forgotten what he is—"

"Going all the way down to Diego, eh, Mr. Merlin?" said the wiry *chicano*. He was trying to rub some of the grease off his hands. The filthy rag he was using already appeared incapable of taking on any more of the tacky blue-black gunk.

"Yeah. So you'll understand, Hector, when I say the J.J.'s got to be in tiptop shape."

"*Ciertamente!* You want to open her up, please?"

Frank nodded and moved over to where the J.J. rested, just inside the rolled-up armor-grille entrance

41

to the big garage. He slid into the deep pile of the driver's bucket, flipped the three keys on the combination ignition, and then jabbed the hood-release switch. As soon as the hood started up he climbed out, leaving the keys in the *On* position. Hector was already bent over the car's power plant, staring intently into the works.

"Well, Mr. Merwin, from what I can see your engine at least is in excellent condition, yes, excellent! You want me to fill 'er up?"

Frank nodded wordlessly. He wasn't at all surprised at the mechanic's rapid inspection of the engine. After all, the J.J. had been given the best of professional care and the benefits of his own considerable work since he'd purchased her. Hector did not look up as he set about releasing the protective panels over the right-side .70 caliber.

"If I may ask, how do you plan to go?"

Frank had the big Meerschaum out and was tamping tobacco into it.

"Hmm. I'll go down Burbank to the San Diego Freeway and get on there. It'd be a little faster to get on the Ventura, but on a trip of this length that little bit of time saved would be negligible and I don't see the point in fighting the interchange."

Hector nodded approvingly. "Quite wise. You know Mr. Merwin, you've got two pretty bad stretches on this trip. Very iffy. I read—about your son. I sorrow. The *jornada de la muerte* comes eventually to all of us."

Frank paused in lighting the pipe. "Couldn't be helped," he said tightly. "Bob didn't realize what was —what he was getting into, that's all. I blame myself too, but what could I do? He was eighteen and by law there wasn't anything I could do to hold him back. He simply took on more than he could handle."

One of Hector's grease monks had wheeled over a bulky ammo cart. The mechanic waved the assistant off and proceeded about the loading himself. Frank appreciated the gesture.

"A Cad, wasn't it?"

"It was." He was leaning over the mechanic's shoulder, better to follow the loading process. Never could tell what you might have to do for yourself on the road. "What are you giving me? Explosive or armor-piercing?"

"Mixed." Hector slammed down the box-load cover on the heavy gun. It clicked shut, locked. He moved away to get a small, curved ladder, wheeled it back. At the top he began checking over the custom roof turret. "Both, alternating sequence. True, it's more expensive, but after all your son's car was destroyed by a Marauder. A black one?"

"Yes, that's right," said Frank, only mildly surprised. "How'd you find out?"

"Oh, among the trade the word gets passed along. I know of this particular vehicle, I believe. Owner does a lot of his own work, I understand. That's tough to tangle with, Mr. Merwin. Might you be thinking of—"

Frank shrugged, looked the other way. "Never know who you'll bump into on the roads these days, Hector. I've never been one to run from a dogfight."

"I did not mean to imply that you would. We all know your driver's combat record, Mr. Merwin. There are not all that many aces living in the Valley."

He gestured meaningfully at the side of the car. Eleven silhouettes were imprinted there. Four mediums, four compacts—crazy people. Gutsy, but crazy. Two sportscars—kids—a Jag and a Vet, as he recalled. He smiled in reminiscence. Speed wasn't *everything*. And one large gold stamping. He ran his hand over the impressions fondly. That big gold one, he'd gotten that baby on the legendary drive out from Indianapolis, back in '83—no, '82. The Imperial had been rough and, face it, he'd been lucky as hell, too young to know better. Ricochet shots were always against the odds, but hell, anyone could shoot at *tires*! So he'd thought twenty-odd years ago. Now he knew better—didn't he?

He wondered if Bob had tried something equally insane.

"Yes, well, you watch yourself, Mr. Merwin. A Marauder is bad news straight from the factory. Properly customized, it could mount enough stuff to take on a Greyhound busnought."

"Don't worry about me, Hector. I can take care of myself." He was checking the nylon sheathing on the rear tires. "Besides, the J.J. mounts a few surprises of her own!"

It was already warm outside, even at five in the morning. The weather bureau had forecast a high of of 101° for downtown L.A. He'd miss most of that, but even with air control and climate conditioning things could get hot. He turned on the climate-cool as he backed the blue sedan out of the garage, put it in Drive and rolled toward the Burbank artery.

It was still too early for the real rush hour and he had little company on the feeder route as he moved past Van Nuys Boulevard toward the Sepulveda on-ramp. A Rambler at the light was slow in getting away at the change of signal. He blasted the horn once and the frantic driver of the heavily neutral-marked vehicle made haste to get out of his way. Theoretically all cars on the surface streets were equal. But some were more equal than others.

The Sepulveda on-ramp was an excellent one for entering the system for reasons other than merely being an easier way to pass through the Ventura interchange. Instead of sloping upward as most on-ramps did, it allowed the driver to descend a high hill. This enabled older cars to pick up a lot of valuable acceleration easily and also provided the driver with an aerial overview of the traffic pattern below.

He passed the commuter car park at the Kester Trans station. It was just beginning to fill as the more passive commuters parked their personal vehicles in favor of the public Trans. He felt a surge of contempt, the usual reaction of the independent motorist to milk-

44

footed driver's willfully abandoning their vehicular freedom for the crowding and crumpling of the mass-transit systems. What sort of person did it take, he wondered for the umpteenth time, to trade away his birthright for simple sardine-can safety? The country was definitely losing its backbone. He shook his head woefully as his practiced eye gauged the pattern shifting beneath him.

Mass Trans had required and still required a lot of money. One way in which the governments involved (meaning those of most industrial, developed nations) went about obtaining the necessary amounts was to cut back the expensive motorized forces needed to regulate the far-flung freeway systems. As the cutbacks increased it gradually became accepted custom among the remaining overworked patrols to allow drivers to settle their own disputes. This custom was finalized by the Supreme Court's handing down of the famous Briver *vs.* Matthews and the State of Texas decision of '79, in which it was ruled that all attempts to regulate interstate, nonstop highway systems were in direct violation of the First Amendment.

Any motorist who didn't feel up to potential arguments was provided a safe, quiet alternative means of transportation in the new Mass Trans systems, most of which ran down the center and sides of the familiar freeway routes, high above the frantic traffic. Benefits were immediate. Less pollution from even the fine turbine-steam-electric engines of the private autos, an end to many downtown parking problems in the big cities—and more. For the first time since their inception the freeways, even at rush hour, became negotiable at speeds close to those envisioned by their builders. And psychiatrists began to advise driving as excellent therapy for persons afflicted with violent or even homicidal instincts.

There were a few—un-American dirty commie pinko symps, no doubt—who decried the resultant proliferation of "argumentative" devices among high-powered autos. Some laughable folk even talked of an "arms" race among automakers. German cars made their biggest incursions into foreign markets in decades. Armor plating, bulletproof glassalloy, certain weaponry—how else did those nuts expect a decent man to Drive with Confidence?

He gunned the engine and the supercharged sedan roared down the on-ramp, gathering unnecessary but impressive momentum as it went. Frank had always believed in an aggressive entrance. *Let 'em know where you stand right away or they'll ride all over you.* The tactic was hardly needed in this instance—there were only two other cars in his entrance pattern, both in the far two lanes.

He switched slowly until he was behind them, looking into rear- and side-view mirror carefully for fast-approaching others. The lanes behind were clear and he had no trouble attaining the fourth lane of the five. Safer here. Plenty of room for feisty types to pass on either side and he could still maintain a decent speed without competing with dragsters. He pushed the J.J. up to an easy seventy-five miles per, settled back for the long drive.

He spotted only two wrecks as he sped smoothly through the Sepulveda Pass—about normal for this early in the day. The helicrane crew were probably in the process of changing shifts, so these wrecks would lie a bit longer than at other, busier times of day.

His first view of action came as he approached the busy Wilshire on-ramps. Two compacts squared off awkwardly. The slow lane was occupied by a four-door Toyota. A Honda coupe, puffing mightily to build speed up the on-grade, came off the ramp at a bad position. It required one or the other to slow for a successful entrance and the sedan, having superior position, understandably refused to be the one. Instead of taking the quiet course, the Honda maintained its original approach speed and fired an unannounced broadside from its small—.25 caliber, Frank judged—window-mounted swivel gun. The sedan swerved crazily for a moment as its driver, startled, lost control for a

46

few seconds. Then it straightened out and regained its former attitude. Frank and the cars behind him slowed to give the combatants plenty of lane space in which to operate.

The armor glass was taking the attack and the sedan began to return fire—about equal, standard factory equipment, he guessed. They were already reaching the end of the entrance lane. Desperately, refusing to concede the match, the coupe cut sharply at the nose of the sedan. The sedan's owner swerved easily into the second lane and then cut tightly back. At this angle his starboard gun bore directly on the coupe. A loud bang heralded a shattered tire. With a short, almost slow-motion bump, the coupe hit the guardrail and flipped over out of sight. In his rearview mirror Frank could just make out the first few wisps of smoke as he shot past the spot.

Now that the fight was over, Frank floored the accelerator again, throwing the victorious driver a fast salute. It was returned gracefully. Considering his limited stuff, the fellow had done very well. He'd handled that figure C with ease, but the maneuver would have been useless against a larger car. Frank's own, for example. Still, compact drivers were a special breed and often made up for their lack of power, engine, and fire in sheer guts. He still watched *Don Railman and his Supersub* religiously on the early Sunday Tele, even though the ratings were down badly from last season. He'd also never forget that time when a *Weekly Caripper's Telemanual* with old Ev Kelly had done a special on some hand-tooled Mighty Mite, low bore, cut down, with the Webcor antitank gun cleverly concealed in the front trunk. No, it paid not to take the compacts, even the subs, too lightly.

He passed the Santa Monica interchange without trouble. In fact, the only thing resembling a confrontation he had on the whole L.A. portion of the drive occurred a few minutes later as he swept past the Los Angeles Sub-International Airport rampings.

A new Vet, all shiny and gold, blasted up behind

him. It stayed there, tailgating. That in itself was a fighting provocation. He could see the driver clearly— a young girl, probably in her late teens. About Bob's age, he thought tightly. No doubt, Daddy dear had bought the bomb for her. She honked at him sharply, insistently. He ignored her. She could pass him to either side with ease. Instead she fired a low burst of tracers across his rear deck. When he resolutely continued to ignore her she pouted, then pulled alongside. Giggling, she threw him an obscene gesture which even his not-so-archaic mind could identify. He jerked hard on the wheel, then back. Her haughty expression disappeared instantly, to be replaced by one of fright. When she saw it was merely a feint on his part, she smiled again, although much less arrogantly, and shot ahead at a good hundred miles per.

Stupid kid better watch her manners, never live to make 20,000 miles. Maybe he should have given her a lesson, burnt off a tire, perhaps. Oh, well. He had a long way to drive. Let someone else play teacher.

He became quiet and watchful as he left Santa Ana and entered the Irvine area. There was little commuter traffic here and only a few harmless beachers this early in the day. He saw only one car in the Cad's class and that was an old yellow Thunderhood. Wasn't sure whether or not to be disappointed or relieved as he pulled into the San Clemente rest stop for breakfast. He could have eaten at home but preferred to slip out without waking Myrtle. He'd have a couple of eggs, some toast and jam, and enjoy a view of the Pacific along with his coffee despite the low clouds which had been rolling in for the last twenty minutes. He hoped it wouldn't rain, even though rain would cut the heat. Weather was one reason he always avoided the safer but longer desert routes. Thundershowers inland were forecast and even the best tactical driver could be outmatched in a heavy downpour. He preferred to be in a situation where his talents could operate without complications wished on him by nature.

A few warm drops, fat and heavy, hit him as he left the diner. It had grown much darker and the humidity was fierce. Still, Irvine was behind him now. Best to make speed down to Diego and get home before dark.

He had only the well-policed Camp Pendleton lanes ahead and then the near-deserted Oceanside to La Jolla run before he'd hit any real traffic again. Contrary to early predictions, the California population had spread inland instead of along the largely state-owned coast. If he'd had sense to buy that hundred acres near Mojave before the airport had gone in there . . .

On the left he could see the old Presidential Palace shining on its solitary hill. He waved nostalgically, then speeded up slightly as he approached the Pendleton cutoff.

The drizzle remained so light he didn't even bother with wipers. Pendleton was passed quickly and he had no reason to stop in Oceanside. Soon he was cruising among rolling, downy hills, mellow in the diffused sunlight. A few cattle were the only living creatures in evidence, along with a few big crows circling lazily overhead in the moist air. Once a cycle pack roared noisily past, long twenties damp with dew. Two tricycles headed up the front and rear of the pack, but the ugly snouts of their recoil-less rifles were covered against a possible downpour. They took no notice of him, rumbling past at a solid ninety-five miles an hour. He had no wish to tangle with a gang, not in this empty territory. A good driver could knock out three or four of the big Harley-Davidsons and Yamaharas easily enough, but the highly maneuverable bikes could swarm over anything smaller than a bus or trailer with ease, magnifying the effect of their light weaponry.

Maybe he could buy some land out here. He gazed absently at the green-and-gold hills, devoid of housing tracts and supermarkets. Not another Mojave, maybe, but still . . .

A sharp honking snapped his attenion reflexively to his mirrors. He recognized the license of the big black coupe almost at the instant he identified the make and model. *You're south of your territory, fella,* he thought grimly. His hands clenched tightly on the wheel as he slid over one lane.

The Cad pulled up beside him, preparatory to passing. He judged the moment precisely, then tripped a switch on his center console. The portside flame thrower erupted in a jet of orange flame. The Cad jerked like a singed kitten. Instantly Frank cut over to the far lane, putting as much distance as possible between him and the big car, staying slightly ahead of the other.

A long dark streak showed clearly on the coupe's front, a deep gash in the tire material. The Cad would have trouble if it tried any sharp moves in his direction now, and Frank saw no problem in holding his present position. Now he could duck at the first off-ramp if need arose. He activated the roof turret, an expensive option, but one which had proven its worth time and again. Myrtle had opted for the big grenade launcher, but Frank and the GM salesman had convinced her that while showiness might be fine for impressing the neighbors, on the road it was performance that counted. The twin fifties in the turret commenced hammering away at the Cad, nicking big chips of armorglass and battle sheathing from its front.

Frank was feeling confident until a violent explosion rocked him nastily and forced him to throw emergency power to the steering. Frightened, he glanced over his shoulder. Thank God for the automatic sprinklers! The rear of his car above the left wheel was completely gone, as was most of the rear deck. Twisted, blackened metal and torn insulation smoked and groaned. A look at the Cad confirmed his worst fears and sent more sweat pouring down his shirt collar. No wonder this Marauder had acquired such a reputation! In place of the standard heavy Cad machine guns, a Mark IV rocket launcher protruded from the rear trunk! Fortunately the shot had hit at a bad angle or he'd be missing a wheel and his ability to maneuver would have been drastically, perhaps fatally, reduced. He did an *S* just in time. Another rocket shrieked past his bumper.

The turret fifties were doing their job, but it was slow, too slow! Another rocket strike would finish him and now the Cad had its big guns going, too. He wished to hell he was in the cab of a big United Truckers tractor-trailer, high above the concrete, with another driver and a gunner on the twin 60mm's. A crack appeared in his rear window as the Cad's guns concentrated their fire. He turned and twisted, accelerated and slowed, not daring to give his opponent another clear shot with those Mark IV's.

Chance time, Frank, baby. Remember Salt Lake City!

He cut hard left. The Cad cut right to get behind him. At the proper (yes, yes!) second he dropped an emergency switch.

The rear backup lights dropped off the J.J. At the same time a violent *crrumpp!* threw him forward so hard he could feel the cross-harness bite into his chest. Fighting desperately for control and cursing all the way, he slammed into the resilient center divider with a jolt that rattled his teeth, two wheels spinning crazily off the pavement, then cut all the way back across the five lanes. Fighting a busted something all the way, he managed to wrestle the battered sedan to a tired halt on the gravel shoulder.

Panting heavily, he undid the safety harness, staggered out of the car, bracing himself against the metal sides. Behind him, a quarter mile or so down the empty road, a thick plume of roiling black smoke billowed up from a pile of twisted metal, plastics and ceramics, all intertwined with bright orange flame. The big bad black Cad was quite finished. He took one step in its direction, then stopped, dizzied by the effort. No driver could survive that inferno. In his eagerness to get behind the sedan, the Cad's driver had shot over at least one, possibly both of the proximity mines Frank had released from where his backup lights had been. Maybe revenge was an outdated commodity today, but he still felt exhilarated. And Myrtle might complain initially but he knew damn well she'd be pleased inside.

He became aware of something wet trickling down his cheek, more than could have come from the sporadically dripping sky. His hand told him a piece of his left ear was missing. The blood was staining his good driving blouse. Absently he dabbed at the nick with a handkerchief. His rear glass must have gone at the last possible minute. A look confirmed it, showing two neat holes and a third questionable one in his rear window. Umm. He'd had closer calls before—and this one was worth it. At least there'd be one license plate to lay on Bob's grave.

He sighed. Better stop off in Carlsbad and get that ear taken care of. Damnation, if only that boy had paid some attention in Driver's Ed. Eighteen years old and he'd never learned what his old man had known for years.

Be safe. Drive Offensively.

The Emoman

Every kind of drug is available on the street market. Pick you up, put you down, carry you off to never-never land—name it and it's being dealt on your local corner.

Someday someone's going to eliminate the chemical middleman.

This is the story of two people and how three of them died.

By and large, they were pretty nice people.

But it's not a very nice story.

"I've come to buy some anger," called up the too-young man. He sat himself down on a metal sawhorse and waited.

"Indeed?" replied the man working up and across from him.

"Indeed," answered the too-young man.

The gentleman working across from the too-young man and his metal sawhorse was engaged in an anomaly. He was repairing a boat. This in itself was not terribly unusual. It was a common enough activity in boatyards. But he was driving metal pinions into the

53

boat's hull with a hand-held hammer. This, instead of using an automatic arm.

What was more, the hull of the craft appeared to be made of natural celluloid materials instead of plasticine, metalloy, or ferrosponges. This ship was not new. Its hull was badly in need of a new coat of paint.

From the back the man did not seem especially arresting. This impression changed when he paused, straightened, and turned on his ladder to face the other.

He stood slightly over average height but seemed taller. Leonine, well built, lithe. The lines in his face seemed put there by a drunken cartographer. Each led to some strange valley, forbidden city, or unfathomable abyss of the soul.

For all of that he was not ancient. The streaks of black in his otherwise iron-gray hair were plentiful and not the product of cosmetics. In back the hair was gathered into a single pigtail by an odd arrangement of leather bindings. A single solid-gold ring pierced his right ear. He had thick gray eyebrows that had been intended for a much larger man. They shaded equally gray eyes. His nose was long and slightly hooked. His mouth and lips were thin and clenched tightly. His whole expression was full of star space and vinegar.

"What makes you think I could sell you anger, feller me lad?"

"You are the man they call Sawbill," said the too-young man. It was not a question.

"I'm the man some call Sawbill. I'm often called other things and many of them are better. Some are worse. Sawbill will do."

Facing Sawbill, the too-young man was not all that young. The gulf between them, though, was one that some people might have called age.

His metallic red jumpsuit flashed in the morning sun. "Then you're the one I want, all right. I am not without resources. Or brains. I've checked on you thoroughly. Oh, very carefully, very quietly. You needn't worry at all."

"I wasn't. But go on." Sawbill was rummaging through a small keg of metal pinions, variously shaped and sized.

"You weren't easy to locate—I'll give you that. But I knew how to find you. It's all a matter of asking the right question in the right places. And if you have money and know a few people in expedient locations —on the Port immigration board, for example—you can find out just about anything. I want to make a purchase, Sawbill."

The boat had a low-lying central cabin. A bird thing perched on the edge of it. The bird's rainbow-hued crest bobbed up and down like a metronome. Its tail was of bright golden feathers and the rest of it was dull, crushed, velvety gold. The thing fluttered down to land on Sawbill's right shoulder. Dipping and bobbing, it surveyed the new arrival. The rainbow crest feathers flashed in avian Morse.

The too-young man stared with interest at the bird-thing. He was no ornithologist, not even an amateur. But he was well read. Enough to know that this bird was not native to Thalia Major. (It might have come from Thalia Minor, but he doubted it because . . .)

"Well, feller me lad, who wants to buy anger— what's your moniker?"

"Moniker?"

"Handle. Wing. Name. Pseudo-corporeal psychic verbal inculcation. What have you been conditioned to call yourself?"

"Jasper Jordan. And it's my real name, not an alias. See, I have no desire to hide things from you. I want this all to be very open. That's a fascinating pet you have."

Sawbill carefully aligned a nail, drove it home with two solid, short raps from the hammer. He spoke without pausing in his work or looking back.

"It's a pim-bird from Tehuantepec. The things are sacred to the Indians who inhabit the planet's two continents. They are called pim-birds for convenience. Of the natives—not of the birds, who have nothing to say in the matter. Their real names are much longer and even incorporate a short snatch of song. You wouldn't understand it, because the natives themselves don't. It's a very old song. A rough terranglo translation begins *Tears of the sun* . . . and flows from there. This particular pim-bird supposedly contains the soul of the great emperor Lethan-atuan, who—depending on which legend you prefer to believe—at one time ruled with the most beautiful Queen Quetzal-ma half this galaxy or a cluster of three small islands off the coast of the continent Col. Just now it happens to be hungry. It is said by the Indians that if the souls of the emperor and his queen are ever reunited, they will once again rule the galaxy. Which is one reason the natives permitted me to take him off-planet. They rather like their present system of rule and frown on the idea of long-dead emperors returning."

He turned and pointed the hammer at Jordan. "So you want to buy anger, hmm? What kind of anger?"

"There are different kinds?"

Sawbill picked up another couple of nails. "Different kinds? There are so many different kinds as there are foolish young men in the universe. There's uncertain anger, which is dark pits filled with thorns. There's jealous anger, which is honey and syrup all blended together and spoiled. There's the anger of unhappiness, which is the texture of polished chalcedony. There's the anger of helplessness, which is like sour milk to a babe. There's the anger of ignorance, which is the space between the stars. And the anger of creative genius, which is the grandest anger of them all and more than the sum of any two others. But I can't sell it to you because I'm always well out of it."

"That's not the kind I want," said Jasper Jordan. "I have money and I'm not offensive to look upon. I need something to boost me down the road a bit. To activate the navigational gyro in my spirit. To move me."

"Then you don't need anger; you need a psychiatrist," Sawbill replied evenly.

"I don't want to change the way I feel. I want to indulge in it, to glory in it. I didn't come for what I need. I came for what I want. What I want is anger. Good strong, biting, cleansing, wave-breaking, glass-shattering anger. The mate of hate. Seven-league-boot anger. Do you understand?" He was not quite pleading.

"Why, surely," said Sawbill, driving home another nail. "That's called righteous anger and I always keep plenty of that in stock. Come aboard."

Jasper Jordan followed Sawbill up a small boarding ladder and into the bowels of the old sloop. The pimbird, which might have been an emperor at one time—and then again, might not—looked down at them and whistled: *Ee-kwoo, ee-kwoo, ee-kwoo-hoo . . .*

Jasper Jordan seated himself in an undisciplined old chair in the spacious central cabin.

"You wait there," Sawbill said softly, "while I get what you want." He disappeared forward.

Jordan looked around. The decor was esoteric—indeed, eccentric. Most of the furnishings were made from natural woods. Some were dark-grained and highly polished, others as brown as raw bacon. For sheer color chromoplate had them beat hollow. For tactile beauty it was no contest.

The chair in which he sat was worlds removed from the late-model automatic fluxator in his office, the one that molded itself to every contour of his body. But somehow this collection of springs and stuffing flattered his backside quite well.

Sawbill returned. He sat down opposite Jordan and placed seven tiny capsules on the table between them. Each was clearly numbered. Jordan leaned forward.

"As you can see, there are seven pills," began Sawbill. "They are to be taken in sequence, an hour apart.

No closer than that, timewise. A thousand credits apiece. You have your card and meter with you?"

Jordan nodded. He reached into a pocket, brought out both. After making the necessary adjustments he handed the card to Sawbill.

"What happens after I've taken them all?"

"An hour after you've taken the seventh pill you'll have thirty-six t-standard hours of what you want. That I promise you." Sawbill registered the exchange of credit on his own battered cardmeter, handed the card back to Jordan. Then he sat back in his chair and took out a pipe. He began stuffing it with tobacco.

Jordan reset his card while Sawbill spoke. "If anyone should ask, you've never seen me before and you never will again." Jordan didn't look up. "You will have the anger to enforce the drive to do what it is you desire to do. Provided you don't run into someone with a stronger reserve of the natural stuff than what I've given you. Most unlikely that there is anyone on this planet who can resist the force those seven capsules are going to put in your head.

"You're a peaceable-seeming young fellow. Those are usually the types who seek me out."

"Mine is a case of a strong emotion seeking a stronger one," muttered Jordan. He pulled out a small quartz vial and carefully deposited the pills in it, one by one.

Sawbill leaned forward suddenly. He put a gnarled hand covered with gray fuzz on Jordan's slimmer, smoother one. He stared hard and searchingly into the other's eyes.

"You've no idea what you're getting into, feller me lad. Before you go I want to know what you intend these capsules for. I want to know why you want them. I want to know the details. I want the ramifications, the exigencies, the history you call up your desire from. I want all that before I let you go."

"Well," Jordan began uncertainly, "there is a woman—"

"Ah," said Sawbill, removing his hand and sitting back. "That will do."

The hull of the sloop had been repaired, sanded, and refinished to be as smooth as the waves it would slide over. Now it was receiving a new coat of fresh, resistant red polymer. Thalia Major had performed another couple of pirouettes on its axis. Thalia Minor had, too. But, of course, that didn't matter, because . . .

A tall young man arrived in the boatyard. He asked a few pointed questions and paid a few small bribes. He was very composed. Soon he was looking up at Sawbill. Sawbill was leaning over the back of the boat, painting the rudder. He used a brush, not a sprayer.

"Are you the one they call Sawbill, who sells emotions?" asked the tall young man composedly.

"Impossible," replied Sawbill sadly, pausing in his painting.

"I'm Terence Wu," said the tall young man. He was elegantly dressed in a black-and-white semiformal suit. He wore his straight black hair in an Iroquois cut—a wide bushy brush ran down the center of his skull. He had high cheekbones, a wide grin, and small black eyes. Judging by the ring on his left hand, a ring that had been cut from a single large sapphire and caught the light of the sun like a siren, he also had a great deal of money.

"I want to buy some anger," said the tall young man.

"What kind of anger?" Sawbill asked, returning to his painting. He caught a spot lower down that he had missed earlier.

"The kind of anger that lets you slash and cut without hesitation," said Terence Wu tightly. "The kind that makes other men look to their feet and cats sweat." The rich young man's hands were tightly clenched, nails impressing palms. He was most earnest. "The kind that the padres do not approve of. That kind of anger."

Sawbill indicated the ladder. "Then come aboard, feller me lad, come aboard."

Wu relaxed slightly and started for the ladder. "Then you have that kind of anger?" he asked.

"Why, surely," replied Sawbill, dipping the brush in a can of clear polymer debonder. "That's the anger of revenge and I always keep plenty of that in stock."

He took another look at the way the photon magnet on the man's finger disorganized the light of the fading sun. "It will cost you three times seven thousand credits, feller me lad."

"That's perfectly agreeable," said Wu evenly, stepping onto the deck.

Sawbill indicated the way down. "May I inquire why you should wish such anger?"

"Well," began Wu, hesitantly, "there's a woman—"

"Ah!" said Sawbill understandingly.

"—and she's been taken from me. I want her back."

"Of course," murmured Sawbill as he followed the young man down.

Forward, the pim-bird observed the ocean devouring the sun-ball and said, *Ee-kwoo, ee-kwoo, ee-kwoo-hoo* ...

He was stacking the last strands of new dylon rigging when a voice from below said, "Hello."

Sawbill looked over the railing. The too-young man stood below. Jordan's face was pale, haggard, worn. His suit, blue this time, was badly rumpled, as was his manner.

"Hello on board," he said rather shakily, evidently not seeing Sawbill.

"Evening," said Sawbill.

"Look—I know I promised not to see you again, but I've got to talk to you."

"Do you?" asked Sawbill, turning back to his waxing. He dipped a hand in the pot of wax and continued running the new line through his fingers. "But I don't have to talk to you."

"Dammit to hell!" came the whining yelp from the

ground. "You got me into this. You've got to help me. Please." The voice paused. "You've got to sell me another dose!"

"I don't have to sell you anything," Sawbill replied quietly. He stopped at a section of line that seemed a little frayed, gave it an extra coat of wax.

"I can make trouble for you——"

"So can a bumblebee——" Sawbill sighed, "if his coordinates in relation to the center of the universe do not coincide with mine. But come on board and I'll listen to you."

Jordan climbed on board. He was panting heavily. His visage was not a comforting thing to look upon. His face was dirty. He wiped absently at a particularly greasy spot under one eye. The gesture had the effect of redistributing the muck evenly across his cheek. He slumped into the pilot's seat behind the many-spoked wheel and groaned.

"I've had other things on my mind," he said.

"Were you satisfied with what you paid for?" Sawbill asked.

For a moment Jordan seemed to brighten. A combination of feelings, none of them holy, came into his eyes.

"Yes. It was everything you promised. But afterward—why couldn't you have given me a stronger dose, one for longer than thirty-six hours?"

"I gave you the maximum for a person of your type."

"How do you presume to know what 'type' I am?" Jordan asked belligerently.

Sawbill looked up from his waxing. "If I'd given you a stronger dose or told you to take the seven at slightly shorter intervals you would have been harmed —you might even have died."

"I don't believe you."

Sawbill shrugged and went on with his waxing. After several minutes Jordan pleaded, "What can I do?"

"Don't beg, don't cry, and don't whine. I could sell

you another kind of emotion that would cure those tendencies, too. But you would resist. So tell me what happened. Why do you find it necessary to acquire more anger than is good for a man at one time?"

"There's this girl—" began Jasper Jordan.

"That's the substance, the body, the core, the hub of the thing." said Sawbill. "Now supply me the tinsel, the sprinkles on top of the sweetcakes, the things that metamorphose your need into leeches."

"She's the most beautiful girl on Thalia Major."

"Not in the universe?"

"Don't mock me. I don't know the universe. I only know Thalia Major. And Minor, of course, but that doesn't matter. We were in love—"

"How long have you known her?"

"Three weeks," Jordan said defiantly. When Sawbill did not comment he continued. "Everything was fine. We were going to be married."

"Did she finally agree to marry you?"

"It went without saying. As I said—everything was fine until several days ago. Then I found out she was seeing another—man, I suppose I must call him. She didn't deny it. She admitted she was meeting this putrid, low . . . I couldn't understand why. But I couldn't convince her to break it off. He had hypnotized her. I'm a very mild, you might even say a tame, individual. I didn't have the force of personality to confront him. We're all very civilized here on Thalia Major."

"Yes," said Sawbill encouragingly.

"I just wanted to warn him off, to tell him to leave us alone. Not to confuse her anymore. So I came to see you. Everyone knows about you Emomen—even if you are hard to find."

"We like it that way."

"Well, the beginning went just as I had hoped—exactly as I had imagined it would. Better, even. I was a terror—although I don't remember the details very well, I'm afraid. I completely overpowered him spiritually and mentally. He couldn't take it. He vowed never to see her again. And he meant it. I could tell. I was irresistible. Then—yesterday—he confronted me in my office. We had a terrible row. He was a madman! I had never seen a human being behave so. I was reduced to—jelly. He was an elemental force. I tried to stand up to him but I couldn't. I found myself babbling apologies for ever having looked at Jo-ann. You can't imagine what it was like. I've never confronted anything like that before. Helpless. And he recorded the entire thing, the whole humiliating experience.

"And then, last night I tried to sneak over to see her. To try to rebuild myself in her eyes at least partially. Praying all the while, of course, that I wouldn't meet that giant, that godlike devil again. I saw them taking the lift up to her apartment—and went out and got drunk. Then it came to me to come back here. You've got to give me something stronger this time— something that will last. Something that will enable me to push him away once and for all."

Sawbill finished washing the wax from his hands. He sat back against the bulk of the cabin. He became absorbed in an inspection of the rear hatchway.

After a long while he asked bluntly, "Why should I become a participant in this? Perhaps he is the better man for her than you. Maybe matters are best left this way."

"It's his father's money that's blinded her! The family name is . . . well, no matter. But the father is one of the richest men in Barragash. I work hard— I'm well off, yes. But not in that class. I can compete with him and better him in everything except the matter of credit."

Sawbill was adamant. "I will sell you nothing stronger. I gave you your maximum dosage. And that's all you can have."

The too-young man was desperate. "Then at least sell me the same, the same seven again. You owe me that."

Sawbill grunted and wiped his hands on his pants. "It will cost you double this time."

"Yes, yes, anything—" He was like an eager puppy. "I promise—if this doesn't do it I will give her up to him. I'll move to another city. Perhaps to another planet. I might even go to Thalia Minor. Who knows? But in any case I will not trouble you again."

On a high mast the pim-bird was sobbing for the moon.

Sails furled, the little sloop sat on the water. Sawbill had the mainsail ready and was preparing the spinnaker when the peaceforcers came for him.

The man on the dock was short and plump. He had a benignly optimistic face and scraggly brown hair that was fighting a rearguard action.

A green aircar waited at the far end of the dock. It had the oak tree symbol of the peaceforcer emblazoned on its side. Two uniformed men stood against it, chatting.

"Pretty little ship," said the man on the dock.

"Yes, it is," said Sawbill. "Used not to be. Is now." He was wrestling with the sail locker. The pim-bird fidgeted and bobbed on his shoulder. It moved to the top of his head, then dropped down to the shoulder again, eying the short man.

"I'd like you to come with me for a bit, Sawbill. I'm Inspector Herrera."

"Nice for you, I guess."

"Usually it is, but not today."

"I was just about to go out for a month or so. I'm trying to get away from people and civilization for a while. A vacation—you understand?"

Herrera nodded. "I do. Really, I do." He seemed honestly sympathetic. "But I'd still like you to come with me."

"If I decline?" Sawbill asked, straightening. "No doubt those gentlemen by your car will hurry down here with things short, metallic, and unesthetic. To persuade me?"

Herrera sighed. "No, Sawbill, they will not. You've probably heard before that we are very civilized, here on Thalia Major. One of those men is a driver—and all he is going to do is drive. The other is a secretary."

"And all he will do is sec?"

"Please don't make light of this. It's difficult enough for me as it is. I cannot compel you."

"Meaning I'm not under arrest, right?"

"As you are well aware I have no grounds for an arrest. Wish I did. But I suspect you will come with me —out of curiosity if for no other reason. I will not delay you long—a moment or two out of your vacation is all I request."

Sawbill hesitated. Then he tied down the sails and climbed down to the dock. He and Herrera started toward the aircar.

"Where are you going to go, Sawbill?"

"The Marragas Islands, then south to the Anacapa atolls. I'd like to put in there for a bit. I understand most of the reefs around there are still uninhabited and rarely visited. Good fishing, too."

"So I hear," said Herrera. "Most folk around here go north for their vacations. To Three and Ark and Jumbles—pleasure towns. Where all their surprises can be arranged for them. All the entertainment galactic ingenuity can provide. And build."

There was a lot of blood in the room, which was done in blue and gold. The red blood contrasted strangely. The electric curtains were drawn back, admitting the sun. They were for effect only, since the glass was fully polarized. The sunlight gave added obscenity to the stains.

What was left of the body of the girl was sprawled across the back of the couch, facing the open window. She had been torn apart. Her insides were strewn across half the room. Her face, Sawbill could see, probably had once been pretty, possibly even beautiful.

Terence Wu was also in the room. All over it. A bit here, a fragment there. Sawbill could make out an arm protruding from under the couch. Nothing was attached to the arm. A leg dangled from the mantel over the quaint, wood-burning fireplace.

The corpse of Jasper Jordan was in the bathroom, slumped over the rim of the sunken oval tub.

Herrera was watching Sawbill closely.

"According to what we've been able to piece together with the help of the building computer, Jordan broke in some time around three in the morning. Probably he just wanted to talk to the girl. For some reason she had forgotten to set her doorseal. When he came in he found them on the rug. There, in front of the fireplace." Herrera pointed. "He didn't even try to talk to them, is my guess. Could be he'd taken something. Blood analysis and tissue evaluation show the presence of complex hormones in his body. Puzzled the lab boys for quite a while. They're not used to seeing that kind of stuff."

Herrera watched Sawbill steadily.

"A fast check on Jordan's credit count revealed the recent transfer of the rather surprising sum of twenty-one thousand credits to one individual. You."

"This whole procedure is quite illegal," injected Sawbill mildly.

"Oh, to be sure, to be sure," said Herrera. "Our information cannot be used in court—and obviously is not going to be."

"I have tapes of the transaction, too."

"I'm sure you do," replied Herrera. "And I've no doubt it was all done with the greatest respect for the letter of the law."

"Quite."

"I'm going to have to compose some sort of explanation for the faxpax and for relatives. These people were no bums. Three nominally respected citizens have died here. Just for my own information and to satisfy my morbid curiosity, what did you sell him?"

"Anger."

"I see. Anger." Herrera looked around and took in the wholesale carnage. "A little anger did all this?"

"Ordinarily it would not. You must believe that."

"Oh, sure. Yeah."

Sawbill shrugged. "I agree with you. When Jordan walked in on Wu and the girl I don't think he'd taken a thing. Knowing the sort he was I expected him to try reason after what I'd told him."

"I'll bet you did."

"I mean that! Otherwise I wouldn't have sold to him. Neither man was inherently vicious. I warned Jordan enough against taking the seven. But when he came in and found them making love he obviously went berserk. The seven integrals of the star should be taken an hour apart. That's leaving a quarter-hour safety limit, which I never mention. A half-hour is the real danger point. He must have downed them all at once. The result is unimaginable to most men. Overwhelming. Few minds could handle such an abrupt release. He couldn't. But I was correct about his innate mental control and discipline."

Herrera gestured angrily around them. "You call this control?"

"Yes! He had enough sense left to kill himself. He did kill himself?"

"We took the knife back to the lab," admitted Herrera.

"What he was undergoing was to normal anger as a nova is to a normal sun. A less controlled individual would have stumbled from the room and gone to kill a hundred people in an orgy of release."

"I don't understand how any drug can boost an emotion like that," murmured Herrera, shaking his head.

"It doesn't 'boost' the emotion—or add to it or multiply it," Sawbill said. "That's the common mistake everyone makes. They don't consider the other—those who don't want to believe it. The drug removes the natural safeguards a man's mind has built up to protect and regulate his natural self. It breaks the seal holding air in the tank, doesn't pump more air into it. It removes a million years of evolutionary barriers man has carefully erected to hold back the blackness that lives inside him. Taken properly it does so in the smallest way. It isn't dangerous, just effectively awesome. Few men can resist the tiny blot of animal self so set free.

"But when all the safeguards are removed, like this . . ."

"I think I see," whispered Herrera.

"May I leave now?"

"What? Oh, yes, you can go. Get out of my sight." Sawbill paused at the door.

"What about the girl?"

"How do you mean? Oh, I understand. What you might expect. She was playing one off against the other. Jordan was a little more naive than Wu, I suspect. I hope she enjoyed it." Herrera paused. Then: "I checked you with Central and Customs, hoping I could get you on illegal entry. No such luck. I see you got your doctorate in endocrinology from the University of Belem. That's on Terra, isn't it?"

Sawbill nodded. He was halfway out of the room.

"One other thing," Herrera said hurriedly. "I've never met one of you before. Tell me, is it true what they say about you Emomen?"

"What do they say about us Emomen?"

"That you haven't any true emotions of your own? That you're so tied up in playing God that you've lost your own capacity to feel? That your humanity's atrophied?"

"Oh, there's no doubt about it," said Sawbill. He closed the door quietly behind him.

Space Opera

Sometimes a science-fiction story is the coming together of seemingly diverse elements. You may have one idea which in itself is insufficient on which to hang a story. And another, seemingly unrelated idea.

Unrelated? Listen, in science fiction, *everything* relates. Including a preoccupation with the less intellectual aspects of current daytime entertainment, the arrogance of humanity, and the relaxed indifference of that rare personality who just wants to get on with the job at hand.

Put them all together and you've got a . . .

—————————————————————————————————————

The biggest drawback in the gleaming functional desk, Commander Cleve reflected, was its damnable imperviousness. Since it was composed of diamondlike silicone plastic, his nails could only scrape futilely across the smooth surface, and at the moment, he was in the mood to mark something.

On the other side of the desk, Lieutenant Vander-

meer shifted slightly in his seat. He recognized the
commander's mood and was uncomfortably aware of
the convenient target he made for any localized may-
hem the commander might choose to commit.

Cleve stopped trying to make an impression on the
desk and looked up.

"I won't let that pipsqueak do it. I refuse!"

"Yes sir," said Vandermeer. Vandermeer was a fine
lieutenant. He always said just the right thing.

"Exceptional stupidity requires foresight, planning,
and careful preparation to be properly effective. But
this fellow Himpel . . . Hurmal . . ."

"Hinkel, sir."

"Yes, this Hinkel's talent for improvising really remarkable idiocy on the spur of the moment is astonishing. And I fear the Council may support it! Perhaps
I shall simply join his sphere of insanity. It may be the
only solution."

"Yes sir."

"What?"

"I . . . I mean, no sir."

Cleve sighed and slumped in his genuine starfox,
red and silver hand-rubbed mahogany swivel chair.
"It's not an *unreasonable* request, is it, Lieutenant?
After all, this is the third expedition to Titan. It's not
as if anything really *newsworthy* were happening.
We're only here to set up a small life-support station for the next three expeditions. And for the
miners. A few simple solidosemis, habitats, an oxy-
conversion plant . . . stuff like that. Why bring along
a big newscast crew with a caster as big as Hurkel?"

"Hinkel, sir. As I understand it, the ISA and Ad-
miral Howard thought it would give us some excellent
publicity, sir. What with the current furor over funding
and all, a few dramatic location shots of exotic Titan
and Saturn, added to Hinkel's prestige, should produce
ratings that—"

"Ratings!" Cleve roared, purpling. "I'm deathly sick
of hearing about Hickey's goddamn, God-awful, got-
verstunken, gder . . . gef . . . !"

"Easy, sir. You know what Dr. Galeth said about your blood pressure, particularly in a low-grav environment."

"Yes, Lieutenant, yes, yes. It's just that I cannot, I purely cannot, permit this man to interfere in any way with the negotiations. The Murrin are an utterly unfamiliar quantity. They could react in an infinitude of ways to anything we say, do, hint at, or even the way we walk. I cannot risk jeopardizing man's first meeting with an intelligent alien race for the sake of . . . of *ratings*." The last word was given the accent usually reserved for ultimate loathsomeness—most often senators who voted against ISA funding and apricots, to which the commander was violently allergic.

Bronislaw Hinkel chose that moment to present himself.

Vandermeer intercepted the diminutive telecaster at the door, blocking him from the commander's view.

"Ah, good morning, Peter! Is the commander busy?"

"Actually, sir, regulation four-two-six-el-ay governing watches between oh-nine-hundred and—"

"Oh, let him in, Lieutenant! Could anyone mistake that dulcet warbling, the pride of post-quickies, the cereal packed in total vacuum, and Channel Three?"

"Thank you, Emmett." Hinkel skipped adroitly past the lieutenant, who closed the door and wished for an attack of partial deafness.

Cleve, however, appeared determined to remain civil. Perhaps, the lieutenant thought hopefully, the commander was rationing his daily quota of bile.

Bronislaw Hinkel was a familiar figure to nearly a billion telecast addicts. An impressive figure who represented votes. Even now, off the air, every strand of his famous wavy gray hair knew its proper place. The short, brush mustache was trimmed and protruded just the correct distance above the strong lips. The dark brown eyes under the heavy salt-and-pepper brows imparted at once sincerity, knowledge, and comfort.

"Well, what can I do for you this time, Mr. Hinkel?" Cleve said pleasantly.

"As long as you brought the subject up, Emmett, there really are one or two things about the upcoming meeting that—"

Cleve interrupted, still calm. "Is there something wrong with the plans for the upcoming *meeting*, Mr. Hinkel?"

"Nothing that can't be corrected easily enough," said Hinkel, cheerfully.

"How reassuring."

"Yes. Now Bess—that's my chief camerawoman, you know—"

"No, I didn't know."

"Uh. Well anyway, one thing she simply insists on is that we locate at least one crew between the *Reykjavik* and the alien. It's necessary in order for us to be able to properly document the full drama of your departure from the ship, and all. Ideally, of course, we'd need another crew similarly placed with respect to the alien ship. I don't suppose you'd okay that?" He ended on a hopeful note.

"No, I'm afraid . . ."

"Well, don't let it trouble you, Commander! I have instructed my staff not to get underfoot in any way— barring what needs to be done to perform required journalistic activity, of course."

"That's certainly a considerable relief to me, Mr. Hinkel. It means that you'll react favorably, quietly, when I inform you that I cannot permit a crew to be stationed between the *Reykjavik* and the alien vessel. No . . ." Cleve raised a hand to still the incipient protest, ". . . allow me to explain.

"If your crew assumes any position, at a respectable distance, between here and the Murrin ship, it could conceivably come into the line of fire from the *Reykjavik*'s weaponry."

"The same situation your greeting party will be in, Commander."

"Quite true. Those gentlemen, however, will be present because they are essential to the success of the operation." Cleve left the obvious correlation unsaid.

"Should you assume a position anywhere near the *Reykjavik,* any emergency maneuvering the ship would be impelled to perform would incinerate your crew instantly! As for newsmen's risks, I am compelled to remind you that you are along on this mission on sufferance. Your safety and well-being are solely my responsibility."

"Bull! First, I'm along because my reputation warrants it and Channel Three's worldwide facilities wangled it. And as to *newsmen's risks,* as you so quaintly put it, my crews and I have indeed faced far greater risks than this!"

"Nevertheless, I—"

"Okay, okay! Spare me the officialese. I'll have only two crews, both set up at a good distance from the *Reykjavik.* They'll manage with telephotos."

Hinkel reached into the leather case on his lap and pulled out a thick stack of brightly colored papers. "Now. Win Hunter, my chief writer, has come up with what I think are some really socko suggestions for the actual ceremony of contact. You know, *greeting* the mysterious aliens, and all. If you'd care to peruse them, I'm sure . . ."

Cleve's chair was displaying marked evidence of a highly localized seismic disturbance. Vandermeer moved quickly forward.

"Um . . . Commander, I was thinking . . ."

"Relax, Lieutenant. I'm quite . . . quite all right," Cleve said, reaching out and gracefully accepting the proffered suggestions.

"One other thing, Emmett," Hinkel said. "When we film the actual moment of contact . . ."

The Commander sighed. He knew this would come up. "Sir, I fear that once the Murrin commander and his party leave their ship, I cannot permit additional filming to take place."

It was Hinkel's turn to sit speechless.

"Your equipment, both the portables and that ghastly heavy big job, bear an unfortunate likeness to ray projectors. Which, in a sense, they are. The Murrin are no doubt as unfamiliar with our technology as we are with theirs. Witness that insane assemblage of angles out on the plain. Yet it seems to carry them from star to star.

"Our exchange of language has been hampered by the lack of experience and trained people on our side. However, it is now sufficient to permit several things. One of these is this first official meeting, a big deal with the Murrin. Among the details they suggested be implemented was the obvious one of neither group carrying or presenting weapons."

"If that's the case," said Hinkel slyly, "then how do you explain your objection to our shooting angles by complaining that they'd interfere with your 'line of fire'?"

"As stated, neither group will display weaponry. At no time will the *Reykjavik*'s lasers be in evidence. I'd bet that the Murrin ship is far better armed. The important thing is that no portable weapons be visible. For psychological and practical reasons."

"Granting all your reasoning, which I do not, isn't the import of this moment, the need to have everyone on earth a part of it, enough to outweigh a few ethereal maybes on your part?"

"There are other reasons."

"Name *one!*" Hinkel snapped.

Cleve allowed his voice a bit more customary bark, and Vandermeer winced. "All right! Let's suppose— just suppose—that I permit you to telecast the whole business, from start to whatever finish, from close-in? We know little of Murrin technology. We know even less of their psychology and sociology, of what they might regard as proper and what they might interpret as offensive. Might they not be curious as to your functioning on the periphery of the encounter?

"Disregarding, for the moment, an infinitude of possibilities of alien reactions ranging from spirit-stealing, to unimaginable phobias, let's say that they perceive exactly what you and your crew are doing."

"If they're half as clever as you seem to think they are, they ought to," said Hinkel.

"So," said Cleve, leaning back and in his chair, "consider this. Telecasting or otherwise recording or broadcasting such a meeting could violate any number of formal taboos, rules of protocol, ambassadorial dignity. Need I go on? It's happened on Earth, before. Why couldn't it happen here, worse?"

"You mean," said Hinkel, "our broadcasting the meeting might insult them somehow?"

"I don't know, Hinkel. I don't know. Look, for the last time, please try to understand my position—*our* position." Vandermeer noticed that long grooves had appeared in the soft wood of the pencil the commander was holding.

"This is the first meeting between mankind and another intelligent race. From what my improvised linguist and philologist and part-time amateur xenologist tell me, that's not the case with the Murrin. Apparently they have encountered at least two other space-going races prior to finding us. You see? They have an established procedure for this! We don't. We'll be judged not only according to how we act, but how we act in comparison to at least two other intelligent species. We haven't the same basis for establishing common ground that they have. If we only had one thing completely in common, everything else could proceed in logical sequence. But we don't. So we must take care to do the right thing at every second, until that first commonality is established. The most crucial moment in the human race's history, sir!"

"Precisely why it must be simulcast," said Hinkel.

"Precisely why I cannot permit the risk of turning this into a circus!"

Hinkel was honestly shocked.

"*Circus!* Do you have the infernal gall to sit there and call the 25th Hour—the highest-rated newscast for five consecutive years, winner of over a hundred prizes for journalistic excellence—a *circus*?"

"Goddamn it! I just *said* it, didn't I? Yes, and with a special vote for exceptional cretinism to the lead elephant!"

Hinkel rose with great dignity. "I see." His voice approached a verbal equivalent of zero Kelvin. "Thank you, Commander, for making your feelings in this matter perfectly clear. Good day."

He left.

Cleve snapped the abused pencil in two and threw the halves at the ceiling. "Well, that tears it!" he said.

"I could instruct engineering not to allow his people transfer facilities for Earthside beaming, sir," offered Vandermeer hopefully.

Cleve rubbed both eyes, tiredly. "No, no . . . let's not be so overt, Lieutenant. Let him contact his influential friends. If the idiots, dirtside, think he should be allowed to cover this meeting, they deserve whatever results result. I pray the Murrin react favorably. No, better they don't react at all! Now go away. Oh, here . . ." He handed Vandermeer the script Hinkel had given him. "I can do one thing. Find a Disposall, Lieutenant, and file this. Discreetly, of course."

"Yes, sir."

The Murrin, as the scrambled videocasts revealed, were a large, ursoid race, clearly mammalian. They resembled the terran brown bear in a fortunate number of respects. Fortunate, because it alleviated Hinkel's first fear. Namely, that the extrasolar visitors would turn out to be ten-foot-wide spiders with slavering fangs and green eyes. Fuzzy aliens inspired little xenophobia.

The Murrin had been on the homeward leg of a normal exploring trip. They'd been examining the planets of the sol system one by one. While circumnavigating Saturn, they'd passed close to Titan while the *Reykjavik* was passing information toward Mars station. They had presented nothing but a friendly continence since the initial contact.

Still, Cleve reflected, there was no mistaking the cautious, defensive approach the aliens had used, coming in low over the horizon and with little warning. A carefully developed military tactic, using mountains as cover. While they might be all for exchanging dirty stories over a beer, they weren't quite ready to hail the terrans as long-lost lodge brothers.

Perhaps they were just naturally cautious. On the other hand, it was conceivable that someone had taken a potshot at one of them before. In any case, they'd dropped in on the *Rey* before anyone could have loaded even a blowgun.

Which was just as well.

So the two ships squatted across the narrow valley from each other while the amateur linguists on the *Reykjavik* and the professional ones on the alien ship tried to talk turkey with the help of several miles of electronic circuitry.

Being prepared for the chance of happening onto another intelligent race, the Murrin acquired basic English a good deal faster than the terrans could pick up guttural Myll. The aliens had given every indication of being highly pleased at discovering another intelligent species (if a bit blasé about the whole thing). Particularly in such an otherwise unpromising system, thought Cleve as he adjusted his exoskin.

Of course, outward manifestations of friendliness were exhibited by numerous terran carnivores—prior to making the kill. The Murrin might play buddy-buddy, but they weren't foolhardy, either. Besides their defensive approach, the lethal-looking objects which projected toward the *Rey* from the alien's midship line were excellent proof of that. The *Rey*'s single big industrial laser looked puny by comparison.

The human party was assembled in the now airless lock, ready for surface EVA. They were composed of a select group of scientists, officers, and engineers. For purposes of negotiation, Cleve had been granted what amounted to emergency ambassadorial status by the Council.

There were three other members in the party. One interpreter, one chaplain (against Cleve's wishes), and one volunteer ensign whose sole assignment was to slam both hands together should the Murrin exhibit obvious signs of irrational bellicosity. Said action would trip several circuits, which would speed both groups rapidly on to the next plane of existence.

As expected, Hinkel's broadcast clearance had come through, along with a gruff statement from Admiralty which stopped just syllables short of being a reprimand.

The lieutenant at Cleve's side—not Vandermeer, who had been left in command of the ship—recited for the last time the short list of names. Subdued replies of "Here!" answered each. When that was completed, everything was completed. Cleve tried to think of something appropriate to say, failed, and led the men down the ramp to the surface.

A few might have wished for trumpets and dancing girls, but the natural setting was quite inspiring enough.

Sharp hills rose on either side of the narrow vale. At the far end of the valley, the awesome bulk of Saturn was just rising. The acute angle at which they viewed the rings showed gold, speckled with black gaps. The planet itself was all rose and swirling butter clouds.

In the Saturnlight, the frozen atmosphere of Titan glittered ice-blue. Cleve dimmed his visor a grade. Millions of miles from home was no place to go snowblind. Here and there, lichens—of as yet unclassified varieties—and a few incredibly tough low scrubs poked up through the powdered crystals.

Language difficulties and the lack of proper structures simplified the meeting arrangements. Whenever they felt ready (letting us work up to it, Cleve thought), the terrans were merely to leave their ship and proceed en masse to a point halfway between ships. There they would be met by a party from the alien craft.

Sooner than anyone expected, the halfway point was reached. For more than several minutes, nothing happened. For once, no one stared at the shining glory of Saturn. All eyes were fixed on the alien craft. Curious, Cleve switched over to the frequency Hinkel was using for his broadcast. He hurriedly switched it off. The man's style was definitely hypnotic. It was hard not to relax and pretend that he was an observer of what was about to happen, and not a prime mover.

The Murrin ship was bright yellow, twice as long as the *Reykjavik*, and bulked at least five times the mass. In similar tense situations, Cleve would have been moved to crack a joke, hoping to ease the tension. Now, he just swallowed. He doubted Columbus had joked, nor had Armstrong, nor Mallard.

Fear was not a factor. He was too consumed with curiosity. What would it actually be like to meet something that had matured under another sun? And intelligent, besides. What would be his reaction those first few seconds? Disgust? Terror? Worship? And what would provide that first, all-important commonality?

A port opened in the side of the alien ship. A single figure detached itself from the dark opening and moved rapidly toward them at a waddling gait.

Cleve analyzed it and prayed that no one would be insane enough to laugh at the comical method of locomotion. Those same waddling feet might contain long, needle-sharp claws especially designed for chastising disrespectful inferiors. He had a sudden, horrible thought that the Murrin might be telepathic, but dismissed it almost as quickly. They'd given no indication of it, and, if they were, there was absolutely nothing that could be done about it.

Soon the alien was standing in front of him. He could have reached out and touched the maroon metal suit. Surprisingly, the creature was nearly a foot shorter than Cleve's six-two, but it was built far stockier. From inside a transparent plastic or glass helmet, two jet-black eyes stared up at him.

No time like the present, he thought, and held out both hands palm up. The psychologists had told him this ought to express trust, friendship, and a hearty welcome. Cleve hoped so.

The alien reacted by removing a roll of paper-thin metal from a jacket pouch and slapping it in Cleve's outstretched right hand. It spoke rapidly over the preset wave-length.

"I am Crift, Apprentice-to-Talker." The commander noticed that Hinkel and one of his camera crews were slowly edging closer from the left. He silently damned Hinkel, the inventor of the camera, the film, the lens, and all channels two through sixty-eight.

The alien continued: "Captain Othine extends his regrets that he cannot join you for as yet," the alien hesitated for a moment, then continued: "for approximate timeparts yours, two, yes two. Crew and captain are absorbed entirely whole in crucial broadcast from home planet now by way of interstellar relay."

The ursoid then indicated the rolled metal, which Cleve had gripped unconsciously.

"The Dryah. Official greeting, us-to-you, it is. Extends friendship, hello, et ceteras. Also explanation in depth for awkward delay. Also apologies, in depth, appended. Okay? Must excuse I now, please, thank you, forgive."

The creature turned abruptly and headed at high speed back toward his ship.

They stared dumbly after the departed alien until the vast craft swallowed the single dark opening in its side. One of the engineers, who had completely forgotten his assignment (which was to observe the details of the alien's suit), said, "Well!" He repeated it several times.

That was the signal for a mild explosion of intersuit communication, mostly inane. Cleve examined the roll of metal, found its function anything but esoteric. It was a simple scroll, in clean English block lettering. He read.

"Excuse me . . . make way, please . . . pardon us, there . . ."

Leading two sound men, a gaffer, and the camera, Hinkel was making his way toward Cleve. Now that the actual contact was completed the telecaster apparently felt perfectly at ease cutting in on the heretofore forbidden frequency.

He panted breathlessly, and needlessly, since his suit's self-regulating respiratory apparatus would not permit him to get out of breath. It sounded quite dramatic.

Halting in front of Cleve, he made an indecipherable gesture, in place of having a microphone to wave under the commander's helmet.

"Commander Zachary S. Cleve, we are now both on intersystem hookup. Three billion humans are awaiting your first words at this historic moment. The presidents of all nations as well as the entire membership of the Council are awaiting the first results of mankind's initial face-to-face meeting with another intelligent race!"

Cleve finished the scroll and rolled it up. He looked absently at Hinkel. Then, very much to the surprise of the ship's officers in the party, he grinned a disarmingly boyish grin.

"Ladies and gentlemen," he began. "As far as it has gone, the first contact with the race that call themselves the Murrin has been successful. They express their hopes for long-term friendly association between species to our mutual benefit. Details will be explained in a second meeting which will take place in about two hours. In addition, a common basis for understanding has been transmitted."

He started to turn toward the *Rey.*

"Commander," said Hinkel. "We all saw that the Murrin sent only a single representative to meet your party. Is this their accepted procedure?"

"Why no, it is not," replied Cleve, his grin widening. "There appear to have been extenuating circumstances."

"Is that what the ship's commander said?" pressed Hinkel.

"Sort of, and it wasn't the ship's commander. It was an interpreter. An apprentice interpreter." The grin was charming.

Hinkel feigned surprise, then concern.

"That seems rather odd, Commander Cleve. Did they—it—give a reason for proceeding in such a manner?"

"Matter of fact, they did. One which you in particular, Mr. Hinkel, ought to understand and sympathize with. It seems they could not spare the time to meet with us just now because the entire crew is absorbed in taking in a broadcast from their home planet."

"Incredible! Think of it, ladies and gentlemen! A beamcast across light-years! Something important enough to draw them into postponing this delicate moment between species; important enough to be boosted at heaven knows what cost across trillions of miles of naked vacuum! Commander, did the alien reveal the nature of this broadcast to you? And if so, are you at libery to repeat it?"

"I don't see why they'd mind," said Cleve. He was watching Hinkel, not the three billion pairs of eyes the camera represented.

"As near as I can make out, the commander of the alien vessel, his entire complement, the contact team, everyone, are deeply immersed in the two thousand four hundred and twenty-sixth episode, segment, or quadrant of something entitled 'At Nest With the Vorxes.'

"It would appear, ladies and gentlemen, that the human race has been temporarily pre-empted." And he turned and walked back to the ship.

The Empire of T'ang Lang

When I heard Steve Goldin was putting together an anthology of stories which would deal with only the alien's point of view, I tried to think of the most alien being imaginable. I was sidetracked immediately by the alien universe thriving in my backyard.

In your backyard, too, if you ever bother to look.

For my central character, I chose the most obviously self-confident, independent, handsome, intelligent-looking inhabitant of that pocket universe. If you've ever met T'ang Lang, or any of his cousins, you'll know immediately who I mean.

If not, you're not looking over your shoulder hard enough.

It was not the sun that woke T'ang Lang. Concealed as he had been for the night, the sun would be well into the heavens before he rose. It was the growing warmth of the air, passing maternally across his body, the heat in the soil, the pitch-change in the world. In a hundred ways, he smelled Day.

Which was as well. Sunrise was not the best time to move a-hunting. The night-men were long asleep, the day-folk not yet stirring.

In truth the sun had been skyward for some time. Nearby, two of the city-builders were inspecting the shell of a small armored Crawler. The Crawler had given out recently. Probably it had failed to return to its resting place in time and was caught by the night. Not fragile, it still had not coped with the extreme change in temperature by daybreak, young as it appeared to be.

It would have been a pretty prize for the city-dwellers. But they saw T'ang Lang awake. They were not cowards, no: not the city-builders. But they were wise. They turned and ran, leaving the ruined Crawler for whoever might chance on it. Wise ones took no chances with T'ang Lang. He was not famed for his pleasant humor.

He, of course, had no interest in the dead thing. A being of his temperament disdained such carrion. He would kill for himself.

It was true that the city-dwellers thrived—in their own fashion. Their superefficient towns and cities exploited the possibilities of the environment better than anyone. But it seemed a pitiable way to live. All city-builders were enslaved by their own system, their precious regimen. T'ang Lang had never tried one of their well-fortified centers. He could do so if he wished, of course. But such was not the way of his folk, as it was not their way to build cities.

He yawned, if such it could be described. Jerkily, he climbed to his feet. It had been rather a wet night. He could *erma* the dampness in his joints. Carefully he washed his face, cleaned his eyes, then preened himself, making sure his sensors were clear of grime and dirt. As befitted his talents, T'ang Lang was a fastidious killer.

He did this without bothering to glance behind, unconcerned. T'ang Lang did not feel much need to guard his rear. There were none in his realm who would try him unless terribly, terribly desperate. Only the Great Sky People troubled him. They could drop down almost silently, without warning. An unsporting way to fight. But most of the sky-folk he feared not at all.

The Rite of Clean Knives followed. Each stiletto had to be kept honed and spotless. It was important to make a clean penetration the first time. T'ang Lang took great pride in his skill. True, even he missed now and then. But not often. And when he struck home, his victim always died. He rinsed his mouth and cleared some mud from his feet. It *had* been a damp night.

He stretched, and looked around. His magnificent senses could *erma* movement and life all about. It was a fertile, green world. The vibrations in the earth beneath his feet, the odors trundling past on the humid breeze—he could read them all. The sun was getting higher, the air hotter, he hungrier. There was little wind. A good day for hunting.

Should he stay and wait for clumsy grounddwellers? It was not a particularly good place. And the city-folk would rarely approach him. What to do?

Well, it was a lovely day to bask in the sun. Why not combine both? And there was always more challenge to hunting the sky-folk.

There were several great light-eaters about, in addition to the one whose body he'd borrowed for shelter. On a whim, he sauntered casually over to the next one, testing the footing around its somnolent body. The night's dew had left it chill and moist here. But T'ang Lang, an expert and experienced climber, would have no trouble. He began to wend his way upward.

This particular light-eater rose about a hundred times T'ang Lang's height. But he was not subject to vertigo. Heights held no more fear for him than his neighbors. He had other reasons for not climbing to

the very top. The platform there was usually un-
stable. So while it afforded a better view of his lands,
the increased wind and smaller blind made prey
harder to come by, strikes more difficult.

He rose slowly, patiently, without the hurry that
afflicted most climbers. Others who shared the light-
eater's body gave him plenty of room.

About twenty body-lengths up, he passed a Retiarius. The gladiator had snuggled himself comfortably
across the way. He waved to T'ang Lang as the other
passed. T'ang favored the creature with a long stare,
putting only token power into it. He was clever with
his net, was the Retiarius. But it was not intended for
the likes of T'ang Lang and the Retiarius knew it.
Even despite it, T'ang could still kill the gladiator and
shred his precious net.

T'ang moved higher. For a moment, a plump tube-
man crossed his path. But the clumsy being was moving rapidly in the opposite direction. He was on a far
platform with too much open space between them.
Perhaps it sensed T'ang Lang's presence. Perhaps not.
T'ang stared hard at it, opening his mind and focusing
the strange power behind his mesmeric eyes. But the
tube-man was out of range and knew it.

It turned once, to glance back at where T'ang
fumed impotently on his temporary platform. The ultimate insult.

For a moment, maybe, T'ang Lang was angry.
Then he sighed. Let the tube-man have his one moment of triumph. If ever he came within range of the
smallest and lightest of T'ang's weapons, he would die
faster than he would be born.

It was not long thereafter that T'ang located what
he wanted. An open platform, with the sun to one
side, well-screened from above but open below and in
front. A cluster of foodstuffs rested just ahead, on a
slightly lower level. They would serve as excellent
bait, attracting fliers and airborne city-folk.

Perhaps a young one would drift by, propulsors

humming, straining with the awkward unit to stay no-ground. Close by.

T'ang Lang settled himself, making an elaborate ritual out of it. Once set, he would not move again until it was time to kill. He tested the footing of the platform, found it pleasantly firm. T'ang was old and knowledgeable. This would be a good place. He carefully spread out and arranged his weapons, ready for instant use. Then he assumed the *Ben-na,* the position of contemplation. For T'ang was also something of a philosopher and had no intention of wasting away his waiting time.

It had been claimed by others, probably even the city-folk, that if T'ang's people had ever decided to pool the wisdom they'd accumulated over the millennia, they could form the most destructive society their world had ever known.

But there was a spark in T'ang Lang, an unquenchable streak of individualism that precluded any such cooperation. Fraternizing was discouraged. Besides, were they not rulers individually? How much better than to submit to a central authority, as the city-builders had done! T'ang's people knew they were superior. And each considered himself superior to his brother.

A small base on which to try and raise a social order.

T'ang found much of interest and pleasure in the harmony of the world. The sun rained down steadily, wombishly warmthful. An occasional breeze trekked across his platform. Across the great Green Plain that was the most dominant physical feature of his world, other light-eaters were busy at their work.

Placid and content in their stolid existence, they were rulers in their own way. But they could be killed. T'ang had yet to meet anyone who could not. Probably even the sun could be killed, but it was even further away than the end of the Green Plain. The opinion was held by some that the light-eaters were the stupidest of all living creatures. Another school thought them the most intelligent. Assuredly they were dedicated pacifists. The light-eaters themselves did not contest these arguments either way.

Possibly this in itself was a sign of that very disputed intelligence.

T'ang Lang wondered, and stared.

One of the lancers flashed by. The lancer-folk owned the finest propulsive systems on T'ang's world. Superbly engineered, they could move at tremendous speed across the sky. Their equally amazing detection systems could spot prey many thousands of body-lengths away. They were capable of twisting, diving attacks few could avoid.

Once, their ancestors had been lords of the planet. Time had changed things and they had slipped back. But they were still a formidable factor in T'ang's world. Despite their speed and ability, though, T'ang would make short work of one if it darted too close.

The sky-man knew it. After a sharp glare at T'ang, he gunned his propulsors and shot off in search of prey of his own.

Yes, a good day to be alive and emperor.

There were many of the sky-folk about, cavorting in the downy-warm air. None flew near T'ang Lang. T'ang was not anxious. He'd fed well the previous day. For the nonce he was mildly satisfied. High karma.

The great light-eater, the Bodikiddartha, rose many thousands of body-lengths above T'ang's present platform. Soaring toward the sun, it stood quietly on the other side of the Green Plain, breathing. Someday T'ang would cross that plain and climb the great bulk. If only to see the world on the other side.

Perhaps—a slip of motion caught his eyes. So intent had he been on the panorama in front of him, he had failed to notice the approach of a *cyuma,* a castle-man, to the cluster of foodstuffs.

It hadn't spotted T'ang.

With infinite slowness, slower than the planet aged, he shifted his head to gain a better view. The torpid creature seemed concerned only with the foodstuffs.

The castle-men were glamorous and daring, skilled weaponeers with their deadly rapiers. They had speed and agility to support their arrogance. Some believed themselves kings of the world.

And T'ang Lang? They found it convenient to avoid him.

It was an adolescent castle-man. He was edging uncaringly about the foodstuffs. Preparing to gorge himself, no doubt. Who would dare attack one of the castle-folk?

T'ang leaned gently forward. He had gone into killing mode. Now nothing in the universe could distract him until he struck. The castle-man grew until it swallowed the world, became the world. And it was going to die.

Knives at the ready, always ready. Superbly crafted and designed, they could penetrate with such speed and force that sometimes a victim would expire of shock.

The castle-man was stupid. His inferior genes would not be saved for transfer to others of his kind. No one would grieve for him.

T'ang Lang struck.

The castle-man shrieked once as he was hit. T'ang struck with such power that several blades pierced clear through the castle-man's body. With easy strength, T'ang automatically absorbed the recoil. He pulled the mortally wounded youth toward him. Desperately, writhing and squirming, the castle-man shifted his rapier. He jabbed, missed, and jabbed again.

To the majority of inhabitants in T'ang's world that rapier was death. Even the Moving Mountains, whose size would seem to protect them, feared that blade.

It hit once, skidding harmlessly off T'ang's gleaming armor. It was a last pass.

T'ang inspected his pinioned, helpless victim. His method for the coup de grace was efficient and rarely varied. He went for the skull. The castle-man was lucky. He died instantly. Others had not been so fortunate. T'ang was not especially concerned whether or not his victims were dead before he began eating.

The flesh of the castle-man had been good, juicy, and succulent, if spare. Having completed his meal, T'ang absently shoved the cleaned skeleton off the side of his platform. He did not bother to watch it go crashing to the earth below.

He finished cleaning his utensils, ascertained once more the position of the sun, and set himself again.

It was late afternoon, almost evening, when the encounter took place.

Two of the Moving Mountains came into view. Although they were not as tall as the light-eater T'ang sat upon, they massed many, many more times. Only the Bodikiddartha itself was greater.

T'ang had thought occasionally about the Moving Mountains. Were they intelligent? It seemed not. They moved about too much, with a great deal of wasted motion and energy. The city-builders were as active, but there was visible purpose behind everything they did. Not here.

Their great, mooning eyes were simple. None possessed a thousandth of the power of concentration T'ang could muster. He had seen them several times before, but they had not seen him. He feared only their clumsiness.

But today, with the sun dying near the horizon, it was to be different. Perhaps he still could have avoided them. Perhaps not. Each massed many million times his body weight. And although they could not move nearly as fast as T'ang, they had great reach. Still, it was their bulk that was most impressive.

T'ang never doubted the force of his mind. He would not run and scramble to avoid them! He'd picked his platform and he was going to stay there. If they wished a confrontation, so be it. *He* would not be the one to run and hide! He was T'ang Lang, the killer, emperor.

They saw him together, it seemed. In their ponderous, clumsy way they turned (so slow, thought T'ang, so slow!) and stared across at him. From his high platform, T'ang could return their stare eye to eye.

Those faces—monstrous, distorted, bloated things! Obscenities beyond imagining! T'ang did not flinch at the nightmare visions. Soft and flabby, surely for all their size they could not be much in the way of warriors.

Could they communicate, perhaps? He chose the smaller of the two Mountains, thought at it:

CAN YOU THINK? WHAT DO YOU MAKE OF THE UNIVERSE? ARE YOU IN HARMONY? FOR ALL YOUR SIZE I FEAR YOU NOT. COME AND FIGHT, IF YOU WILL.

NO? YOU HAVE CROSSED THE GREEN PLAIN, I HAVE SEEN YOU DO IT. WAS IT FOR A PURPOSE? OR DO YOU ALWAYS WANDER AIMLESSLY? I AM T'ANG LANG, THE KILLER! STAY AND FIGHT, OR GO IN PEACE.

The Moving Mountain made no answer. Definitely, T'ang Lang was not impressed. In fact, he was by now a little bored. He still had hunting to do and these great, ludicrous beings obscured his vision. Did they mean to stand there forever?

The sun, now that was impressive. The Bodikid-dartha was impressive. But these? They were simply big. Fagh!

The smaller Mountain of the two leaned forward, ponderously. Its bulk shut out the sun. A great mis-shapen limb extended itself toward T'ang's platform.

So it was to be battle after all? Come, then! T'ang steadied himself. All the power of his mind was directed outward in one great withering blast of mental energy.

The limb paused, hesitated. The huge saucer-shaped eyes blinked. Slowly, the limb was retracted. The Mountain looked at its companion for a moment. Then the two turned and lumbered off across the Green Plain, their size devouring the distance.

T'ang had won.

Giver of light and warmth, and sun had sunk lower in the sky. It was dragging the heat down with it. T'ang could sense the approaching chill. It crawled at his back armor.

He'd made another kill, a late one. A tube-man, this time, though not the same one he'd seen earlier. It had been fat and plump, a good meal.

Perhaps he would rest among the platforms of this light-eater tonight. It was a good spot.

He thought again on the Moving Mountains. Could he have been wrong? Mightn't they be intelligent, after all? If only he could compare thoughts with another emperor! Or even an empress. But that was quite unthinkable—for now, at least.

He sighed and turned, working his way back toward the heart of the light-eater. Intelligent or no, T'ang did not feel sanguine about the possibilities of contact.

It pained him.

A Miracle of Small Fishes

Arguments between materialists and religionists occasionally get round to the question of "miracles." Are they truly the products of divine dispensation, as the religionist would claim, or are they merely coincidental sequences of perfectly natural events, as the materialist might argue?

It's a fine, fine line, and sometimes the obvious answer isn't all that obvious. Sometimes both theologian and rational apologist find their certitude wavering ever so slightly.

Only one person doesn't question the reasoning behind a miracle—the beneficiary.

These days the old purse seiner had the long dock pretty much to itself. Few fishing boats were left in San Quintin; and only one went out with any regularity. But Grandfather Flores was fortunate. The dock was kept in good repair for the powerful cruisers and sailing yachts of the rich men from Mexico City and Acapulco, and for the wealthy Norteamericanos who made San Quintin a quaint overnight stop on their journeys.

He waved to Josefa, then vanished into the little

cabin below the bridge. Moments later he reappeared and tossed the line over the side. He could still vault the ship's rail, and did. But the vault was lower than it had once been, the hand on the rail taking more care in its grip. And he did not bend as easily as before when he stooped to make fast the line to the rusty red cleat.

Grandfather had a long brown face, with smooth lines in it like the crinkled sand dunes in the Desert Vizcaino to the south. His hair was nearly all gone gray now, and when he smiled his teeth flashed many colors besides white. But the light in the back of his eyes still winked as regularly as the old buoy marking the bay entrance. And although Josefa was no longer a baby, but a fine slim girl of nine, the powerful muscles under the stained shirt could still lift her a thousand meters high for a friendly shake, bring her close for a warm kiss redolent of garlic and onions.

Josefa preferred Grandfather's breath to the new-linen smell of roses in the church garden. He did not take her hand as they walked into town—that would have been unseemly. But he slowed his pace carefully so that she would not have to run to keep up.

Grandfather's body was cold steel—until he coughed. Then the sun dimmed a little and the shadows of the houses moved closer.

"How was the fishing today, Grandfather?" She knew the answer, but any break in this ritual would have worried him.

"Not too bad, *querida*. A few yellowtail, some bonita, one good shark—"

"And the sardines, Grandfather?"

He shook his head and smiled sadly. "No, *querida*, the sardines did not come this week. Perhaps it is too early in the season for them."

He coughed then, a long dry rasp like burning eucalyptus. To Josefa that was more horrible than any scream. She gave no sign of this, but waited until it was finished and Grandfather had resumed the walk.

No, it was too early in the season for the sardine.

It had been too early in the season since before the second great war of the nations. Then San Quintin and the other villages along the coast had supported many fishing boats. The men had gone out every morning in season and returned with fine, smelly catches, for the beautiful and delicious California sardine had spawned from Mexico to Alaska.

But there had been too much fishing, especially by the Norteamericanos of Monterey and San Francisco. Were not the schools of sardine never ending, like the buffalo and passenger pigeon? Then suddenly there were no sardines. The long purse seines brought up only free swimmers and last survivors. And not all the demands of the markets or the rise in prices could entice the sardine back. For many, many years after that there were none at all.

Now there were more sardines than ever before. But not for Grandfather's net. The great fishing fleets of Alta and Baja, California, trapped them all past the Bahia de Todos Santos, far to the north.

Josefa had never seen the great fleets. But the young men of the village, sons of fishermen's sons, went every year to work on them. Grandfather's little *Hermosa* would be only a lifeboat for such ships, and not a very big one at that.

Grandfather could have gone too. At least, he could have gone a few years ago, before the cough had come to weaken him so much. But he would not go like the others.

"That is not fishing," he told them, wagging a knobby finger at those who would listen. "That is manufacturing." And he would tell Josefa to look for the difference between the bread her mother baked in the little brick oven at home and the pale white things Diego's store kept on its shelves for the tourist boats. She did not understand, really, but since Grandfather said it was so, there must be some truth in it.

"Perhaps the sardines will come next week, Grandfather."

"Perhaps," he replied, nodding down at her.

Another attack of the cough came, and this time
it bent him over and he had to put a hand against
a wall for support. Josefa wanted to scream. Instead she looked away to where a dog was sniffing
at a mousehole. Grandfather stopped coughing, forced
a grin at her.

"That was a bad one. But I know how to handle
it. You must roll with the cough, the way the *Hermosa*
rolls with the big seas in a storm. Now I think it is
time for you to go home, *querida*."

"I would rather go with you, Grandfather, and
make the tea for you."

"No." He bent to kiss her in the parting of the night-
black hair that fell to her waist. "Your mother and
father would not like it. Go home now, and maybe I
will see you tomorrow. I will have some splices to
make in the net and you can help."

He turned and walked away from her, a tall, proud
silhouette against the evening sunset. But he was only
a shell. Josefa could remember, just two years ago,
when Grandmother had left them. That had weakened
Grandfather more than the cough. Soon the seas would
grow too high for him to roll with. Then he would join
Grandmother in the little family plot behind the
church.

She ran home, but she did that often, these days.

Thousands of kilometers to the north, past huge
smoking cities and lime-colored cliffs, past thousand-
year-old trees and day-old babies, a billion young
sardines swam idly in a cool deep sound and waited
without awareness of their impending destiny.

Father Peralta permitted himself a quiet, inward
smile of satisfaction. It had been a good mass and a
fine sermon. Now he would listen to the simple con-
fessions of his simple people, and then maybe he
could get some work done with the new books that
had been sent by the university.

He settled himself comfortably in the box. There

had been a big celebration in the village two nights ago—a wedding—and a small fight had broken out. Nothing serious, but unusual for San Quintin. This day would be longer than most.

The voices he knew. Martin, Benjamin, Marceal, Carmen, little Josefa Flores . . .

"Father, María Partida got a new dress last week. I envied her for it."

"Perhaps you just admired it, *niña*"

"No, Father. I desired it badly."

Father Peralta thought. The Flores were not as well off as some of the other villagers.

"This is a small thing, *niña*, that will pass quickly. Do not worry on it."

There was a pause from the other side. A long pause.

What is it, child?"

"Last week, Father, José and Felipe—"

José and Felipe. Peralta knew them. Good boys, made a little wild by too much money too soon. And those motorcycles, ay!

"—they laughed at Grandfather when he was going out to fish. I thought some terrible things about them, Father."

"Why were they laughing, child?"

"They said Grandfather would catch more fish at the market than he would with the *Hermosa*. They called it a hotel for worms and said the only way to fish was with the new ships they use at Ensenada and San Diego."

"And how did your grandfather respond to this?"

"He ignored them, Father. He always ignores such things and pretends they do not bother him. But I know. It's not the poor fishing he minds so much, I think. But the laughter hurts him inside. Even his friends wish he would go to Diego's and sit with them on the porch and play checkers and watch the tourists."

Peralta smiled. "I know your grandfather, *niña*. He is not one to sit on a porch and spend his days staring at the sun. Now, you must not hate José and

Felipe, or the others. They laugh because they are still young and do not know better. Since the big fishing fleet makes work for all, few in the village the age of José and Felipe have known hard times. They cannot understand why your grandfather would never work for another man, for a salary. When they are older they will understand.

"You must try to understand now, *niña*."

"I think I do, Father," she replied quietly, after another pause. "Father, why don't the sardines come south anymore?"

Father Peralta considered. How could he explain the economics of managed migration and spawning and factory-ship mechanics to a nine-year-old girl?

"They do not come anymore, *niña*, because the great, great engines make much better livings for them in the north, at special times and places. And the big ships are so good and smart that they take all the fish above Ensenada before they can swim this far south."

"But there must be so many fish, Father," she said. "Surely some must swim pass the nets?"

Peralta shook his head, realized foolishly that the girl couldn't see the gesture.

"No, *niña*, none get through. The big boats and the fishermen on them are too good for that."

"If Grandfather could only make one more catch," came the small voice. "Just one more catch—before the cough takes him. Then he could laugh, too. And José and Felipe and all the others would have to say they were wrong."

"I'm afraid that would take a miracle, *niña*."

"Then I will pray for a miracle!" The words were excited and determined, with just a shading of grandfather's steel in them. "I will light candles and pray to San Pedro for one more catch for my grandfather."

Peralta smiled. "And I will pray for that, too, child."

It was a blistering hot day, and there were many hot days in San Quintin. But when all the others had left the church, even the widow Esteban, a small angel with hair and eyes of Indian obsidian was still there, praying in front of the altar. And when Father Peralta looked in from his study that evening, she was still there.

Finally he walked over to her, made her straighten her dress, and sent her home before she would worry her parents. Yes, she had prayed well, and perhaps San Pedro would be kind.

But, he cautioned her, San Pedro was a very busy saint.

He returned to his study and pulled close to his desk, opening a thick book. He began to write.

"Again we can see that the primitive hieroglyphs of the aboriginal inhabitants of Baja California are in no way . . . in no way—"

He stopped, rolled the pen between his fingers and sat back in the stiff chair, thinking. The book that had already taken six months to accumulate lay in a pile of paper to one side—the manuscript that none but a few elderly professors and graduate students in far places would ever bother to read. Then he looked out the window, toward the serrated silhouette of the Sierra San Pedro Martir. He pulled a fresh sheet of paper from the virgin pile, considered briefly.

He began to write.

The crowd had grown smaller year after year. Now, barely a decade after fireworks and television crews had shed lights on the program's beginning, only a pair of minor functionaries from the mayoral offices in Seattle and Victoria, a few news photographers and the fisheries men were there to observe the ceremonial opening.

The chief engineer checked his watch against the wall chronometer and took a bite out of his sandwich.

"Okay, Milt . . . might as well open 'er up."

The fourth engineer nodded easily and threw the switch. A few flashguns conjured memories of Christmas. Milt obligingly reopened the switch and threw it again for the photographers' benefit.

Grumbling about the inclement weather and hoping

they could make it home before dark, the newsmen shuffled away. The representative functionaries exchanged signatures on the traditional scrolls and went their separate ways—one to his wife, the other to his mistress. The fourth engineer performed a routine check of dials and meters to ensure that the closing of the switch opened what the manuals claimed it would, and he went to try and rewire the lamp he had promised his spouse he would fix. Then the chief engineer returned to the gustatory pleasures of ham sandwich and pickle. All was quiet again.

Nor was there visible change offshore, either. No bubbling and heaving, no seething disturbance of the halcyon surface. But below . . .

Instead of being recycled by the station's own cooling plant, the heated seawater of the Port Hardy Fusion Station was being returned directly to the ocean. Water that mollified terrible energies was forced out half a hundred nozzles in Davy Jones' locker. Disruption and a great upwelling commenced on the abyssal plain below. Water and nutrients rose as the sun set.

Bacteria and phytoplankton floated delirious in the sudden confluence of sunlight and nutritive material from the depths. Multiplication and growth took place exponentially, until the sea resembled a thick soup.

Sun retired and moon clocked in for a night's work. Up with the moon came the zooplankton: minute crustacea, tiny crabs and shrimps with unpronounceable names, miniature fish larvae—all intent on a morphean orgy of feeding.

And orgy it was, for tonight food abounded in unnatural concentration. Brilliantine specks of life shot hysterically through the murky waters, reproducing and growing with nonhuman desperation. A million billion translucent monsters swam, all wriggling antenna and claws and phosphorescent eyes.

To the north, a few quarter-meter-long shining fish impinged on this cauldron of infinitesimal life, darted into it, and gorged themselves. Others nearby noticed the change in feeding pattern, turned, and followed.

Still others further north, leaders of schools small and great, came also.

A mountain of finned silver began to move south.

The Charlotte Sound Plankton Pod was devoured quickly, but the engines of Cape Flattery Station promptly took over, catalyzing their own section of ocean. The station lit and warmed and fueled the cities of Olympia, Tacoma, Seattle, Bellingham, Everett, and most of Washington State. Now it employed the sweat of its primary function to play god with small universes. Even this mass of life, too, was consumed.

But the hand of production was passed on as each pod did its job, vanishing sequentially down uncountable hungry maws, moving the growing mountain south down the finest coast in the world.

Astoria Station . . . School coming! Coos Bay . . . School coming! Crescent City and Ukiah, San Mateo and San Luis Obispo and Santa Barbara.

El Pueblo de la Nuestra Señora de Los Angeles . . . School coming!

"Well, what does the system bring today, Mendez?"

Archbishop Estrada stared back out the window, felt the surge of loving and cursing and wheeling and dealing of millionaires and beggars that was the life of Mexico City. He took in a deep, heady draught of the still clear moutain air, not smog-choked yet, by God, that eddied down from the slopes of slumbering Popocatépetl.

Gustavo and the other stalwarts on the antipollution board deserved recognition. A commendation or something, yes. He turned from the window.

At two meters and a solid hundred kilos, the archbishop was a giant of a man. In his casual slacks and shirt he was an imposing executive. In his churchly robes of office, he seemed a biblical visitation.

"Mendez, make a note. A plaque should be prepared on which the church recognizes and applauds the contribution of the Air Pollution Board of Mexico

City, making particular note of the activities of chairman Gustavo Marcos."

"Yes, sir. Your mail, sir."

"Thank you, Mendez."

The secretary put the stack of letters and brown manila envelopes on the archbishop's desk. Estrada glanced down at his watch. Plenty of time to bless the new elementary school and still make the meeting of the Urban Renewal Commission.

Most of the mail looked the usual. Requests for information, blessings, money, advice, praises for the active role the archbishop was playing in city affairs, damnations for the active role the archbishop was playing in city affairs.

He went through them rapidly, occasionally putting one aside for more personal scrutiny. His secretary could handle most of these. An invitation from the Colombian ambassador to a formal diplomatic dinner, a letter from a certain lady in Guadalajara . . .

Then he came to the letter from San Quintin.

"I'll be damned! Oh, sorry, Mendez," he said hurriedly at the stunned look on the young man's face. "Don't take it seriously." He lowered his voice, muttered to himself in surprise.

"Madre de Dios, a letter from Father Peralta!"

He slit the unlucky envelope with sharp anticipation. He'd known Father Peralta since they had played together on the university's champion soccer team. What a pro! Peralta had a brain as fast as his feet. True, he, Estrada, had risen much farther and faster in the church hierarchy. Peralta had chosen to take over the tiny church in San Quintin and pursue his scholarly anthropology.

Ah, well. He read. There were the expected greetings and small talk, all the pleasure and entertainment inherent in a predictable letter. Then . . .

"By the way, Luis, there's an old fisherman in the village who persists in going out with a rotting purse seiner every week, despite the fact that Fisheries Control has been harvesting nearly 300 kilometers north of here for years now. He's a good fellow, but stubborn as a brick and too set in his ways to change.

"As you can imagine, his antics serve as a large source of humor for the rest of the village, most of it good-natured joshing. He's got a granddaughter though, the most exquisite little thing you ever saw, who absolutely dotes on him. I see no harm in the relationship, but the parents wish she wouldn't see so much of the old man, considering her impressionable age and his terminal illness.

"Love, however, doesn't subscribe to the rules of reason. I tried to explain to her, very simply, why her grandfather can't catch sardines anymore. All I did was get her to spend most of a hellishly hot day on her knees in the church, praying to San Pedro for one last catch for her grandfather. I told her it would take a miracle, not thinking she'd take me at my word.

"Then our days at school came back to me. If I remember right, you and Martin Fowler himself were quite good friends. I didn't know the man—never even met him. Only read about him in the school paper. But it occurs to me that if anyone can do anything to fulfill even a little part of this child's dream, even if it's only dumping a few dozen sardines in her grandfather's fishing grounds by airdrop, it would be Fowler.

"Of course, I realize that I'm presuming on a friendship that may not even exist any longer. Indeed, one that may not have been that close at all. But it was the only thing I could think of. And if anyone ever deserved a miracle, even a small one, it is this Josefa Flores.

"Now, come out to San Quintin some time and get away from the noise of the city and the cardinal's griping. I'll show you the Painted Caves and some of the most beautiful, peaceful desert country you ever saw, you old reprobate.

"Sincerely, Francisco Peralta."

The archbishop looked at the letter for a long time. Then he put it in the Answer pile. He picked up the next envelope and started to slit it open, but his eyes and mind were elsewhere. Back and forth, back and forth ran the opener along the top of the fresh envelope When Mendez's voice broke the silence, he did not look up.

"Sir, there's a man here from the Ministry of State to see you. Something about an official briefing for to-night's dinner."

Estrada continued to draw lazy abstracts with the opener on the back of the envelope, staring at a point within his desk. It was quite impossible, of course. Quite.

"Tell him," he told his secretary, "that I'll see him in an hour."

The mountain was in the Channel of Santa Barbara now, moving steadily south. The Point Vincente power plant initiated pumping, boosting the phytoplankton cycle twentyfold. In a little while the mountain would hit the major booster field off San Onofre. Then they would really begin to move.

Martin Fowler steadied himself, his eyes never moving from the target. He considered his position, then moved a step closer. Gripping the powerful club in both hands, he swung downward with all his strength.

"I think you've sliced into the rough again, Marty," said Wheeling noncommittally.

Fowler said a bad word, slung the club back in his bag. The two men took hold of their carts and started down the fairway. They could have ridden in comfort. But, as Wheeling said, walking was the only exercise to golf—might as well get remote-controlled clubs and play from bed as ride a cart. Other men followed.

After a while, Wheeling looked over at his younger friend, spoke comfortingly.

" 'Course, there's nothing unusual about me taking money from you, Marty—it's only natural that those of us with God-given talent should teach the amateurs. But you usually manage to argue the point. What's eating you—Petterson?"

"You have a devious and evil mind," countered the director of the North American Fisheries Control. "If that old crank and the cat-food freaks would just give me leave to open a partial gate—five minutes, that's all I want, just five lousy minutes! You should see the projected five-year figures. The second-year catch alone—"

"If any of the folks on the commission who lean to your way of thinking heard you refer to another United States senator, their peer, as 'that old crank,' they wouldn't give you a crack big enough to let a sick salmon through, let alone your precious gate."

"I know, Dave. I won't tell if you won't. Oh, the senator's not a bad person, personally. But so damned obstinate!"

"Why, Marty! I would think you'd have worked in Washington long enough to know that senators are born obstinate. That's why they gravitate toward becoming senators. Too obstinate and stubborn and bullheaded to go into something sensible when they mature, like plumbing or home videonics."

"But, dammit, Dave, all the indications—everything the computers and the guys in the office have been able to put together—point to the Islas San Benitos as the perfect spot for establishing the first yellowtail fishery. All we have to do is attract a natural seed crop there in the first place. You know we can't plant an ocean locale the way we do Lake Ontario or Tahoe. The tuna would never spawn there, they'd just swim away. We've got to generate a major influx of food fish."

"And that's just your problem, Marty," agreed Wheeling, deciding on a seven-iron. "Senator Petterson has constituents who depend on those food fish. Existing yellowtail don't vote, let alone imaginary ones."

"But anyone who can just take the time to analyze

our figures, Dave—" He stopped and watched with distaste as his companion's ball landed short, bounced over the shoulder and onto the green. They moved to search for his own ball.

"Well, you'd better think of something fast if you expect to get that gate this year," warned Wheeling. "Last I heard, the School was passing L.A."

"Newport Beach," Fowler grumbled. "Look, you be there at the committee meeting tomorrow."

Wheeling eyed his friend with a compassion that reached beyond sympathy for his bad lie. "You never give up, do you, Marty? I'm telling you, you can bury Petterson under a ton of influence and favorable figures. But all the maybes and probablys and could-bes in the world won't convince a politician with hungry people to feed—"

"Ah, here it is," interrupted Fowler, parting the grass. He evaluated the situation, then chose an iron. Wheeling peered toward the distant green.

"You've got a shot at it, but it won't be easy. Take it from me. I've played this course."

"I know. Maybe I should give up trying logic and reason. Oh, you mean the pin. That too. Funny, it's the damnedest thing, but I got a letter the other day from a chap I haven't seen in twenty-five years. Went to school with him. Full of the usual reminiscences, what's happened to mutual acquaintances, what hasn't happened to mutual acquaintances, how the world's changed and how it should have and how we had nothing to do with it in spite of all our dreams.

"You know, at one time my greatest ambition was to become a resort hotel magnate? Another Conrad Hilton? Until I got too interested in the land I was supposed to blister with high-rises and planted swimming pools.

"Well, there was this postscript—cute little story about some kid he didn't even know. Should have just smiled and forgotten it, but the darned thing kept me up half the night, sitting and thinking, till Majorie killed the light. Silly stuff, but—"

He hefted the club, stepped up to the ball.

"If it's something you think can get you past Petterson, I'd like to hear it."

Fowler paused, looked back over his shoulder. "See? No reason, no logic, and I finally got you interested. Come to the committee meeting tomorrow." He put his head down and took a vicious swipe at the ball.

"Okay, I'm hooked," confessed Wheeling, watching the white moon sail into the distance. "I shouldn't, but you got me fair and square." He looked back at his friend, eyed him evenly. "Looks like you're trapped."

The committee room was small and informal, with a stately atmosphere and sense of history hand-worn into the rich wood paneling. There was just enough room for the long committee table and the modest guest gallery under the high window.

A single old pane let in sunlight and a respectable view of the mall. Wheeling quietly took a seat near the back of the gallery, on a bench that was made before the term "built-in obsolescence" was known. The gallery was practically deserted.

A small knot of youngsters sat at the far end and below him—early junior high or late elementary school by the looks of them, with their teacher. Though kids grew up so fast these days it was hard to tell. Question them about their favorite water hole, and they were likely to give you a lecture on spatial physics or oceanography. A couple of tired, bored-looking reporters and a few tourists completed the audience. Wheeling smiled and nodded politely to the newspapermen, then looked up.

Fowler sat at the near end of the thick walnut table. He kept running a hand through what was left of his sandy brown hair while he conferred with a neatly dressed subordinate from his department.

The children quieted, and the committee filed in, took their seats at the end of the table opposite the director. Fowler turned, saw Wheeling, and grinned. Wheeling gave back the high sign and smiled in what he hoped was an encouraging manner.

Senator Vincente of Coahuila, Senator Kaiser of Oregon, Senator Brand of Maine, Senator Petterson of New Jersey, and Minister Stanislaus of Newfoundland.

Petterson opened the meeting in her usual no-nonsense, let's-get-on-with-it tones.

"The Committee for Maritime Resources, Organic, is now in session. Let's get cracking, gentlemen."

To look at her you'd think Senator Diana Petterson was the favorite grandmother of some Midwest farming clan. And, indeed, she was. She also had a command of the English language that could bend nails, a relentless questing mind that had given more than one cocky freshman senator the holly-gobbles on the floor of Congress, and devotion to the basic needs of human beings that was sufficiently uncompromising to have put her in the Senate for her fifth consecutive term.

The lawyer-type on Fowler's left stood, rustled a sheaf of forms and computer printouts. The paper sounded loud in the chamber. He cleared his throat and began dryly to recite facts and figures.

Production of pompano here, king crab fishery there, oyster take from Chesapeake off such and such percent, edible kelp harvest up so and so many tons . . .

Wheeling found himself looking elsewhere. The schoolchildren sat politely, storing material for the homework certain to come. The two reporters had turned on their recorders and gone to sleep. He found himself becoming engrossed in the antics of a fat bumblebee that had somehow blundered into the building and was now popping against the windowpane, trying to regain the cleaner sunlight outside. How like some Congressmen, Wheeling reflected.

Half an hour later the reciter concluded his report. The reporters turned over their cassettes, and the children shifted in their seats. The fortunate bee had escaped.

"Mr. Fowler, if there is no other new business, this committee can proceed to the matter of this year's final appropriations, and we can wind up this meeting early."

"Beg your pardon, Madam Senator, but there is the outstanding question of my formal request for a temporary gate in the season's Pacific Coast sardine take."

One of the other senators groaned.

"Really, Mr. Fowler," admonished Petterson, "you've assaulted us with this request at every meeting for over a year now!"

"I realize that, Senator," agreed Fowler amiably. "Nonetheless, I wish to submit the proposal again. If you wish, I can quote the section of proceedings regulations which—"

"I am fully conversant with the rules of procedure for this committee, Mr. Director, as are my fellow senators. If you *will* persist in this inexplicable masochism, we are compelled by courtesy to indulge you. But permit me to say that I have no reason to believe your proposal will be met by any more receptive an audience this time than in the past. However, I suppose each administrator is entitled to one private aberration. Begin.

"But please have the grace to be as brief as possible. Most of us have important work to do." She did not have to stress the "us" to make her point.

Fowler rose. He had only a single sheet of notes in front of him, and he rarely referred to it. He had no need to. He had made this speech many times before.

He spoke about the history of the North American Fisheries Control, now concluding its first decade. For the first time, Canada, Mexico, and the United States had organized together to properly manage and exploit the living resources of the sea. He related how excess heat and water from offshore and onshore fusion and fission plants had been used to drive nutrients from the ocean floor up to the surface, thus generating controllable and unprecedented population booms among commercially valuable surface-dwelling fish.

He told how the Alaskan king crab industry, once in danger of being fatally overfished, had been managed to the point where it could now support the hungry fleets of six nations and would still increase year by year.

How the cost of Maine lobster had been cut to sixty cents a half-kilo, while lobster fishermen made more money than ever. How the neglected waters off the Yucatán Peninsula now supported the largest natural sponge industry in the world.

And finally, he outlined how the research at Fisheries Control had advised him that the world's largest yellowtail fishery could be created off the Bahia Sebastian Vizcaino only if enough food fish could be provided to meet the tuna as they were herded northward.

"And to do this," Senator Petterson concluded for him, "you propose to sacrifice perhaps a hundred thousand tons of one of the finest food fishes in the world, the California sardine."

"Not sacrifice, Madam Senator. The sardines would spark the first artificial spawning area for the most popular food fish in America. We can improve existing yellowtail fisheries, but the production from one managed and controlled by us from its inception would be a dozen, eventually perhaps a hundred times greater!"

"How much will your dream cost the consumer, Mr. Director?"

"Research postulates at most a slight rise in the cost of basic sardine and sardine products."

"Slight!" Petterson's gray hair bobbed. "Mr. Fowler, do you have any idea how many people in my home state alone exist on minimal incomes? People for whom a 'slight' rise in food costs translates into a catastrophic effect on basic nutrition. People for whom seafood—in particular the sardine—is the only source of bulk protein?"

"Chances are good that none of them would ever be affected, Senator."

"Chances." She nodded knowingly. "Now we come down to it. I will not gamble with hungry people's bellies."

She smiled magnanimously, a smile which had come to be quite familiar to Fowler.

"But I tell you what, Director. I'm willing to take a reasonable risk. I like to be considered progressive. All you have to do is guarantee this committee a ninety-percent probability of success for your tuna ranch, and I'll vote aye with the rest of 'em."

"You know our agency isn't experienced enough to guarantee a ninety-percent chance of success, Madam Senator, but—"

"Then that's done with! I won't risk the well-being of thousands of humans on a radical new plan concocted by idle scientists who've probably never eaten an algaeburger in their overpaid lives." She grimaced with distaste and looked past Fowler to the placid form of Wheeling. "Not for anyone!"

She looked around the table. "And neither, I venture to say, will any of my fellow committee members."

There was a long pause. Fowler glanced down at his single paper. When he felt the senators were about to fidget, he resumed, a calculated note of anger just coloring his tone.

"Then if you won't do this for me, Senators, and you won't do it for the men of Fisheries Control, maybe you'll do it for Josefa Flores."

"Josefa Flores?" echoed Petterson, looking wary. "Who, pray tell, is Josefa Flores? I'm afraid I don't know the lady."

"That's not surprising," continued Fowler. "She

doesn't exactly wield strong influence in Congress. Or in the Canadian Parliament or in the National Assembly. You see, she's only nine years old.

"Her grandfather is a fisherman—or was, until in our combined wisdom we took away his livelihood, and . . ."

Wheeling perked up, sat straighter on the hard bench. This promised to be more entertaining than the bumblebee. For the first time the young school-children stopped squirming and paid attention. The pair of newshawks woke up and hurriedly restarted their recorders, leaning forward intently like wolves who've just crossed a new scent. Wheeling could almost see little neon lights flashing: *Human interest—human interest! . .*

Fowler told the committee about little Josefa Flores, about her dying grandfather and the fish that didn't come anymore—and about her one wish: that before he died, her grandfather should enjoy one last taste of his youth by taking an honest day's catch of the sardine. Here was a story that even survived Fowler's unabashed emotional embroidery. He kept telling it until the banging of Senator Petterson's gavel drowned him out.

"Will you sit down, Mr. Fowler?" she finally shouted.

Smiling, Fowler sat.

"Now, then," the lady senator began firmly, attempting to regain control of the meeting, "you may, of course, say whatever you like in support of your proposal, Mr. Fowler. It is so stated in the rules. But we are apparently now dealing with private lives and personal experiences of absurdly emotional overtones, which should not casually be aired in public. I therefore declare that the committee should recess for private consu—"

"Never mind, Dee," interrupted Senator Kaiser. He jerked his head toward the back of the room. "They've already left."

Wheeling looked down to the seats vacated by the departed reporters.

Petterson sighed slightly, then directed an unhappy glare at Fowler. He looked back innocently, for all the world a balding cherub in a sharkskin suit. A similarity, Wheeling reflected approvingly, that clearly went deeper than the weave.

"I confess I fail to understand your insertion of high school melodramatics into what is, by your own admission, a matter of science, Mr. Fowler. Your statements do not reflect credit on your department."

"Your pardon again, Madam Senator, but may I remind you that the department had nothing to do with fixing a location for the sardine catch, and therefore it bears no responsibility for this elderly gentleman's sad existence. As a matter of fact, it was your committee—I beg your pardon, its ancestor—that settled on the U.S.–Mexican border. A decision which should have been made on the basis of solid scientific evidence, but which in actuality was decided by the insertion of melodramatics in the form of political maneuvering."

Petterson watched him finish, then commented dryly, "I'm not entirely satisfied that your description of this person's situation is all that you make of it, Mr. Director."

Fowler crossed mental fingers and blessed the air conditioning. "It can, of course, be verified, Senator. Any independent news team investigating—"

"Oh, I hardly think that's necessary," put in Senator Kaiser with admirable speed. "We all have great confidence in the accuracy of Mr. Fowler's research people."

Fowler knocked wood with those mentally crossed fingers, said quietly, "Then may I propose that that ability be put to a vote, Senators?"

"Oh, we can do that tomorrow, or even next week," continued Kaiser. "No need to take up with such a small matter now."

"Excuse me, Charley," said Minister Stanislaus, "but I do think there is need."

Petterson stared around the table, examined each face individually. "I see. Very well. You all know my views on the matter, gentlemen. You've heard Mr. Fowler's—yet again. I think a simple show of hands will suffice.

"All those against?"

Two hands shot up, Petterson's and Kaiser's. They stayed up a long time, millennia it seemed to Fowler. But no third hand joined them.

Petterson kept her hand up while she bestowed a motherly smile on each of the three unvoting congressmen—a motherly smile that held promises of murder and total destruction if at least one other palm didn't expose itself. To their credit, the three remaining senators sat firm.

Finally she caved in—her arm was getting tired— and tried one last ploy.

"Abstentions?"

No hands went up. She didn't even bother to call for the affirmative vote.

"Congratulations, Mr. Fowler. Your proposal for a five-minute gate in this year's California take is hereby approved by vote in committee. Five minutes and not one second more. Rest assured the gate will be independently monitored." She rapped the table once, formally, with the gravel.

"This committee stands adjourned until tomorrow at one o'clock, at which time appropriations and additional business will be discussed and considered.

"And off the record, Mr. Director," she whispered out of earshot of the recording secretary, "I hope for your sake that the researchers in your department are more accurate in their predictions than the political pollsters who have been predicting my defeat in every congressional election for the last twenty-five years."

When the children had finished applauding and the

tourists and senators had left, Wheeling walked down to join his young friend.

"Ready for a drink, Marty?"

Fowler let out a long sigh. "Now there's a prediction I know I can fulfill. But first I've got to call the Coast and then make a stop at the office and tell the staff in person. They've worked for this even harder than I have. It's a great thing."

"Sure," said Wheeling. "Tell me, was that sob story on the level, or something you cooked up?"

Fowler grinned. "It was and it wasn't. I had to rely entirely on the information in that friend's letter. But I think it's probably legit, though I had a bad moment when Petterson seemed ready to press for more facts. Anyway, this fellow isn't in a position where one has to make up stories to get by."

They rounded a turn in the hall, started down the well-worn stairs, smoothed and polished by the shoes of hundreds of lawmakers present and past.

"Frankly," Wheeling confessed, "I didn't think you'd pull it off. Dramatic appeal and all."

"I wasn't sure, either. But it helps if you've got a story to work with that you'd like to believe in."

"That's a fact," agreed Wheeling. "Also a help that Brand and Stanislaus are up for re-election this year. And the timely appearance of those two fellows from the *Post* and *Time*."

"Sure, all that contributed, Dave," agreed the director as they turned down the next hall and nearly bumped into a Secret Service man. "But frankly, if you had come to a hearing before now, I might not have had to wait ten months to push this thing over."

"Sorry, Marty. You've got to remember that I'm retired, and I don't like to be accused of meddling. Not my place, even from a distance. But that letter was something different. Figured it couldn't hurt to sit in the back of the bus and smile a little in the right places.

"Now, you make that phone call and we'll have that drink. And then I'll beat you another eighteen holes."

"Not today," replied Fowler, cracking a broad smile. "I feel so good that I don't think I'd even have any compunctions about walloping an ex-president."

He took from his coat pocket the little communicator that linked him with his office and beeped for his aide.

"Sherrie, get me Papadakis."

Aristophanes Papadakis paced the outside bridge of the factory purse seiner *Cetacean* and surveyed the darkness. Occasionally a smoke-serpent appeared around the stem of his meerschaum and vanished wraithlike into the crystal Pacific night.

The lights of the fleet formed uncertain trails of light on the calm black water. For a change, the Pacific seemed inclined to live up to its name.

When the School came through tonight, fishing conditions would be perfect.

He tried to pick out the other ships of the flotilla. The *San Cristóbal, Quebec, Typee, Carcharodon, Scrimshaw*—the pride of the fishing fleets of three nations. Each vessel a food-processing factory in itself, dozens of them, scattered starboard, port and aft in orderly rows. As flagship the *Cetacean* rode point, awaiting the southern charge.

And best of all, here was a great armada that would meet a charge with no guns, and fought only hunger.

"Captain?"

"Eh?" Papadakis turned from the floating city. "What is it, son?"

"Sir, sonar reports that they're inside the kilometer mark." The young officer's voice held barely repressed excitement.

"Be here soon, then. Good! Are all the other captains informed of my instructions concerning the gate?"

"Yes, sir," replied the other. "The communications mate on duty said to compliment you on your final instructions, sir. Said they were explicit and evocative beyond the call of duty."

"Did he now?" Papadakis smiled around the pipe stem. Mitchell and he had come up together, fishing off the municipal pier for rock cod and an occasional gift of halibut.

"Any man who closes his seine before the gate has been run gets packed in olive oil and shipped off with the first catch."

He turned away, stared back down into the secretive waters. Wondered how Fowler had been able to pull it off. Sardines were fine to catch, and good eating, but yellowtail—now that was a noble fish. After a while he became aware that the new officer was still standing in the floorway.

"Well, come in or out, son. Can't salt half a peanut."

"I'm sorry, sir," the youth replied, coming outside, "but this is my first actual catch—outside academy drills, of course. Tell me, can you see them when they go by?"

Papadakis made a sound, chomped hard on the pipe.

"Nope. More's the pity, too. Oh, the caravaners can, they and their porpoises. But they're so busy chasing off sharks and groupers and other predators that they've got no time to spend admiring things. Got better uses for their lights. Trying to cut a blue shark out of a school at night in this plankton stew is near impossible even with sonar. Couldn't do it without the porps."

A voice came from within the bridge.

"Two minutes, Cap'n." Papadakis acknowledged this information by grunting louder than usual.

"Isn't it exciting, sir?"

"Exciting? Just fish, son."

The youth stayed quiet for a minute. Then, "Sir, I know what the book says—it seems silly—but can you really feel them?"

"Oh, sometimes, sometimes not. Doesn't happen too often. Depends mostly on surface conditions. Then too, they've got to pass fairly close under your keel. The *Cetacean* and her cousins are *big*. Conditions got to be just about perfect."

"They're just about perfect tonight, aren't they, sir?"

"Yep," Papadakis spared an inquiring glance for the moon. Full. Good! Tonight they could use all the light they could get. Course, the moon was always full for the catch. Migration set it up that way. The crews would be working till daylight.

"You know, sir, it's still kind of mind-boggling when you think of it. I mean, a half a year's preparation and driving, all leading up to a single night's catch." The ship rocked to port, shifting gently back to starboard. Water patted at the waterline. "It's overwhelming, sir."

Papadakis sighed, looked at his watch. He knocked the dottle from his pipe and fed the sea dead tobacco.

"Odd sort of wave, sir. Must be getting rough further out."

"That was no wave, sonny." "Pappy" Papadakis bit firmly into the well-worn stem. "That was a million tons of sardine racing south and eating like nobody's business."

He turned and headed for the interior bridge, checked his watch again. "Let's go. In five minutes you're going to start the busiest night of your life. And wait till the main School gets here. Then you better grab something and hang on tight."

The sun mixed paint with the ravines and peaks of the Sierra San Pedro Martir. Josefa Flores walked down the slight slope toward the old pier.

But there was something odd this evening. There were many people gathered around the pier, and not just tourists. Market-owner Diego was there, as were her friends Juana and María, and many others.

Then she saw the *Hermosa*, chugging slowly and painfully toward her mooring place at the pier's far end, a white stormcloud of seagulls and terns escorting her. She saw how close the old boat's sheer dipped to the water. She began to move faster, and as she got closer she could see the old man standing straight and proud on the tiny bridge, and the sun also made color with his teeth.

She was on the pier, the boards click-clacking under her soles as she ran and yelled, pushing past the people, not caring if she bumped the wealthiest Norteamericano in the world into the bay.

"Grandfather, Grandfather . . . !"

His hands smelled of fish when he picked her up, but they were good at brushing away tears.

Dream Done Green

Where do you get your ideas?

That has to be the question most often asked of writers, and writers of science fiction in particular. I tend to the answer the great writer-artist Carl Barks gave when his character inventor Gyro Gearloose inquired of a nondescript bird as to why it sings, and the bird replied, "Oh, maybe I'm glad, maybe I'm sad, maybe I'm a little mad."

But there are exceptions. A farmgirl in Maryland wrote me once and happened to mention that her favorite books were about horses, and science fiction. Why, she wondered, weren't there more science-fiction horse stories?

I wondered too, and so . . .

The life of the woman Casperdan is documented in the finest detail, from birth to death, from head to toe, from likes to dislikes to indifferences.

Humans are like that.

The stallion Pericles we know only by his work.

Horses are like that.

We know it all began the year 1360 Imperial, 1822 After the Breakthrough, 2305 after the human Micah Schell found the hormone that broke the lock on rudimentary animal intelligence and enabled the higher mammals to attain at least the mental abilities of a human ten-year-old.

The quadrant was the Stone Crescent, the system Burr, the planet Calder, and the city Lalokindar.

Lalokindar was a wealthy city on a wealthy world. It ran away from the ocean in little bumps and curlicues. Behind it was virgin forest; in front, the Beach of Snow. The homes were magnificent and sat on spacious grounds, and that of the industrialist Dandavid was one of the most spacious and magnificent of all.

His daughter Casperdan was quite short, very brilliant, and by the standards of any age an extraordinary beauty. She had the looks and temperament of a Titania and the mind of a Baron Sachet. Tomorrow she came of legal age, which on Calder at that time was seventeen.

Under Calderian law she could then, as the oldest (and only) child, assume control of the family business or elect not to. Were one inclined to wager on the former course he would have found planty of takers. It was only a formality. Girls of seventeen did not normally assume responsibility and control for multimillion-credit industrial complexes.

Besides, following her birthday Casperdan was to be wed to Comore du Sable, who was handsome and intelligent (though not so rich as she).

Casperdan was dressed in a blue nothing and sat on the balustrade of the wide balcony overlooking Snow Beach and a bay of the Greengreen Sea. The aged German shepherd trotted over to her, his claws clicking softly on the purple porphyry.

The dog was old and grayed and had been with the

family for many years. He panted briefly, then spoke.

"Mistress, a strange mal is at the entrance."

Casperdan looked idly down at the dog.

"Who's its master?"

"He comes alone," the dog replied wonderingly.

"Well, tell him my father and mother are not at home and to come back tomorrow."

"Mistress"—the dog flattened his ears and lowered his head apologetically—"he says he comes to see *you*."

The girl laughed, and silver flute notes skittered off the polished stone floor.

"To see me? Stranger and stranger. And really alone?" She swung perfect legs off the balustrade. "What kind of mal is this?"

"A horse, mistress."

The flawless brow wrinkled. "Horse? Well, let's see this strange mal that travels alone."

They walked toward the foyer, past cages of force filled with rainbow-colored tropical birds.

"Tell me, Patch . . . what is a 'horse'?"

"A large four-legged vegetarian." The dog's brow twisted with the pain of remembering. Patch was extremely bright for a dog. "There are none on Calder. I do not think there are any in the entire system."

"Off-planet, too?" Her curiosity was definitely piqued, now. "Why come to see me?"

"I do not know, mistress."

"And without even a human over h—"

Voice and feet stopped together.

The mal standing in the foyer was not as large as some. La Moure's elephants were much bigger. But it was extraordinary in other ways. Particularly the head. Why . . . it was exquisite! Truly breathtaking. Not an anthropomorphic beauty, but something uniquely its own.

Patch slipped away quietly.

The horse was black as the Pit, with tiny exceptions. The right front forelock was silver, as was the diamond on its forehead. And there was a single streak of silver partway through the long mane, and another in the black tail. Most mal wore only a lifepouch, and this one's was strapped to its neck. But it also wore an incongruous, utterly absurd hat of green felt, with a long feather, protruding out and back.

With a start she realized she'd been staring . . . very undignified. She started toward it again. Now the head swung to watch her. She slowed and stopped involuntarily, somehow constrained from moving too close.

"This is ridiculous! she thought. *It's only a mere mal, and not even very big. Why, it's even herbivorous!*

Then whence this strange fluttering deep in her tummy?

"You are Casperdan," said the horse suddenly. The voice was exceptional, too: a mellow tenor that tended to rise on concluding syllables, only to break and drop like a whitecap on the sea before the next word.

She started to stammer a reply, angrily composed herself.

"I am. I regret that I'm not familiar with your species, but I'll accept whatever the standard horse-man greeting is."

"I give no subservient greeting to any man," replied the horse. It shifted a hoof on the floor, which here was deep foam.

A stranger and insolent to boot, thought Casperdan furiously. She would call Patch and the household guards and . . . Her anger dissolved in confusion and uncertainty.

"How did you get past Row and Cuff?" Surely this harmless-looking, handless quadruped could not have overpowered the two lions. The horse smiled, showing white incisors.

"Cats, fortunately, are more subject to reason than many mal. And now I think I'll answer the rest of your questions.

"My name is Pericles. I come from Quaestor."

Quaestor! Magic, distant, Imperial capital! Her

anger at this mal's insolence was subsumed in excitement.

"You mean you've actually traveled all the way from the capital . . . to meet me?"

"There is no need to repeat," the horse murmured, "only to confirm. It took a great deal of time and searching to find someone like you. I need someone young . . . you are that. Only a young human would be responsive to what I have to offer. I needed someone bored, and you are wealthy as well as young."

"I'm not bored," Casperdan began defiantly, but he ignored her.

"I needed someone very rich, but without a multitude of ravenous relatives hanging about. Your father is a self-made tycoon, your mother an orphan. You have no other relatives. And I needed someone with the intelligence and sensitivity to take orders from a mere mal."

This last was uttered with a disdain alien to Casperdan. Servants were not sarcastic.

"In sum," he concluded, "I need you."

"Indeed?" she mused, too overwhelmed by the outrageousness of this animal's words to compose a suitable rejoinder.

"Indeed," the horse echoed drily.

"And what, pray tell, do you need me for?"

The horse dropped its head and seemed to consider how best to continue. It looked oddly at her.

"Laugh now if you will. I have a dream that needs fulfilling."

"Do you, now? Really, this is becoming quite amusing." What a story she'd have to tell at the preparty tomorrow!

"Yes, I do. Hopefully it will not take too many years."

She couldn't help blurting, "Years!"

"I cannot tell for certain. You see, I am a genius and a poet. For me it's the dream part that's solid. The reality is what lacks certitude. That's one reason why I need human help. Need you."

This time she just stared at him.

"Tomorrow," continued the horse easily, "you will not marry the man du Sable. Instead, you will sign the formal Control Contract and assume directorship of the Dan family business. You have the ability and brains to handle it. With my assistance the firm will prosper beyond the wildest dreams of your sire or any of the investors.

"In return, I will deed you a part of my dream, some of my poetry, and something few humans have had for millennia. I would not know of this last thing myself had I not chanced across it in the Imperial archives."

She was silent for a brief moment, then spoke brightly.

"I have a few questions."

"Of course."

"First, I'd like to know if horses as a species are insane, or if you are merely an isolated case."

He sighed, tossing his mane. "I didn't expect words to convince you." The long black hair made sailor's knots with sunbeams. "Do you know the Meadows of Blood?"

"Only by name." She was fascinated by the mention of the forbidden place. "They're in the Ravaged Mountains. It's rumored to be rather a pretty place. But no one goes there. The winds above the canyon make it fatal to aircars."

"I have a car outside," the horse whispered. "The driver is mal and knows of a winding route by which, from to time, it is possible to reach the Meadows. The winds war only above them. They are named, by the way, for the color of the flora there and not for a bit of human history . . . unusual.

"When the sun rises up in the mouth of a certain canyon and engulfs the crimson grasses and flowers in light . . . well, it's more than 'rather pretty.' "

"You've already been there," she said.

"Yes, I've already been." He took several steps and

that powerful, strange face was close to hers. One eye, she noticed offhandedly, was red, the other blue.

"Come with me now to the Meadows of Blood and I'll give you that piece of dream, that something few have had for thousands of years. I'll bring you back tonight and you can give me your answer on the way.

"If it's 'no,' then I'll depart quietly and you'll never see me again."

Now, in addition to being both beautiful and intelligent, Casperdan also had her sire's recklessness.

"All right . . . I'll come."

When her parents returned home that night from the party and found their daughter gone, they were not distressed. After all, she was quite independent and, heavens, to be married tomorrow! When they learned from Patch that she'd gone off, not with a man, but with a strange mal, they were only mildly concerned. Casperdan was quite capable of taking care of herself. Had they known where she'd gone, things would have been different.

So nothing happened till the morrow.

"Good morning, Cas," said her father.

"Good morning, dear," her mother added. They were eating breakfast on the balcony. "Did you sleep well last night, and where did you go?"

The voice that answered was distant with other thoughts.

"I didn't sleep at all, and I went into the Ravaged Mountains. And there's no need to get excited, Father" —the old man sat back in his chair—"because as you see, I'm back safely and in one piece."

"But not unaffected," her mother stated, noticing the strangeness in her daughter's eyes.

"No, Mother, not unaffected. There will be no wedding." Before that lovely woman could reply, Casperdan turned to her father. "Dad, I want the contract of Control. I intend to begin as director of the firm eight o'clock tomorrow morning. No, better make it noon . . . I'll need some sleep." She was smiling faintly. "And I don't think I'm going to get any right now."

On that she was right. Dandavid, that usually even-tempered but mercurial gentleman, got very, very excited. Between his bellows and her sobs, her mother leveled questions and then accusations at her.

When they found out about the incipient change-over, the investors immediately threatened to challenge it in court—law or no law, they weren't going to be guided by the decisions of an inexperienced snippet. In fact, of all those affected, the intended bridegroom took it best. After all, he was handsome and intelligent (if not as rich), and could damn well find himself another spouse. He wished Casperdan well and consoled himself with his cello.

Her father (for her own good, of course) joined with the investors to challenge his daughter in the courts. He protested most strongly. The investors ranted and pounded their checkbooks.

But the judge was honest, the law machines incorruptible, and the precedents clear. Casperdan got her Contract and a year in which to prove herself.

Her first official action was to rename the firm Dream Enterprises. A strange name, many thought, for an industrial concern. But it was more distinctive than the old one. The investors grumbled, while the advertising men were delighted.

Then began a program of industrial expansion and acquisition unseen on somnolent Calder since the days of settlement. Dream Enterprises was suddenly everywhere and into everything. Mining, manufacturing, raw materials. These new divisions sprouted tentacles of their own and sucked in additional businesses.

Paper and plastics, electronics, nucleonics, hydrologics and parafoiling, insurance and banking, tridee stations and liquid tanking, entertainments and hydroponics and velosheeting.

Dream Enterprises became the wealthiest firm on Calder, then in the entire Stone Crescent.

The investors and Dandavid clipped their coupons

and kept their mouths shut, even to ignoring Casperdan's odd relationship with an outsystem mal.

Eventually there came a morning when Pericles looked up from his huge lounge in the executive suite and stared across the room at Casperdan in a manner different from before.

The stallion had another line of silver in his mane. The girl had blossomed figuratively and figurewise. Otherwise the years had left them unchanged.

"I've booked passage for us. Put Rollins in charge. He's a good man."

"Where are we going?" asked Casperdan. Not why nor for how long, but where. She'd learned a great deal about the horse in the past few years.

"Quaestor."

Sudden sparkle in beautiful green eyes. "And then will you give me back what I once had?"

The horse smiled and nodded. "If everything goes smoothly."

In the Crescent, Dream Enterprises was powerful and respected and kowtowed to. In the Imperial sector it was different. There were companies on the capital planet that would classify it as a modest little family business. Bureaucratic trip-wires here ran not for kilometers, but for light-years.

However, Pericles had threaded this maze many times before, and knew both men and mal who worked within the bowels of Imperial Government.

So it was that they eventually found themselves in the offices of Sim-sem Alround, subminister for Unincorporated Imperial Territories.

Physically, Alround wasn't quite that. But he did have a comfortable bureaucratic belly, a rectangular face framed by long bushy sideburns and curly red hair tinged with white. He wore the current fashion, a monocle. For all that, and his dry occupation, he proved charming and affable.

A small stream ran through his office, filled with trout and tadpoles and cattails. Casperdan reclined on a long couch made to resemble solid granite. Pericles preferred to stand.

"You want to buy some land, then?" queried Alround after drinks and pleasantries had been exchanged.

"My associate will give you the details," Casperdan informed him. Alround shifted his attention from human to horse without a pause. Naturally he'd assumed . . .

"Yes sir?"

"We wish to purchase a planet," said Pericles. "A small planet . . . not very important."

Alround waited. Visitors interested in small transactions didn't get in to see the subminister himself.

"Just one?"

"One will be quite sufficient."

Alround depressed a switch on his desk. A red light flashed on, indicated that all details of the conversation to follow were now being taken down for the Imperial records.

"Purpose of purchase?"

"Development."

"Name of world?"

"Earth."

"All right . . . fine," said the subminister. Abruptly, he looked confused. Then he smiled. "Many planets are called Earth by their inhabitants. or discoverers. Which particular Earth is this?"

"*The* Earth. Birthplace of mankind and malkind. Old Earth. Also known variously as Terra and Sol III."

The subminister shook his head. "Never heard of it."

"It is available, though?"

"We'll know in a second." Alround studied the screen in his desk.

Actually it took several minutes before the gargantuan complex of metal and plastic and liquid buried deep in the soil beneath them could come up with a reply.

"Here it is, finally," said Alround. "Yes, it's available . . . by default, it seems. The price will be . . ." He named a figure which seemed astronomical to Casperdan and insanely low to the horse.

"Excellent!" husked Pericles. "Let us conclude the formalities now."

"Per," Casperdan began, looking at him uncertainly. "I don't know if we have enough . . ."

"Some liquidation will surely be necessary, Casperdan, but we will manage."

The subminister interrupted: "Excuse me . . . there's something you should know before we go any further. I *can* sell you Old Earth, but there is an attendant difficulty."

"Problems can be solved, difficulties overcome, obstructions removed," said the horse irritably. "Please get on with it."

Alround sighed. "As you wish." He drummed the required buttons. "But you'll need more than your determination to get around this one.

"You see, it seems no one knows how to get to Old Earth anymore . . . or even where it is."

Later, strolling among the teeming mobs of Imperial City, Casperdan ventured a hesitant opinion.

"I take it this means it's not time for me to receive my part of the dream again?"

"Sadly, no, my friend."

Her tone turned sharp. "Well, what do you intend to do now? We've just paid quite an enormous number of credits for a world located in obscurity, around the corner from no place."

"We shall return to Calder," said the horse with finality, "and continue to expand and develop the company." He pulled back thick lips in an equine smile.

"In all the research I did, in all my careful planning and preparation, never once did I consider that the location of the home world might have been lost.

"So now we must go back and hire researchers to research, historians to historize, and ships to search and scour the skies in sanguine directions. And wait."

A year passed, and another, and then they came in small multiples. Dream Enterprises burgeoned and grew, grew and thrived. It moved out of the Stone Crescent and extended its influence into other quadrants. It went into power generation and multiple metallurgy, into core mining and high fashion.

And finally, of necessity, into interstellar shipping.

There came the day when the captain with the stripped-down scoutship was presented to Casperdan and the horse Pericles in their executive office on the two hundred and twentieth floor of the Dream building.

Despite a long, long, lonely journey the captain was alert and smiling. Smiling because the endless trips of dull searching were over. Smiling because he knew the company reward for whoever found a certain aged planet.

Yes, he'd found Old Earth. Yes, it was a long way off, and in a direction only recently suspected. Not in toward the galactic center, but out on the Arm. And yes, he could take them there right away.

The shuttleboat settled down into the atmosphere of the planet. In the distance, a small yellow sun burned smooth and even.

Pericles stood at the observation port of the shuttle as it drifted planetward. He wore a special protective suit, as did Casperdan. She spared a glance at the disconsolate mal. Then she did something she did very rarely. She patted his neck.

"You mustn't be too disappointed if it's not what you expected, Per." She was trying to be comforting. "History and reality have a way of not coinciding."

It was quiet for a long time. Then the magnificent head, lowered now, turned to face her, Pericles snorted bleakly.

"My dear, dear Casperdan, I can speak eighteen languages fluently and get by in several more, and there are no words in any of them for what I feel. 'Disappointment'? Consider a nova and call it warm. Regard Quaestor and label it well-off. Then look at me and call me disappointed."

"Perhaps," she continued, not knowing what else to say, "it will be better on the surface."

It was worse.

They came down in the midst of what the captain called a mild local storm. To Casperdan it was a neat slice of the mythical hell.

Stale yellow-brown air whipped and sliced its way over high dunes of dark sand. The uncaring mounds marched in endless waves to the shoreline. A dirty, dead beach melted into brackish water and a noisome green scum covered it as far as the eye could see. A few low scrubs and hearty weeds eked out a perilous existence among the marching dunes, needing only a chance change in the wind to be entombed alive.

In the distance, stark, bare mountains gave promise only of a higher desolation.

Pericles watched the stagnant sea for a long time. Over the intercom his voice was shrunken, the husk of a whisper, those compelling tones beaten down by the moaning wind.

"Is it like this everywhere, Captain?"

The spacer replied unemotionally. "Mostly. I've seen far worse worlds, sir . . . but this one is sure no prize. If I may be permitted an opinion, I'm damned if I can figure out why you want it."

"Can't you feel it, Captain?"

"Sir?" The spacer's expression under his faceglass was puzzled.

"No, no. I guess you cannot. But I do, Captain. Even though this is not the Earth I believed in, I still feel it. I fell in love with a dream. The dream seems to have departed long ago, but the memory of it is still here, still here . . ." Another long pause, then, "You said 'mostly'?"

"Well, yes." The spacer turned and gestured at the distant range. "Being the discovering vessel, we ran a pretty thorough survey, according to the general directives. There are places—near the poles, in the higher elevations, out in the middle of the three great oceans—where a certain amount of native life still survives. The cycle of life here has been shattered, but a few of the pieces are still around.

"But mostly, it's like this." He kicked at the sterile sand. "Hot or cold desert—take your pick. The soil's barren and infertile, the air unfit for man or mal.

"We did find some ruins . . . God, they were old! You saw the artifacts we brought back. But except for its historical value, this world strikes me as particularly worthless."

He threw another kick at the sand, sending flying shards of mica and feldspar and quartz onto the highways of the wind.

Pericles had been thinking. "We won't spend much more time here, Captain." The proud head lifted for a last look at the dead ocean. "There's not much to see."

They'd been back in the offices on Calder only a half-month when Pericles announced his decision.

Dream-partner or no dream-partner, Casperdan exploded.

"You quadrupedal cretin! Warm-blooded sack of fatuous platitudes! Terraforming is only a theory, a hypothesis in the minds of sick romantics. It's impossible!"

"No one has ever attempted it," countered the horse, unruffled by her outburst.

"But . . . my God!" Casperdan ran delicate fingers through her flowing blond hair. "There are no facilities for doing such a thing . . . no company, no special firms to consult. Why, half the industries that would be needed for such a task don't even exist."

"They will," Pericles declared.

"Oh, yes? And just *where* will they spring from?"

"You and I are going to create them."

She pleaded with him. "Have you gone absolutely mad? We're not in the miracle business, you know."

The horse walked to the window and stared down at the Greengreen Sea. His reply was distant. "No . . . we're in the dream business . . . remember?"

A cloud of remembrance came over Casperdan's exquisite face. For a moment, she did—but it wasn't enough to stem the tide of objection. Though she stopped shouting.

"Please, Per . . . take a long, logical look at this before you commit yourself to something that can only hurt you worse in the end."

He turned and stared evenly at her. "Casperdan, for many, many years now I've done nothing but observe things with a reasoned eye, done nothing without thinking it through beginning, middle, and end and all possible ramifications, done nothing I wasn't absolutely sure of completing.

"Now I'm going to take a chance. Not because I want to do it this way, but because I've run out of options. I'm not mad, no . . . but I *am* obsessed." He looked away from her.

"But I can't do it without you, damn it, and you know why . . . no mal can head a private concern that employs humans."

She threw up her hands and stalked back to her desk. It was silent in the office for many minutes. Then she spoke softly.

"Pericles, I don't share your obsession . . . I've matured, you know . . . now I think I can survive with just the memory of my dream-share. But you rescued me from my own narcissism. And you've given me . . . other things. If you can't shake this psychotic notion of yours, I'll stay around till you can."

Horses and geniuses don't cry . . . ah, but poets . . . !

And that is how the irony came about—that the first world where terraforming was attempted was not some sterile alien globe, but Old Earth itself. Or as the horse

Pericles is reputed to have said, "Remade in its own image."

The oceans were cleared . . . the laborious, incredibly costly first step. That done, and with a little help from two thousand chemists and bioengineers, the atmosphere began to cleanse itself. That first new air was neither sweet nor fresh—but neither was it toxic.

Grasses are the shock troops of nature. Moved in first, the special tough strains took hold in the raped soil. Bacteria and nutrients were added, fast-multiplying strains that spread rapidly. From the beachheads near the Arctic and in the high mountains flora and fauna were reintroduced.

Then came the major reseeding of the superfast trees: spruce and white pine, juniper and birch, cypress and mori and teak, fir and ash. And from a tiny museum on Duntroon, long preserved Sequoia and citrus.

Eventually there was a day when the first flowers were replanted. The hand-planting of the first bush—a green rose—was watched by the heads of the agricultural staffs, a black horse, and a ravishing woman in the postbloom of her first rejuvenation.

That's when Pericles registered the Articles. They aroused only minor interest within the sleepy, vast Empire. The subject was good for a few days' conversation before the multitudes returned to more important news.

But among the mal, there was something in the Articles and accompanying pictures that tugged at nerves long since sealed off in men and mankind by time and by choice. Something that pulled each rough soul toward an unspectacular planet circling an unremarkable star in a distant corner of space.

So the mal went back to Old Earth. Not all, but many. They left the trappings of Imperial civilization and confusing intelligence and went to the first mal planet.

More simply, they went home.

There they labored not for man, but for themselves.

And when a few interested humans applied for permission to emigrate there, they were turned back by the private patrol. For the Articles composed by the horse Pericles forbade the introduction of man to Old Earth. Those Articles were written in endurasteel, framed in paragraphs of molten duralloy. Neither human curiosity nor money could make a chip in them.

It was clear to judges and law machines that while the Articles (especially the phrase about "the meek finally inheriting the Earth") might not have been good manners or good taste, they were very good law.

It was finished.

It was secured.

It was given unto the mal till the end of time.

Casperdan and Pericles left the maze that was now Dream Enterprises and went to Old Earth. They came to stand on the same place where they'd stood decades before.

Now clean low surf grumbled and subsided on a beach of polished sand that was home to shellfish and worms and brittle stars. They stood on a field of low, waving green grass. In the distance a family of giraffe moved like sentient signal towers toward the horizon. The male saw them, swung its long neck in greeting. Pericles responded with a long, high whinny.

To their left, in the distance, the first mountains began. Not bare and empty now, but covered with a mat of thick evergreen crowned with new snow.

They breathed in the heady scent of fresh clover and distant honeysuckle.

"It's done," he said.

Casperdan nodded and began to remove her clothes. Someday she would bring a husband down here. She was the sole exception in the Articles. Her golden hair fell in waves to her waist. Someday, yes . . . But for now . . .

"You know, Pericles, it really wasn't necessary. All this, I mean."

The stallion pawed at the thick loam underfoot.

"What percentage of dreams are necessary, Casperdan? You know, for many mal intelligence was not a gift but a curse. It was always that way for man, too, but he had more time to grow into it. For the mal it came like lightning, as a shock. The mal are still tied to their past—to this world. As I am still tied. Have you ever seen mal as happy as they are here?

"Certainly sentience came too quickly for the horse. According to the ancient texts we once had a special relationship with man that rivaled the dog's. That vanished millennia ago. The dog kept it, though, and so did the cat, and certain others. Other mal never missed it because they never had it. But the horse did, and couldn't cope with the knowledge of that loss that intelligence brought. There weren't many of us left, Casperdan.

"But we'll do well here. This is home. Man would feel it too, if he came here now. Feel it . . . and ruin this world all over again. That's why I wrote the Articles."

She was clad only in shorts now and to her great surprise found she was trembling slightly. She hadn't done that since she was fifteen. How long ago was that? Good God, had she ever been fifteen? But her face and figure were those of a girl of twenty. Rejuvenation.

"Pericles, I want back what you promised. I want back what I had in the Meadows of Blood in the Ravaged Mountains."

"Of course," he replied, as though it had happened yesterday. A mal's sense of time is different from man's, and Pericles' was different from that of most mal.

"You know, I have a confession to make."

She was startled to see that the relentless dreamer was embarrassed!

"It was done only to bribe you, you know. But in truth . . . in truth, I think I enjoyed it as much as you. And I'm ashamed, because I still don't understand *why*."

He kicked at the dirt.

138

She smiled understandingly. "It's the old bonds you talk about, Per. I think they must work both ways."

She walked up to him and entwined her left hand in his mane, threw the other over his back. A pull and she was up. Her movement was done smoothly . . . she'd practiced it ten thousand times in her mind.

Both hands dug tightly into the silver-black mane. Leaning forward, she pressed her cheek against the cool neck and felt ropes of muscle taut beneath the skin. The anticipation was so painful it hurt to speak.

"I'm ready," she whispered breathlessly.

"So am I," he replied.

Then the horse Pericles gave her what few humans had had for millennia, what had been outlawed in the Declaration of Animal's Rights, what they'd shared in the Meadows of Blood a billion years ago.

Gave her back the small part of the dream that was hers.

Tail flying, hooves digging dirt, magnificent body moving effortlessly over the rolling hills and grass, the horse became brother to the wind as he and his rider thundered off toward the waiting mountains. . . .

And that's why there's confusion in the old records. Because they knew all about Casperdan in the finest detail, but all they knew about the horse Pericles was that he was a genius and a poet. Now, there's ample evidence as to his genius. But the inquisitive are puzzled when they search and find no record of his poetry.

Even if they knew, they wouldn't understand.

The poetry, you see, was when he moved.

He

When I wrote the first version of this story, "jaws" were something that took up space between your neck and nose. While the story has undergone considerable rewriting to bring it to its current state, the central figure hasn't changed a bit.

In fact, there's even a nonverbal reference to Him in that notorious novel and movie named after that thing which takes up space between . . . you remember. Our hero, the police chief, is thumbing through several books on sharks. One picture shows a black-and-white photo of four scientists standing together, within one of His jaws.

So while I loved the book and the movie, after researching this story I had to be a bit disappointed in the minnowish size of Mr. Benchley's main character.

He came out of the abyss and out of the eons, and He didn't belong. His kind had passed from the world long ago, and it was better thus for the world, for They were of all Nature's creations the most terrible.

140

He

But still He survived, last of His kind, a relic of the time when They had ruled most of this world. He was old, now, terribly old, but with His kind it showed little. He'd stayed to Himself, haunting the hidden kingdom of darkness and pressure. But now, again, something impelled Him upward, something inside the superb engine of Himself drove Him toward the light, something neither He nor anyone could understand.

Two men died. The reason was basic.

The rain had worked itself out and the sun was shining by the time Poplar reached the station. The building was as unspectacular as the simple sign set into the white stucco.

UNITED STATES
OCEANOGRAPHIC
RESEARCH STATION
DEPARTMENT OF THE INTERIOR
AMERICAN SAMOA

He pushed through a series of doors and checkpoints, occasionally pausing to chat with friends and coworkers. As station director, it was his obligation as well as a pleasure.

The door to his own offices was half ajar. Long ago he'd lost the habit of stopping to admire the gold letters set into the cloudy glass.

DR. WOODRUTH L. POPLAR
DIRECTOR

He paused in front of Elaine's desk. She'd arrived some six months ago, the first crimp in a routine otherwise unbroken for the past five years. His first reactions had been confused. He still was. She swiveled around from her pile of books to face him.

In her mid-twenties, Elaine Shai had tiny, delicate features that would keep her looking childlike into her forties and fifties. Long auburn hair fell loosely in back, framing small blue eyes, a tiny gash of a mouth, and a dimpled chin. In contrast, her unnervingly spectacular figure was enveloped in print jeans and a badly outflanked white blouse. She had a fresh yellow frangipani behind one ear.

She looked great.

The elfin illusion was blurred only when she opened her mouth. Her accent was pure Brooklyn. It had disconcerted Poplar only once, when he'd greeted her on her arrival at the airport. From that point, for all it mattered, she could have chattered away in Twi.

But she bothered him.

"Well, what are you staring at, Tree?"

"You must be using a new shampoo," he said easily. "Your follicles are in bloom."

She grinned, touched the flower lightly. "Pretty, isn't it? He's in your office. I got tired of him staring at the door. Strange old bird. Never took his hands off that package. But you know these small-island Matai better than I do, Doctor. Stuffy."

"Proud, you mean."

She popped her bubblegum at him. That was her one disgusting habit. He pushed open the door to his office.

As always, his first glance was reserved for the magnificent view of the harbor out his back window. He was always afraid he'd come in one day and find a view of downtown New York, the one from his old office at Columbia. Reassured, he turned to greet the man seated in front of his desk.

Standing in front of his chair, he managed to take a fast inventory of the papers and envelopes padding his desk while at the same time extending a greeting hand.

"Talofa," he said.

"Hello, Dr. Poplar. My name is Ha'apu." The oldster's grip was firm and tight. He sat down when Poplar did.

The director stared at the man across from him. On second and third glance, maybe he wasn't so old. That Gauguinish face, weather-beaten and sunburnt, could

have as well seen forty summers as seventy. The few
lines running in it were like sculpture in a well-
decorated home, placed here and there strategically,
for character, to please the eye. The hair was cut short
and freckled with white.

The Matai retained a taut, blocky build. Ropes of
stringy muscle flexed when his arms shifted. He
matched Poplar's 175 cms. in height.

"I've come a distance to see you, Dr. Poplar."

"You sure have, all by yourself, if what they tell me
is true. I'm flattered." He changed to his best fatherly-
executive style, which was pretty sad. "How are things
on Tafahi?"

The old chief shook his head slowly. "Not good.
Since He came."

"I'm sorry to hear that," replied Poplar in what he
hoped was a convincing display of sincerity. Privately
he didn't give much of a damn about daily life on
Tafahi. "Uh . . . who is 'He'?"

"I have heard over the television that you are a
Doctor to the Sea. Is this true?"

Poplar smiled condescendingly. "I can't cure storms
or improve fishing, if that's what you mean." Educa-
tional television had performed miracles in reaching
and teaching the widely scattered Polynesian and Mel-
anesian peoples throughout the Pacific.

It was Ha'apu's turn to smile. "I still think we may
be better at that than you." He turned somber again.
"By Sea-Doctor, I mean that it is your business, your
life, to study what the ocean is, what lives in it, and
why Tangaroa does the things he does."

"That's a very astute summation," replied the director. He felt the sea-god himself would have approved, and his estimation of this man's intelligence
went up a notch.

Ha'apu seemed satisfied. "So I believed. I wanted
to make certain I understood. My mind takes longer to
think things than it once did. What I have brought to
show you . . .," he indicated the small package in his

lap, ". . . could be understood and believed only by such a person."

"Of course," said Poplar, sneaking a fast glance at his watch. He wished the chief would come to the point. Then Poplar could haggle, politely refuse, kindly suggest the chief try the usual tourist markets downtown and wharfside, and he could get to work. He'd found one new shell this morning that . . . But he didn't want to be rude by hurrying the conversation. Some Matai were easily insulted. And he wasn't famous for his diplomatic manner.

Ha'apu was working at the small package. It was tightly bound in clean linen and secured with twine.

"But first you must promise me you will be careful of whom you speak to about this. We have no wish to endure an assault of the curious."

Poplar thought back to the moaning jetliner that had passed overhead this morning, crammed to the gills with bloated statesiders eager for a glimpse of the quaint locals betwixt brunch and supper, and applauded the Matai's attitude. He wasn't all that naive.

"I promise it will be so, Matai."

Ha'apu continued to work deliberately with the knots. "You are familiar with Niuhi?"

"Yes, certainly." He peered at the shrinking pile of cloth and twine with renewed interest. A good carving of Niuhi would be something of a novelty. At least it wasn't yet another dugout or tiki.

"Then you will know this," said Ha'apu solemnly. He removed an irregular shaped object and placed it carefully on the desk in front of the director.

Poplar stared at it for a long moment before he recognized it for what it was. The realization took another moment to penetrate fully. Slowly he reached out and picked it up. A rapid examination, a few knuckle taps convinced him it was real and not a clever fake. It wasn't the sort of thing one *could* easily fake. And besides, even the simplest islander would know he couldn't get away with it. He brought it up to eye level.

"Ye gods and little fishes," he murmured in aston-
shment.

It wasn't a carving.

It was a tooth. And it was quite impossible.

The tooth was almost a perfect triangle. He reached
into his desk and brought out a ruler, laid it alongside
the hard bone. Slightly under 18 cms. long, about 14
cms. wide at the bottom, and over five thick. The base
was slightly curved where it fit into the jaw. Both cutting edges were wickedly serrated, like a saw. He
stared at it for a long, long time, running his fingers
along the razor-sharp cutting edges, testing the perfect
point. A magnifying glass all but confirmed its reality.
That failed to temper his uncertainty.

"Where did you get this, Ha'apu? And are there any
more?" he asked softly.

"This was taken from the wood of a paopao." The
Matai smiled slightly. "There is another."

It took Poplar about thirty seconds to connect this
with what the chief had told him earlier. Einsteinian
calculations aside, he could still add up the implica-
tions. He leaned back in his chair.

"Now Ha'apu, you're not going to try and convince
me that this tooth came out of the mouth of a living
Great White!"

The chief began slowly, picking his words. "The
doctor is very sure of himself. About three weeks ago,
two young men from my village were out fishing an
area we rarely visit, rather far from Tafahi. There is
better fishing in other directions, and closer to home,
but they wished also a little adventure. They did not
return to us, even hours after nightfall.

"All of the men of the village, including myself, set
out to search for them. We were not yet worried. We
knew where they had gone. Perhaps their boat had
been damaged, or both had been injured. There was no
moon that night. One cannot see far onto the ocean at
night by only torch and flashlight. We did not find
them.

"What we did find, floating by a small reef and still

145

anchored to the coral, was the rear half of their pao-pao. It had been snapped in two, Dr. Poplar. That tooth you hold now in your hand was buried in the side of the wreckage. Television and great jet airplanes admitted, Doctor, old beliefs still linger on most of the islands. I am the most educated man in my village and proud of my learning. But this frightened me. We have lived with the sea too long to doubt what might come from it. We put on an exhibition of rowing that could not be matched, Dr. Poplar, in any of the Olympic games.

"It was very quiet on Tafahi the next day. Fishing, a daily task for us, had grown suddenly unpopular. I pointed out there was still a chance to recover the bodies or . . ." he winced, ". . . parts of them. But no one would return to that reef.

"I went alone. It is a small atoll . . . very tiny, not on any but the most detailed of your maps, I should guess. That was where our two men had gone to fish. To the northeast of it, I believe, the ocean bottom disappears very fast."

Poplar nodded. "The northern tip of the Kermadec-Tonga Trench runs across there. In spots the sea floor drops almost straight down for, oh, 3500, 3600 fathoms . . . and more."

"As you say, Doctor. The sun does not go far there. It is where He dwells.

"I anchored my paopao behind the protection of the little reef, safe from the breakers on the other side. It was where the men had anchored. Swimming was not difficult, despite a slight current."

"If you thought you might encounter a big Great White prowling around down there, why'd you go in?" asked Poplar shrewdly.

The chief shrugged. "My family have been chiefs and divers for enough generations for my genealogy to bore you, Doctor. I respect Niuhi and know him. I was careful. Anyhow, someone had to do it. I did not swim too long or too deep. I had only mask and fins and did not use the weights. I also have respect for age, including my own.

"The small lunch I had brought with me did not take long to eat. The afternoon was long, the sun pleasant. I dove again.

"I had given up and was swimming back to the boat when I noticed a dark spot in the water to my left. It was keeping pace with me. The water was clear, and so it must have been far away to be so blurred. It paced me all the way back to the boat. Despite the distance I knew it was Him."

"Mightn't it have been . . . ?" Poplar didn't finish the question. Ha'apu was shaking his head.

"My eyes, at least, are still young. It was Him. I could not be absolutely certain He was watching me. I doubt it. Faster or slower I did not swim. A sudden change of stroke might have caught His attention. But I was glad when I was in the bottom of my boat, breathing free of the sea.

"I waited and watched for a long time, not daring to leave the small shelter of the reef. Once, far away, I think I saw a fin break the surface. If it was a fin, it was taller than a tall man, Doctor. But it might not have been. It was far away and the sun was dropping.

"I have only been truly afraid, and I say this honestly, a few times in my life. To be alone on the sea with Him was terrible enough. To have been caught there in the dark would have frozen the blood of a god. Then I knew the legend was true."

"What legend?" asked Poplar.

"Whoever sees Him is forever changed, Doctor. His soul is different, and a little bit of it is stolen away by Him. The rest is altered forever."

"In what way?" Poplar inquired. Better to humor the old man. He was interested in the damn tooth, not local superstition.

"It depends so much on the man," the Matai mused. "For myself, the sea will never again be the open friend of my youth. I ride upon it now and look into its depths with hesitation, for any day, any hour, He may be come for me.

"My people were surprised to see me. They had not expected me to return."

Poplar considered silently. "That's quite a story you want me to swallow. In fact, it's pretty unbelievable."

"A strange thing for you to say, Sea-Doctor," smiled Ha'apu. "But I do not blame you. Come back with me. Bring a good boat and your diving tools. I will show you what remains of our young men's paopao. And then I will take you to the spot where I saw Him, if you dare. He may have returned to the deeps. Surely this is a rare thing, or He would have been seen before. There must be a purpose for it."

B.S., M.S., Ph.D., he thought hard for a moment. The legend stuff was all bushwah, of course. But the tooth . . . he tried to visualize its owner, and a little shiver went down his spine. This business about soul-changing . . . ridiculous! . . . *he,* frightened of another fish?

"This tooth could be very, very old, you know. They've been found before, like new. Although," he swallowed and cursed himself for it, "not quite of this size. According to the best estimates these creatures became extinct only very recently."

"Creatures? There is only one of *him,*" said Ha'apu firmly.

"You could fake the ruined outrigger," persisted Poplar.

"To what end?"

"I don't know!" He was irritated at his irrational terror. Goddammit, man, it probably doesn't exist! And if it, by some incredible chance, did, it was only another fish.

"Maybe you want to attract those tourists you profess to dislike. Or want to try and wangle some free diving equipment. Or simply want to draw some attention to yourself. Who knows? But I can't take that chance." He took another look at the tooth. "You know I can't, damn you. Where are you staying while you're on Tutuila?"

"With friends."

"Okay, we have a couple of cruisers here at the station. They're not in use just now. Down at the very end of Pier Three. The one we'll use is called the *Vatia.* You can't mistake it. The other, the *Aku-Aku,* is longer and has a flying bridge. Meet me at, oh, ten tomorrow morning, on the pier. If you get there ahead of me, tie your boat to the stern." He stopped turning the tooth over and over, feigned unconcern. Inside, he was quivering with tension.

"May I keep this?" He knew what he was asking. Did the chief?

"There is another still set in the paopao. Yes, you may have this one. For your children, to remind them of when you were young."

"I have no children. I'm not married, Ha'apu."

"That is sad. The other tooth must remain with us. It will not . . ." he said, in reply to the unposed question, ". . . ever be for sale."

Poplar was seeing his name blazoned across the cover and title page of every scientific journal in the world. Below the name, a picture of himself holding the largest tooth of *Carcharodon megalodon* ever found. He might even manage to include Ha'apu in the picture.

He leaned over the desk, began shuffling papers.

"Good-bye till tomorrow, then, Matai Ha'apu."

"Tofa, Sea-Doctor Poplar." The chief gathered up his wrappings and left quietly.

He began going over the supplies they'd need in addition to what was standard stock on board the *Vatai.* Plan on being gone at least a week, maybe two. Get him out of the office, at least.

Elaine walked in, strolled over to the desk and leaned across it. That finished any attempt at paperwork. When she noticed the tooth in front of him, she almost swallowed her gum.

"My God, what's that?"

149

"You're a master's candidate in marine bio. You tell me." He handed it to her.

She examined it closely, and those pixie eyes got wider and wider.

"Some gag. It looks like a Great White's tooth. But that's absurd."

"So was the *coelacanth* when it turned up in 1938," he replied evenly.

"But it *can't* be *Carcharodon!*" she protested. "It's three times too big!"

"For *Carcharodon carcharias,* yes. Not for *Carcharodon megalodon.*" He turned and dug into the loosely stacked books that inhabited the space between desk chair and wall. In a teacher-student situation, he was perfectly comfortable with her.

"You mean the Great White's ancestor? Well, maybe." She took another look at the unreal weapon in her hand. "I found one in Georgia about half this size. And there was a six-incher turned up just a few years ago. Extrapolating from what we know about the modern Great White, *carcharias,* that would mean this tooth came out of a shark ninety fee—"

"Ah-ah," he warned.

"Oh, all right. About, um, thirty meters long." She didn't smile. "Kind of hard to imagine."

"So are sharks attacking boats. But there are dozens of verified incidents of sharks, often Great Whites, hitting small craft. Happens off stateside waters as well as in the tropics. The White Death. The basis for a real Moby Dick, only ten times worse. Not to mention a few thousand years of sea-serpent stories."

"You think one of these might have survived into recent times?"

Poplar was thumbing through a thick tome. "That's what that chief thinks, only to him it's a god and not a shark. The Great White prefers ocean-going- mammals to fish. Probably this oversized ancestor of his fed on the earlier, slower-moving whales. First the whales grew more streamlined, and then man began picking off the slower ones. The sea couldn't have supported too many of these monsters anyway. A megalodon would have a killer whale for breakfast."

"A man-eater as big as a blue whale." She shook her lovely head. "A diver's nightmare."

"The Matai who brought this one in says he knows where there's another, and maybe more."

"Far out. You think I might get my thesis out of this?"

"Well," he smiled, "the chief did say that according to legend anyone who sees Him is forever changed. All you've got to do is spot Him."

"Very funny."

"We leave first thing tomorrow morning, on the *Vatai*. Tenish. Now go and pack." But she was already out the door.

She was not so happy for the reasons Poplar thought.

Tourists waved from the hotel balcony. It had been built at the point where the open sea met Pago Pago's magnificent harbor. Elaine slid her lava-lava down a little lower on one shoulder and waved back coquettishly. Poplar looked up from the wheel disapprovingly.

"Just because naked native maidens went out of fashion forty years ago is no reason for you to feel any obligation to revive the tradition for the benefit of overweight used-car salesmen from Des Moines."

"Oh, foo! For what they charge the poor slobs to stay in that concrete doghouse they're entitled to a little wish-fulfillment."

"Courtesy of downtown Brooklyn, hmm," he grinned in spite of himself. He swung the wheel hard over and they headed south-southwest. The powerful twin diesels purred evenly below deck.

Wreathed in gold-gray clouds, Mt. Rainmaker, all 530 meters of it, watched them from astern long after Tutuila itself had vanished into the sea.

The trip was uneventful, except that Elaine insisted on sleeping stark naked. She also had what Poplar felt was a childish habit of kicking her sheets down to her feet. He considered going over and replacing them, but hesitated. He might wake her and that would be awkward.

Ha'apu was clearly pleased at the situation, and there wasn't anything Poplar could do about it. Well, if she wanted to expose herself, he'd simply ignore her. Clearly she was looking for attention, and he didn't intend to give it to her.

So until he fell asleep, he spent a lot of time staring at the sterile cabin wall that separated him from the sea.

And the other wall remained equally unbroken.

Like most small, low-lying Pacific islands, Tafahi was nonexistent one moment and a destination the next, popping out of the blue ocean like a cork. The white sand beach sparkled in evening sun, devoid of the usual ornaments of civilization . . . beer cans, dog-eared sandals, plastic wrappers, empty candy papers, beer cans.

There was a broad, clear entrance to the small lagoon. Poplar had no trouble bringing the *Vatai* inside. Ha'apu climbed into his paopao, its little sail tightly furled, and paddled ashore. Poplar and Elaine followed in the *Vatai*'s powerful little runabout.

"We're not here just to look for teeth, Elaine," he said abruptly. She stared at him expectantly.

"Ha'apu really thinks—I know it sounds absurd—that this monster is still swimming around somewhere to the east of here. Supposedly it's taken two fishermen along with the front half of their boat. Probably a cleverly faked fraud the villagers have made up, for what purpose I don't know yet. Commercial, probably."

"I see," she replied easily. "Be careful you don't run over any of the local craft when we hit the beach."

For all the surprise she'd shown you might have thought they were here for an evening feast and a casual swim in the little lagoon.

They were on the best of terms with the islanders right from the start. Poplar had rammed the runabout into a beached paopao, spilling them both into the shallow water. Being men of the sea, the villagers thus felt the same sort of sympathy for Poplar that they'd have given any idiot.

When Ha'apu had finally managed to separate himself from his immediate family and Poplar and Elaine had dried out a little, the Matai beckoned them inland.

"The remains of the dugout are in front of my fale, Doctor."

Tafahi was far from being a major island, but it was large enough to support a fair population. A television-FM antenna poked its scarecrow shape above the tallest coconut palm. It jutted from an extra-large fale that served as combination school, church, and town hall.

If the damage to the outrigger had been faked, it was the product of experts. Poplar knelt, ran his hands over the torn edges of the opened hull. Great triangular gashes, each larger than his fist, showed clearly around the shredded edges. Apparently it had been hit —or the hit had been faked to indicate an attack from an angle slightly to port.

"The first tooth was in here . . ." Ha'apu knelt beside Poplar to indicate a narrowing hole in the bottom of the craft, ". . . and the other, here." He pointed, and Poplar saw the other tooth, as large as the one back in his office, still embedded in the side of the outrigger.

"He lost them, as Niuhi and his cousins often do when they attack hard objects," commented Ha'apu in a helpful tone.

"Yeah," agreed Poplar, absorbed in his examination. "Always carries plenty in reserve, though. I wouldn't think his ancestor would be any exception." He squinted up at the sinking sun. It had begun the spectacular light-show sunset that was an every-evening occurrence in the South Seas.

"It's getting late. No point in hurrying to reach that reef tonight. About two hours to get there, you said?"

Ha'apu nodded. "In your boat, yes."

Poplar was a bit surprised. Now was the time the

Matai should have begun his excuses, his hedging. He stood, brushed sand from his pants. "Then if you can put us up, I'd just as soon spend the night here. We've been doing enough shipboard sleeping and we'll be doing more."

"I agree!" said Elaine, rather more loudly than was necessary.

The Matai nodded. "Of course there will be a fale for you."

"With *two* mats," Poplar added.

"Why should it be otherwise, Dr. Poplar?" agreed Ha'apu. If the old chief was being sarcastic, he covered it well. But as he walked away, muttering in Samoan, he was shaking his head slowly.

It wasn't the strange surroundings, nor the hard floor beneath the mat of woven tapa cloth that made Poplar's sleep uneasy. He'd enjoyed some of the deepest sleeps of his life in similar situations. And when he was awakened about midnight by a sudden bumping, he drew a startled breath. His dreams had been full of dark arrow-shapes with mouths like black pits. But it was only Elaine. She'd rolled over in her sleep and was resting against his shoulder, breathing softly. Courteously, he didn't push her away, but it made it harder for him to get back to sleep, which displeased him.

When he awoke the next morning he was covered with sweat.

"This may not be the exact spot, but it is very close," breathed Ha'apu. "I know by the trees."

Since the single minuscule "island" harbored barely six or seven small palms, with but two of decent size, Poplar felt confident the old chief had found the spot he wanted.

They'd anchored in the lee of the atoll. It was small enough so that you could see the surf booming against the coral on the far side.

Poplar kept an eye on Ha'apu while he helped Elaine into her scuba gear. Still no sign of an attempt to keep him from diving. He thought the hoax was beginning to go a little far.

The tanks they'd brought were the latest models. They'd have an hour on the bottom with plenty of safe time. Elaine checked her regulator, he checked his. They each took up a shark stick, but Poplar gave his to Elaine. He wanted both hands for his camera, and she could handle anything likely to bother them.

There was a diver's platform set just below the waterline at the stern of the *Vatai*. Elaine jumped in with a playful splash. He followed more slowly, handling the expensive camera with care.

Both wore only the upper half of a heat-retaining wetsuit. The ocean flowing around his bare legs told him it was a good thing he had. It wasn't cold, but cooler water flowing from the depths of the oceanic trench obviously found its way up here. The thermocline would rise nearer the surface. That would permit deep-sea dwellers to rise closer to the top. Still, it was comfortable and refreshing after the trip on the boat.

Ha'apu watched them descend, and worried.

The water inside the lagoon would be clear as quartz. Even out here, visibility was excellent in all directions.

The underwater world held as much fascination for him now as it had on his first dive, years ago. Much of the mystery was gone, but the beauty of his refuge was ever-present.

For the first few minutes, as they swam parallel to the reef, he couldn't stop himself from turning to look anxiously in all directions. He gave up that nonsense after five minutes. Nothing more impressive than a fair-sized grouper had trundled clumsily across their path. His shark prod now dangled lazily from his belt.

They stopped often for pictures. Even if this were only a pleasure jaunt, it would be nice to bring back something to justify the expenditure and time.

They returned to the *Vatai* ten minutes early. Poplar was feeling hungry and a little discouraged. The tiny reef had been exceptional in its mediocrity. He'd

155

seen hundreds of identical spots during his trips throughout the Pacific and the Caribbean. And he didn't feel like staying another five or six days.

In sum, he was being took. If Ha'apu's plan was to use the two teeth to get a free estimate of the fishing grounds (probably been in the village for years, he thought), it was working admirably. Poplar was definitely being used.

"Did you see anything?" asked Ha'apu politely as he helped Elaine doff her tanks.

"I got a couple of shots of a pretty good-sized Moray. Otherwise, Ha'apu, there's more sea life to be found outside the harbor at Pago Pago or Apia."

"He has frightened them all away," commented the chief knowingly. "Perhaps you will have better luck on your next dive."

"Sure," replied Poplar drily, helping himself to a glass of tea.

By the third day, the attractions of the un-unusual reef had long since paled for Poplar. Even the attraction of swimming through the brilliantly lit water was beginning to feel like work again. Elaine seemed to thrive on it, but, then, there was still something in every crevice to delight her. But he'd seen enough angel fish, brain coral, giant mollusks, trumpet fish, et cetera, et cetera, ad infinitum, to last him another year. And nothing he couldn't see with much less trouble right in the station's backyard.

In fact, except for a peaceful encounter with a poisonous stonefish, the last three days had been about as exciting as a dive in one of Pago Pago's hotel pools.

"Possibly He willl come this afternoon," said Ha'apu.

"I know, I know," Poplar replied irritably. It was just about time to tell the old chief off, find out what he wanted, and return home.

In the many-times-three dives, they'd sighted exactly three sharks. Two small blues and one pelagic white-tip, a seven-footer that had turned and run for the open sea even before Poplar could set his camera for a decent shot. To him they were just three more fish.

They'd go home tomorrow. True, he'd sort of promised the Matai a week. But the longer he stayed away from the office, the more work would be piled up for his return. Although he'd left the pressures of extreme paperwork back in the States and settled into the more agreeable Samoan mode, old habits died hard. As director, he still had certain responsibilities.

He was drifting along just above the sea bottom about half a mile from the boat. His camera had lined on a gorgeous black and yellow sea worm, flowerlike body fully extended. It was the first really unusual thing he'd seen since they'd arrived. A perfect picture ... his light meter shrank by half.

Damn and hell, that was the last straw! Poplar whirled angrily, expecting to see a playful Elaine floating just above and behind him. He'd warned her at least half a dozen times to stay out of the light when he was taking pictures. She'd seemed to think it was fun.

But something else had swallowed the sun.

For a second Poplar, training, degrees, and experience notwithstanding, stopped thinking. He went back to his childhood. When he'd lain in bed at night, the covers up around his chin, staring at where his clothes lay draped over the back of his chair. You wouldn't know the kind of terrifying shapes clothes and chair and night can combine to make in a child's mind. Fear squeezed his spine and his heart pumped madly.

Above him, *Carcharodon megalodon* glided majestically through the clear water, its seemingly unending tail beating hypnotically from side to side, the great pectoral fins cutting the current like hydrofoils.

He turned, saw Elaine drifting alongside. He tugged at her arm. She ignored it. He tugged harder. As though in a dream, she turned to face him. He pointed in the direction of the boat. She nodded, sluggishly following him, half swimming, half towed.

A line from Cousteau ran through his mind, and he tried desperately to swim faster.

"Sharks can instinctively sense when a fish or animal is in trouble."

She shook free from him, nodded at his concerned gaze, and began swimming steadily on her own.

For a while the monster seemed not to notice them. It swam slightly ahead, moving effortlessly. A single gigantic stretch of cartilage, tooth, sinew, and muscle. Poplar stared at it and knew that what Ha'apu had said was true. This was more than a fish, more than a shark. You could feel it in yourself and in the water.

Lazily, it banked like a great bird and came at them.

He turned frantically, gestured to Elaine. The shark was between them and the boat. Trying to outswim it would be like trying to outrun lightning. He'd spotted a long crack in the battlements of the reef. Usually such breaks harbored morays, powerful clams, and poisoners like the stonefish. Right now they seemed like the best of friends, harmless as puppies.

There was no subtlety, no attempt to deceive, in their retreat. They swam like hell.

Maybe He was disinterested in such small prey. Whatever the reason, His pursuit remained leisurely. They attained the safety of the rift. Wedged back in the deep, wide crevice, they still had room to swim freely.

He came straight at them. Poplar had to fight down the urge to scrape frantically at the coral behind him. For the moment, he was afraid the monster would try to bite them out, coral and all. It looked big enough to take half the atoll in one gulp.

At the last moment, He swerved to His right. There was a brief glimpse of a half-open mouth, a cavern big enough to swallow a truck. It was lined with multiple rows of 18-centimeter-long teeth. A wide black eye passed, pure malignancy floating in a pool of red-hot venom. Then there was a long, endless wall of iron-gray flesh rough as sandpaper—darker than the skin of a Great White, some part of him noted—and it was past.

He floated. Elaine prodded him and he could see the terror behind her mask. He wondered if he looked as bad. The great bulk had circled and was beginning a slow patrol of the reef. Not that it was smart enough to consider bottling them up. Clearly it liked the area.

Anyhow, they were stuck.

If the rift had been a chimney, open all the way to the surface, they could have swum upward. Despite the battering of the light surf, they'd have been safer on the reef's jagged top than in the water with Him. But it was closed overhead. To reach the surface, they would have to leave their small fortress.

Minutes passed. They looked at each other without seeing. Each was wholly absorbed in personal thoughts. They'd encountered a terror whose psychological effect was even more overwhelming than its reality. It did not belong to the world of men, this perfect, unmatched killing machine. How puny man seemed, how feeble his invented efforts at destruction.

How frightened he was.

He looked down at his watch. At the rate they were using air, in a few minutes they'd be down to their emergency supply. Elaine prodded, moved her hands in diver's argot. He remained frozen. She grabbed him by the shoulders and shook him. But there was no way he could tell her in sign language of this new problem.

Woodruth "Woody" Poplar was a coward. A physical and moral coward. He knew it, buried it beneath work and joking.

Elaine started tugging at her own tanks. It unfroze him. He grabbed her arms, held them at her side until she finally nodded slowly, calmed.

It took every ounce of courage he possessed to look outside that cranny. He blinked, drifted out further. *He* had disappeared. Poplar glanced in all directions. Nothing.

He beckoned to Elaine. Carefully he made his intentions clear. Megalodon, being as stupid as any modern shark, had doubtlessly drifted off in search of prey that behaved like such and didn't melt into hard, unappetizing coral.

Poplar armed his shark stick . . . a terribly futile-seeming gesture. Elaine did likewise. He had to try twice with his shaking hands before he got the shell armed. The monster was a good 30 meters long and must weigh more tons than Poplar cared to think about. The shark stick might tickle Him. But it was comforting to hold in the crook of one arm.

He pushed away first and they headed for the *Vatai*. Moving fast, they hugged the reef as tightly as they could. He let her get a little ahead, as arranged. That way they'd make less of a blur against the reef. The smaller shapes would be harder for the shark's eyesight to detect against the dark coral.

As they rose gradually toward the surface, leaving the protection of the reef wall, he tried to watch five directions at once. Inside he was oddly calm. What an animal! Nearly a hundred feet of sheer grace and power.

He missed a stroke. Hell, he'd forgotten to take a single picture! Not one lousy shot! All he had by way of proof was the corroborative statement of Elaine—worth nothing in such august publications as the *Journal of Marine Biology*—and a couple of teeth that they'd treat as he first had. He would have cried, but it would have ruined his vision.

The curved bottom of the *Vatai* became visible just ahead and above, its anchor cable hardly moving in the calm sea. The platform occasionally broke the surface. He looked regretfully down at his camera.

An unmistakable shape, a slate-gray torpedo, was coming up fast behind them. This time it wasn't a lazy chase. The attack was as sharply defined as death. Sunlight flashed on teeth that could snap through steel plate.

They swam for their lives. Panic filled him, terror made jelly of his muscles. Only adrenalin pushed him through the clean glass water.

They weren't going to make it. *He* wasn't a fish. He was the devil himself, Beelzebub, all the things that go bump in the night, the terrors of childhood and of little-boy darkness.

Elaine was falling behind. He slowed.

Goddammit, it was only a fish.

He turned and waited. Elaine paused only to give him a stricken look in passing and then was gone. Perfectly calm, he was. Relaxed and peaceful in the cool water. Inside, his one major concern was that no one would be able to record this for the *Journal*. Pity. Then there was no sea bottom, no reef, no sunlight. Only He and me, thought Poplar.

He kicked with every bit of energy in his legs, exploding to his right. He had a brief glimpse of an obscene eye as big as a saucer, a black gullet as deep as a well. It touched him. Consciousness departed as he jabbed with the shark stick.

He doubted, along with the best Biblical referents, that the sky in heaven was blue. But he wasn't going to argue. There was a constriction, a tightness in his throat, that wasn't caused by fear. Elaine was hugging him and crying. It felt like he'd swallowed a cork.

"For Christ's sake let me get some air!" he finally managed to croak. She backed off.

"Damn you, damn you. You scared the hell out of me, you insensitive, you . . . !" She sniffled. Her hair was wet and stringy and she was totally beautiful. "I ran away and left you." The crying broke out again in full force, and she fell onto his chest, sobbing.

"I'm sorry, I apologize for my inconsiderateness. Tell you what, I'll marry you. Will that make up for it?" He rolled over, felt the softness of the mat they'd slipped under him. Someone had removed his tanks and mask.

She pulled away, stared at him in stunned silence. For some reason, this started her crying all over again. They'd removed his fins, too. He wiggled his toes.

Only one set moved.

He sat up slowly and looked down at himself. His

right foot ended at the ankle in a swath of bandages and dried blood. His voice was so even it shocked him.

"What happened?" he asked the old Matai, who had been watching him carefully. He was aware the question lacked brilliance, but at the moment he didn't feel very witty.

"He did not take you, Sea-Doctor Poplar. Perhaps so close to the surface, the sun blinded it at the last moment. Perhaps He lost you against the bottom of the boat."

"You don't believe any of that," said Poplar accusingly. He searched for pain but there wasn't any. Someone had made use of the *Vatai*'s medical kit.

"No, Dr. Poplar, not really. Tangaroa knows why."

Poplar thought of something, started laughing. Elaine looked at him in alarm, but he quickly reassured her.

"No. I'm still sane, I think, 'Laine. It just occurred to me that I can't go stalking around the office like Ahab himself, with only a lousy foot taken. What a cruddy break."

"Don't joke about it," she blubbered, then managed a weak smile. "It will ruin your rhythm at the wedding."

He laughed, too, then slammed a fist against the deck. "We're going back to Tutuila. I'm going to get a ship from the Navy base, somehow, and harpoons. We'll come back here and . . ."

"Poplar," began Ha'apu quietly, "no one will believe you. Your Navy people will laugh at you and make jokes."

"Well, then I'll get the funds to hire a bigger ship, someway. One big enough to haul that thing back on. My God, one day I'll see it stuffed and mounted in the Smithsonian!"

"They'll have to build a special wing," Elaine grinned tightly.

"Yeah. And don't you go putting out any fishing

lines on the way back, you hear? I don't want to lose you on the trip in."

"How about after we get back?" she replied, staring at him.

He looked at her evenly. "Not then, either. Not ever. Hey, you know something? I'm famished."

"You've been unconscious for five hours," she told him. "I'll fix you something." She rose, moved below decks.

"And now you are as I, Doctor, for you have gazed upon Him. He has changed you, and you are no longer yourself as before, and He has taken a piece of your soul."

"Listen, Ha'apu, I don't want to offend you by attacking your religion, but that was just a fish, that's all. A monstrous big fish, but no more. I'm the same sea-doctor, and you're the same Matai, and we're just lucky all I lost was a few toes and such. Understand?"

"Of course, Dr. Poplar." Ha'apu turned, went up to the bridge.

Changed indeed! He crawled over to the low railing near the stern, looked down into the waters. Small fish swam down there, magnified and distorted by the sea. He shivered just a little.

He would have married Elaine anyway, of course. And if she'd been threatened by anything, he'd have stepped in to defend her, wouldn't he? Ha'apu fired the engines and the *Vatai* started to move.

Well, wouldn't he?

Maybe He knew.

Polonaise

This was written for a volume of alternate-history stories, the "What if the South had won the Civil War?" type. I went back a bit further than that, to a period of European history little studied in this country. It all came out of my liking for a writer named Henryk Sienkewicz —and I don't mean his *Quo Vadis?* I'm talking about his other books, the good stuff.

Henryk who? Among other things, he won the Nobel Prize for literature in 1905. And his obscurity is one reason I chose the alternate history I did. Another is the fact that it could have happened.

Then we wouldn't have been stuck with all these American jokes.

"It's a very delicate situation, Michael, very delicate. We cannot afford an incident now, yet if we treat this too seriously it will invite unwanted attention. It all happened so fast. Quite ridiculous, when you view it from a distance."

Framed against the imposing panorama of sun-steamed fog as seen through the massive two-story window, the old man looked terribly tiny and fragile. Now and then a gull or two would sail past the twentieth-floor overlook and gift the men with a peek of sorrowful curiosity.

Beyond, solidifying now as the morning mists burned off the Baltic coast, was the long low spit of land known as the Hel Peninsula. Running parallel to the nothern shore of the Imperial Republic, it formed a surprisingly resistant barrier to the sea.

The flotilla of sightseeing boats was still growing. Like hovering bees they huddled together in anchored expectancy of the launch. Tall dark shapes were taking form off their bows, way down the peninsula. Vertical piers cradling a very different kind of vessel.

Michael Yan surveyed the scene visible on either side of the administrator and shook his head.

The Poles were a gentle people. If any of the boosters misfired, there would be a chance of serious injury to the growing mob of spectators, and considerable national hand-wringing would ensue. It was typical of the King that he'd agonized for days over whether or not to permit outsiders a good view of the launch. And equally typical that he'd given in.

"Can you at least tell me who he is?"

Administrator Longin ran a hand over his white crewcut, fingered the scar over his broken nose where he'd slammed into the computer console on the fourth moon-flight, and turned to face Michael.

"Not he, she. She planned it all very carefully." He nodded appreciatively. "She went straight to the American Embassy and *then* got in touch with us. Basically, she threatened to release the taped information she stole unless we agree to call off the shot and admit on-site inspectors to all subsequent multiple launchings."

"That's *all?* Look, why not let her go ahead and blab to the press? What harm can it do? What can she know? So we plan to launch six ships simultane-

ously to celebrate the King's birthday. So what?"
Longin was shaking his head dolefully.

"It's not as simple as that, Michael. The release of
the tapes we could absorb. The problem is that she's
convinced we've an ulterior motive concealed in the
launch. She should know if we do." Michael's smile
disappeared.

"Why is that?"

"She works . . . worked . . . in your department."

"My . . . ?" He stopped, then continued guardedly,
"What does she think is this 'ulterior reason' behind
the shot?"

Longin sat down behind his desk. "She is quite convinced from her inside knowledge of material being
loaded on board some of the ships, that we are planning to establish a permanent military base on Mars
and claim the whole planet for the Republic."

Michael's grim smile turned to a look of honest
bafflement. "That's the most nonsensical thing I ever
heard. Doesn't she know the Imperial Edicts forbid
acquisition of territory except by vote of independent
peoples? You say she works in my department. I can't
imagine what might motivate any of my people to
jeopardize the King's birthday."

"Not citizens, no. But you have a number of exchange students working for you, do you not?"

"As part of our policy of sharing space science,
yes."

"Any Americans?"

"The Americans, the Americans!" Michael threw
up his hands. "That's all you hear about, the American threat! Just because their newspaper columnists—"

"Do you know those who have access to restricted
files?" pressed Longin softly.

"Oh, John Huxley, Marshall McGregor, and Dana
Canning . . ." He paused, considered a moment. "You
said 'she'? No, that's crazy, Henryk."

"Not as crazy as this situation we suddenly find
ourselves in. I just finished talking to the American
ambassador. Her premise is absolutely mad, as we

know, but she's thrown enough real facts at him to get him unsettled. And we cannot do with prying this close to lift-off."

"No, of course not." Michael considered. "You don't really think the Americans would actually try and *stop* the launch?" Longin leaned back in his chair and gave an expressive shrug.

"Who knows?" His face was sad. "Americans are capable of anything—all that misdirected drive. They're even crazier than the French."

"You'd think we'd never helped them win their independence from England," Michael added ruefully.

Longin nodded. "They never forgave us for that. Charity's never appreciated as much as it's resented. They're suspicious of us because they don't understand us."

"You'd think they'd worry more about the Russian Federalists."

"They might," Longin agreed, "if the Russians ever get strong enough. But we worry them more. According to their philosophy, our government should have collapsed a hundred years ago." He sighed.

"Their ambassador pretends to understand, but of course he doesn't. I tried to explain to him. 'You elect a President,' I said, 'and we elect a King.' And he counters, 'But how can you give absolute power to a new person every five years?' I asked him the same question and of course he gave me that cow-eyed pitying look they all do whenever the subject comes up. Insists the American President doesn't have anywhere near the same kind of power. So I list historical examples for him and he gets all huffy and self-righteous.

"But he can cause real trouble. So that's why you've got to go over there and convince that girl she's got her tape systems crossed. So much planning has gone into this birthday present for the King—too much for the ravings of some neurotic adolescent to ruin it. We could take less orthodox steps to quiet her, but—well, you know that's just not our style. If we did that we'd be exactly the kind of folk she seems to think we are."

Yan spread his hands. "Mars colonization! Honestly! But why me, sir? Why not someone from the Defense Ministry?"

"You know her, Michael. As a friend. None of her tirades included you. We know, we taped them. Either she doesn't believe you're involved, which is unlikely, or else she has a desire not to implicate you, which is better."

"Look, sir . . ." Michael squirmed uncomfortably. "I'm an engineer. I have a fiancée, and I'm just not going to try and seduce some misguided teenager."

"We're not asking you to be nearly so melodramatic about this, Michael. Of course," the administrator murmured, "if you should happen to find the situation developing along apolitical lines, it wouldn't be . . ."

"All right, all right! I'll talk to her. For the project, mind. And for the King, of course."

"Naturally."

"How am I supposed to convince her the launch has nothing to do with Mars? I can't show her secret files."

"No, you can't. You must convince her that the Imperial Republic of Poland has embarked on the exploration of space for the good of all mankind and nothing more, and that we have no intention of deviating from that principle with this launch. Our very strength renders this unnecessary. Just show her the truth, Michael —in a circumspect fashion, of course.

"Consider yourself fortunate. You have only a slightly hysterical young lady to convince, while I am forced to contend with high-pressure Hartford and his horde of foggy-headed foggy bottoms. I'd trade with you anytime."

Michael sighed. "Where do I meet her, and when?"

"We'll set up something on the grounds of the American Embassy." Longin's expression took on overtones of disgust. "She's convinced if she leaves it she'll be cut down in the streets. Does she think Warsaw is Chicago?"

As arranged, she was waiting for him by the Japanese pool in the Embassy garden. The bull-necked Marine at the gate eyed him hostilely, but passed him through. As requested, there was no one with her.

No doubt she was bugged from head to foot, while he was probably walking under the gaze of half a dozen sharpshooters. His neck itched. This wasn't his line at all.

Michael was less concerned with the bugs, since he packed enough antibugging equipment inside his jacket to electronically fumigate a skyscraper. Hopefully their would-be listeners wouldn't interfere, trusting in Dana to report to them later.

She was small, blonde, pretty, quiet: the last woman in the world he would have selected as a self-appointed martyr.

"Hello Dana," he said gently.

"Mr. Yan?" Not Michael, as in the office, but mister.

There was defiance in her voice, in her eyes, in her stance. He didn't know this girl at all. Longin had been wrong.

She was daring him. All right. Her Polish was better than his English, despite her odd accent. She was from Georgia. He remembered because he was always confusing it with Russian Georgia.

He gestured at the bridge leading over the pond and they started off toward it. The ripples on the surface were reflected in the surrounding glass walls of the Embassy buildings. How the Americans loved their glass!

"Dana, I love you." She stumbled and her expression changed drastically. At least he'd put her off her guard.

"You've got a funny sense of humor, Mr. Yan."

"Michael, please. I'm not old enough to be called 'mister.' "

"Michael, if you will. I don't believe—No, wait a minute." She smiled sardonically. "Of course you love

169

me. You also love Maricella, Jean, Don-anna and all
the other girls in the office. You love everybody."

"Yes, that's right. And everyone thinks we Poles
are crazy because we love everybody. It causes us
so much trouble."

"You didn't love the Germans," she reminded him.
He shrugged.

"What were we supposed to do? Nobody else seemed
ready to stand up to the maniac. Fortunately, the Germans declared war on us first. You didn't have to fight
anybody. Why complain? We hated it. War isn't our
style."

She looked at him challengingly, but with a little less
belligerence, he thought. "You make such a big deal
out of it. He was just another petty despot."

Just another petty despot! Michael shuddered. He'd
read the madman's book. It was fortunate King
Yampolsky XIX had recognized the danger and mobi-
lized the armed forces early. The French, English,
Americans, and others showed no inclination to fight,
despite the madman's avowed intentions.

Six long months of war. But the madman had been
killed and a form of democratic monarchy patterned
on the Republic had been established in Germany, with
that popular war hero—what was his name?—oh yes,
Goering, elected first King. Germany had been well-
behaved ever since.

It was the establishment of the Polish form of
government in Germany that really irked the Americans, though. But the Germans had had all examples
to choose from and had chosen the best.

"Dana, this tantrum of yours is understandable, I
suppose. An outsider could read all sorts of things into
those loading specifications. But it's not true, about
Mars."

"Is."

Spoiled child. Typical adolescent American messiah
complex. He stared hard at her and tried to sound
solemn.

"I swear on my honor, Dana, that tomorrow's launch

has nothing whatsoever to do with claiming any planet or moon or setting up any base thereon. We haven't done it on Luna . . . why should we do it on Mars? I'm just an engineer, Dana, I'm not involved with anything like your CIA.

"Why can't you believe me when I swear that we're only interested in preserving the peace of mankind—what peace there is in a world where the Japanese and Brazilians and the Semitic Union all have thermonuclear capability?

"Peace and freedom—don't you see? Poland's had the stablest government in the world for over three hundred years now. Why should we want to jeopardize that by antagonizing your country, or the Russians?"

"It's wrong to slave under a dictator!" she sputtered. "Monarchies are outmoded, archaic, despotic forms of government. No other major power has a king or queen."

"And no other major power is quite as major as the republic, for that very reason. What's wrong with 'slaving' under the highest standard of living in the world? So we have a true king, with absolute power. He serves only for five years. And then we elect a new king, or queen, from the nobles and princes. It works. That's the only rationale I can give you."

"It'll collapse any day now," she insisted, "and then maybe you'll get a real democracy."

"Good God, no! Anything but that, Dana. A 'real democracy,' like yours? Where the legislature is paralyzed, the executive corrupt, the courts logjammed? We've become what we have precisely because we've avoided all that.

"Just as an example, to change the republic's television networks to 3-D hologram, the king signed a proclamation. You're still arguing over who gets what rights, years later. And we've not called on the final check—the Society of Assassins—for 230 years."

She didn't understand. They never would, he thought sadly. An elected monarchy was impossible and therefore could not exist. This did not trouble the Poles.

"Look, don't ruin this launching, Dana. I don't blame you for misinterpreting the data you found. You don't *really* know what all that information means, do you?"

She looked at the Koi, playing near her feet. "Well, not entirely, but there are orders for material that . . ."

"Suppose," he sighed, "I agree to take a lie-detector test? Voluntarily, here, on one of your own Embassy's machines? Would *that* satisfy you?" Longin wouldn't like that, but at this point Michael didn't see what else he could do. If it didn't work, Longin would have only himself to blame.

He'd *told* him he was only an engineer.

She looked uncertain. "You'd do that?"

"Right now, if you want."

"Well, yes, I guess that would do it." She looked confused. "That fueling data . . . I was so *sure*."

"Anyone would be, I guess." He put an arm around her shoulders. "Let's go take that test."

The multiple launch was a great success. The King was pleased, Longin was pleased, everyone connected with Project Polonaise was pleased.

It was two weeks later that his intercom buzzed and a harried secretary reported that there was a hysterical woman in the lobby, screaming Michael's name in juxtaposition with unpleasant words.

"She had a gun with her, too, sir, but it was detected at the gate. The security people have her."

"What does she look like?" He already knew, but the secretary confirmed it.

"The police want to know if you want to speak with her, sir, before she's removed."

"I suppose I should. You might relay appropriate information to the proper offices to see that they initiate deportation proceedings. She doesn't belong here. She's . . . confused. But yes, I will see her."

There was a curious crowd gathered around the security cubby at the entrance to the center. Michael gestured irritably at them.

"There are a hundred men and women in orbit wholly dependent on us here at the Center. Get back to work, now." The crowd scattered back to consoles and desks.

Two large gentlemen were in the room, Dana Canning held firmly between them. Her hair was disheveled, her look wild. All traces of the elfin innocence he remembered so fondly were gone.

"You! You lied to me, damn you!"

"I did not lie to you, Dana."

"You lied to me about the launch!"

"And the detector? Did I lie to it, too?"

"You—you evaded the question!" She tried to kick him and he stepped carefully out of range. The guards tightened their grip on her.

"You never asked it. If you had, I couldn't have answered. I decided to take a calculated risk."

She glanced at him bitterly. "An orbiting station— a missile platform big enough to cover every nuclear station and launch site in the world!"

"Its purpose is primarily commercial and scientific in nature, Dana," he said quietly, "but it is true that the station does possess some military capability."

She laughed. There was no humor in it. " 'Some military capability'! According to the reports on the tube, you've slipped enough warheads up there to destroy any country seconds before a preemptive attack could be launched."

"Ah, and you've hit on it," he confessed. "To a Pole, even the idea of a 'preemptive' attack is enough to bring on a bout of nausea. Don't you see? With the proliferation of atomic arms in the world, somebody had to step in and say 'Don't mess around with your new toy or you'll get spanked.'

"The King and the High Council reluctantly decided that we had to take this burden on ourselves. We're too close to the stars, Dana, to risk crippling ourselves now. Poland hasn't initiated a war against anyone in hundreds of years. The same cannot be said of any other world power, including yours. A critical vacuum has been filled."

"The old story," she spat. "Everyone has only the betterment of mankind on their minds. The rationale of every conqueror since the pharaohs. Why should you be any different?"

He shook his head. She'd never see, never understand. Nor would the Russians, or Chinese, or Kenyans. They'd never understand and they'd always be jealous and there was nothing that could be done about it, nothing at all—except press on.

He turned away, shut out her screaming and insults.

It was something that couldn't be explained, something in the fabric of the people themselves. He'd wanted to show her. The reason why Poland *was* the most powerful country on Earth, why no other country *could* ever hope to equal the Republic.

The Poles were a gentle people, the only ones.

Wolfstroker

Anyone who thinks telekinesis, telepathy, and thought-control are merely science-fictional inventions has never attended a decent-sized rock concert. It's almost a certainty John W. Campbell never did, because his psi-oriented stories in *Analog* would never have been the same.

This is one of those stories where several seemingly unrelated elements suddenly fall into place for the writer, and you have that supreme thrill of abruptly shouting to yourself, "Jesus, where did *that* come from!? I didn't think up that, did I? Oh boy ohboyohboy . . . I wonder what happens next?"

That's what the fans at a concert wonder, too, when the music stops going from ear to brain and instead enters directly into the bloodstream, and you find yourself utterly at the mercy of the electric guitar, bass, organ, and drum. It's possession, body and soul.

A version of this story was published in mangled form by an enterprise called *Coq* magazine. What follows is the first publication of the full, unbutchered text.

I.

You're getting fat, Sam Parker. Too fat and too old. You drink too much, you smoke too much, and you go around with bad ladies, yes. Why don't you wise up, Parker? Cut out the stogies, lay off the liquor, read a good book once in a while.

Why don't you shut up, Sam Parker.

I can't, Sam Parker sighed. I'm you.

He chomped down defiantly on the cheap cigar and gave the dingy exterior of the club another look. Name: Going Higher. Parker shook his head slowly. Going down, more likely, into the depths. Just like him.

The only hint of brightness on the exterior, which fronted on equally drab Pico Boulevard, was the small neon sign that belligerently shouted "Beer on Draft" to the uncaring double-lane strip of tired asphalt. It hadn't been a good week for Mrs. Parker's little boy.

On Monday "Deanna and her Performing Pups" had played their first engagement under his aegis. In the middle of the act, what does one of the rancid bitches do but take a sinking leap into the audience and proceed to put the fang to a couple of hysterical moppets. Sam's abortive relationship with Madame Deanna had dissolved faster than a headache tablet. He escaped partnership in three separate lawsuits only because the apologetic madame had providentially signed her name to their agreement in the wrong place.

And now this.

The January wind poured out of the Hollywood Hills like white wine and stung his cheeks. It had to be warmer inside. He walked down the three steps.

The crowd was a surprise, larger than he'd expected. Considering the near-mystical affectation for dirt and filth by today's generation, he should have known better. He took an empty table in a front corner, forsaken because you had to lean outward to see more than half the performing area that passed for a stage. He put down the stub of his cigar. One fast glance around the club told him all he'd need to know about it and all he'd ever want to.

The "fresh flowers" on the tables might qualify as passable lichens. The nicest thing one could say about the rest of the place was that it wouldn't be hurt by a new coat of paint. Naturally, in keeping with proper atmosphere, it was too dark to see your own pants.

A young man with blond hair like Aryan seaweed appeared at Sam's side, pad in hand. He had a dreamy, disaffected look, probably from trying to study all day and work all night. Sam felt a smidgen of sympathy for him.

"Scotch and soda."

"I'm sorry, sir," the youth murmured. "We don't serve hard liquor. Can I get you a hot cider?"

Saints preserve us, hot cider! Parker would have laughed, only it was bad for his ulcer. That Lipson kid had been so enthusiastic about this place! Well, he nodded imperceptibly, he'd learned his lesson. Last tip he took from that quarter of the "in" people.

"Can I maybe get a Heinekin's?"

"Not on tap, sir."

"That's all right," said Parker thankfully. "A bottle will be fine." The waiter vanished.

You couldn't rightly say the stage lights came on. Rather, the section of club that served for performing became slightly less stygian than the rest. Then the band—he used the term advisedly—moseyed out on stage.

With the possible exception of the lead guitar, they were as sad-looking a group as he'd ever seen. Lead guitar, bass, drums, and yes, it had to be, a xylophone, for God's sake! He almost smiled. Maybe the quiet evening would present him with a chuckle to go with his good beer.

Sam Parker, if you haven't guessed by now, was an agent. Not undercover, but theatrical, which was

harder on body and soul. One of a multitude of busy
ants, forever scrounging the ashcans of talent. Occasionally an ant died. Then he was casually dismem-
bered by his fellows and carried into the hill to be
eaten. Sam had come close a few times, but so far he
was still intact and out among the scavengers. He was
very observant, was Sam. So he didn't miss the unmistakable aura of expectancy that had settled over the
audience. For this schlock group? This skeletal collection of insensate clods? Something didn't smell right.
He found himself getting just a teensy bit excited.

Well, the drummer killed that when he started
things. Sam resisted the melodramatic gesture of putting hands over ears. It was no worse than the performing pups. But if this kid had a real rhythm in his
body he was preserving it for his death throes.

The bass was next, fumbling at his strings like he
was sorting soggy spaghetti. Worse and worse. The xy-
lophonist—Sam still hadn't recovered from that—
joined in. Or rather, he started playing. What he
played bore no relationship—rhythmically, melod-
ically, harmonically—to the bass or drummer. Sam
was ready to go, but he'd only started the beer. He
shut out the disaster on stage and tried to concentrate
on the music in the bubbles.

The lead guitar shuffled up to the single mike. There
was one sad spotlight, which might have been a big
flashlight on a string. He had a face like polished sand-
stone, full of lines that shouldn't have appeared there
for another forty years yet. Straight black hair cut off
at thin, bony shoulders was caught up in a single raw-
hide headband. He wore faded blue jeans, faded from
heavy use and not modish bleaching, a stained flannel
shirt, and boots whose leather had merged forever with
caked earth and gray clay.

A colorless, tired, dead personality, washed up at
the age of twenty-four, maybe twenty-five.

Only in the eyes, something. Eyes, pieces of fine old
obsidian . . . and Gorgon's hair for fingers.

It didn't take a song, or even a stanza for Sam Parker to know. Those long young-old fingers came down and gentled on the strings, the left hand rose and curled vinelike about the top. A finger moved, touched the electric guitar, which made a sound. Near the back of the room a girl moaned.

His name was Willie Whitehorse, and he played like a god.

Sam Parker sat up straight in his cider-damp chair and leaned forward, wheezing a little. It didn't matter that the drummer couldn't carry a simple beat. It didn't matter than the bass had hands like wrought-iron shovels. It didn't matter that the xylophone player ignored the others for his own private limbo. It only mattered that Willie Whitehorse played—and sang.

Sang about what it was like to be like the brown eagle, to be alone. Sang how love was like snow-melt on hot winter days. Sang about smooth rocks and small crowded bird bowers and fresh green holly sprigs, about the crusty feel of tree bark under your palms and the smell of dry firewood and old histories. Sam Parker missed a lot of it, but he missed none of the crowd.

When the black-eyed singer sang happy, the audience laughed, and strangers nudged their neighbors. When he sang sad, the cynical students cried. When he sang angry, just a little, there were frightening mad mutterings from the far blacknesses of the club, and somewhere a glass broke.

He was skinny and tired and all alone up there. But there was something in him and in his music that reached out and toyed with the souls of those who listened; grabbed and twisted and tweaked and hung on tight, tight without letting go, till it had flung them twice round the white moon and back again.

Yes, it even touched Sam Parker. And for thirty-five years nothing, absolutely *nothing* had affected Sam Parker. But there was a strange wildness at work here that passed the ramparts erected by decades of Dorsey

and James and Lombardo to tantalize the little man
slightly.

And right at the finish there was something that
frightened him just a little. It went away fast and he
forgot it soon enough, for now. As he watched Willie
Whitehorse, for just the shortest odd second there was
no guitar in those thin arms, no guitar but instead a
vapory gray outline. Like one of those things everyone
sees out of the corner of their eyes and aren't there at
all when they turn to look at them. A funny outline
that had four legs and a tail, in those arms. Four legs,
a tail, sharp pointed ears, long snout clustered with
coconut-pale teeth, and two tiny eye pits of red-orange
that burned like wax matches.

Beer and bad lighting, of course, and Sam Parker
forgot it quick.

After a while the musicians and applause drifted
away and the stage lights followed. Sam sat staring at
the empty place for a few minutes, thinking. Then he
tapped his vest pocket, heard the faint rustle of the
blank contract he always carried there. He liked to joke
about it, his "soul" contract. If the Devil ever presented
Sam with an offer for same, he wanted to be ready for
him. Know better what he was getting and Satan might
try to back out of the deal.

"Another beer, sir?" Sam blinked and looked around.
The waiter was back at his side, as sleepy and tired as
before.

"What?"

"Would you care for another drink, sir?"

"No. No thanks." Sam shoved back his chair and
stood. He handed the kid a five-dollar bill.

"I'll get your change, sir."

Sam put an arm out. "Hold it, s—pal. I got enough
change. I'm rolling in change. Just tell me how to get
to the dressing room."

The waiter licked his lips, eyed the faded green
paper. "Won't be anyone there, 'cept maybe Whitehorse. His first name's Willie." The bill vanished into
shirt, to be replaced by directions.

II.

He hadn't really expected to find a dressing room in this dump, but damned if there wasn't one. As if unconsciously aware of the incongruity, it partly compensated by having no door.

Someone sat inside on a bench in front of a chest of drawers that had seen good days before the last world war. There was a mirror above it. An electric guitar lay across the chest, like an Aztec maiden readied for sacrifice. Sam hesitated at the entrance, rapped on the inside of the wall.

"Can I come in?" The singer turned and Sam saw the bottle, near empty.

"Can't keep you out," muttered the figure, finishing a long swallow. He choked, wiped his lips with the back of a wrist. This was bad, but it didn't stop Sam.

"Yes you can. Just tell me to and I won't come in."

The singer seemed ready for another swallow, paused, and vested a flicker of interest on Sam. It disappeared before anyone might see it.

"Come in or get lost, as it pleases you. Makes no difference to me."

Sam walked in, sat down in the single wicker chair, facing the singer's back.

"I'll be short and to the point. I'm an agent."

A slight smile touched the corners of the singer's mouth as he turned slowly. There was no humor in it.

"How sad for you."

"That's an opinion others share," Sam agreed. "Sometimes I feel that way myself. You Willie Whitehorse?"

Barely audible around sips of raw sad whiskey. "Yeah."

"You're an Indian?"

That produced the first reply above a mumble. Whitehorse opened his eyes all the way (how black they were!) and glared at the agent. Sam squirmed a little. They seemed to back up to naked space.

"You're a Jew, aren't you?"

"I am," replied Sam, unperturbed.

"Parker your real name?"

"No. My folks changed it when I was small."

The singer shook a little. It might have been laughter. It was probably the liquor.

"Well, Whitehorse is my *real* name, and my folks didn't go and change *it!* And I'm not about to." His gaze was unsteady but defiant. "Guess that makes me just a cut or two above you, don't it?"

Folding his hands over his tummy, Sam replied quietly, "If it pleases you to look at it that way."

The eyes glittered a moment longer. Then they closed tight, like wrung-out washrags, and turned away.

"God damn you," Whitehorse hissed. "Oh, God damn you!"

Pause; quiet. "You got an agent, Willie?"

"No." With satisfaction, "Can't stand 'em."

"I'm not surprised. Most of us are pretty obnoxious."

"And you're different, I suppose?" he sneered.

"I think so. You may come to think so. You know what I think, Willie? You've got talent. A lot of talent." When there was no reply to that, Sam continued

"I'd like to handle you. I think you could be a big star. The biggest, maybe. Get you some respectable sidemen, put together a decent band. Like a chance to work with some guys who can play more than chopsticks, Willie?" Still no reaction. But no rejection either. Encouraged, Sam plunged on:

"I guarantee to get you out of this sump heap, anyway." He sat back, concealing his anticipation with the ease of long practice. "What do you say, Willie?

Only sound the greasy tinkle of the bottle tapping rhythmically against the wooden bench. It was empty and so was the rhythm.

Then, "Sure, why not? At least somebody else ca

fight with the owners for drink money. Stupid bastards, think they all know music . . . Yeah, sure, you can be my agent. What'd you say your name was?"

"Parker," Sam repeated patiently. "Samuel Parker."

"Okay, Samuel Parker. Deal. Manitou help you."

"Fine," said Sam, reaching into his vest. "Now if you'll just sign here, and he—" Whitehorse was shaking his head.

"Huh-uh. No contracts, no papers. If I want to quit, I up and quit. Just like that."

"Where does that leave me?" prompted Sam.

"In hell for all I care. I could give a damn. That's a problem for the Great Spirit, not me. Take it or screw it."

Sam sighed. "I'll take it. Now that that's done with," he stood and extracted a fresh cigar, "what's the first thing I can do for you, to seal our agreement?"

Whitehorse hungrily sucked the last recalcitrant drops from the glass. He gazed at it moodily, hefting it by the neck. When he threw it into the far wall it shattered in a crystalline shower of quick brilliance and cheap wind chimes.

"Get me another bottle."

III.

Without even seeing the hovel Whitehorse was living in, Sam offered the singer the use of his own apartment. Whitehorse refused, but he didn't like riding the bus. So he accepted Sam's offer of a ride home.

On the way Sam nearly blew it.

"You know," he mused conversationally, "I've been thinking about ideas, presentation. Every group's got to have a gimmick to make it these days."

"Yeah," muttered the singer indifferently, staring out the window. "Hey, I know," he turned suddenly. "You're probably thinking that Indians are pretty 'in' right now, huh?"

"Well, I was sort of considering—"

"You were thinking of maybe fixing me up in something real authentic. Beads and buckskin, maybe, with a full war bonnet and moccasins. Call us 'War Party' or something? Hey, how about a handful of fake cigars, too?"

"Not exactly that," Sam countered, aware he'd somehow upset the singer. "There's already a group with a similar name and—"

" 'Come see the real Indian band play the sacred music of the Red Man as you've never heard it before. The new in, now powwow sound—that it, Parker? That's pretty good, ain't it, 'powwow'?" His voice was getting close to a shout.

"Easy, easy," said Sam placatingly, not looking into those volcanic orbs. They ate at something in him. "I didn't mean anything like that."

"No?" screamed Whitehorse. What bothered Sam wasn't the kid's violence. Darned if he didn't seem to be almost crying. Abruptly the singer seemed to collapse in on himself.

"No. Maybe you didn't. I'm sorry." He put his head in his hands and rocked a little on the seat. "Sorry, sorry, sorry. I've taken so much of that, that sickening, sticky, patronizing—" He coughed twice, violently the second time.

"Ought to lay off that stuff," Sam commented, keeping his tone carefully neutral. Whitehorse swayed, laughed a little wildly.

"Think I'm drunk, don't you?"

"No—" began Sam.

"Well, I'm not! Most Indians drink, mister agent Parker. Not 'cause they like this rot. Not that. They drink 'cause most of what they were was ripped away from them by the white man's world before they got born. Liquor blurs over all the empty spaces a little. All those dark wide holes that were once full of beautiful things. And the worse thing is, Parker, that you don't really know what they were, those things. Just a big nothingness feeling that they aren't there anymore.

"No, I'm not drunk, Parker. When I'm drinking I'm sober. I'm only drunk when I'm playing."

Sam slowed and pulled into the curb. He didn't offer to come up. They weren't in Beverly Hills. It took the singer three tries to get the door open.

Sam leaned over from the wheel, looking out. "Remember, Willie. The studio tomorrow. Sure you can find it?"

Whitehorse swayed, turned to face the agent. He held the guitar to him like a mute child. "I'll find it." It was hard to tell whether he was laughing or crying. "Man, I'm an *Indian!* I can find my way to anywhere, don't you know that? Yeah, I'll get there, if I can make it up the stairs." He put his hand to his mouth, blew out.

"Woo, woo, w—!" The third war whoop expired prematurely, subsumed in wracking cough. Sam turned away, embarrassed.

"I'll be there. I'll be there."

IV.

Three young men stood in the concrete womb of the studio and stared impatiently at the white walls, their instruments, and Sam Parker. Sam transferred his gaze to his innocent watch and tried not to let them see how worried he was. He'd told Whitehorse ten o'clock. It was now twelve thirty and the trio was not in good humor.

He couldn't blame them. They were top performers all, maybe the best three unattached musicians in L.A. just now. He'd spent all night begging, pleading, offering his unmarketable soul again, to get them to cancel their other plans and show up here. No, he didn't blame them for being impatient. These guys were *good,* damn good, and Sam knew he couldn't expect them to hang around much longer. The next time he asked for a little more time they would laugh at him.

Meanwhile every half hour in the studio was costing him money, lots of money. Money he didn't have. The only thing that was doing well was his ulcer. He'd been a fool not to drag his discovery home with him, keep him in sight. Damnfool crazy drunken kid! Might have done anything. Might've hopped a plane to anywhere, or more likely a freight.

Every five minutes he'd phoned Whitehorse's apartment, then every ten. The last call had been forty-five minutes ago. If he was still there he wasn't asleep, he was catatonic. Or dead. Sam's hopes and visions were dying just as fast.

Drivin' Jack Cavanack stopped clicking stick on stick and looked up from behind his drums.

"Hey, man, this hotshot of yours better show up real quicklike, or I'm splitting. I got a gig in Seattle tonight and I do not, positively do not, feel like gettin' in there in the dark and cold. Comprende?"

Uccelo plunked his bass for the thousandth time and didn't look up at Parker. "Right on." Vincente Rivera honked a few funky free notes on his harmonica, gazed sympathetically at the harried agent.

"Sorry, Sam, but Jack's right. We all of us have got other things to do than wait around here. This is a favor from me to you, I know. But we been here for too many hours now, Sam. Offhand, I don't think your wonder boy's gonna show."

He snapped open a small black case with red velvet guts and eased his harmonica therein.

"Please Vince . . . Jack, Milo. Give me a chance, willya? Hey, another ten minutes, that's all I ask. Okay? Ten lousy minutes. I'm sure he'll be here. He promised me he would."

Rivera sighed, snapping the latch on the case. "Sam, I think you've been had."

"He was had when he decided on joining his noble profession," came a thin voice from the studio door. Sam spread a relieved grin from ear to ear, but inwardly he was seething.

"Willie!" It came out like a curse. "Knew you'd make it, fella!" Whitehorse walked past Sam, ignored the proferred palm.

"Sure, Sam. Promised." The singer looked only slightly less haggard than he had the previous night.

He found a plug, started to hook himself into the ganglion of his guitar's mechanical lungs, and talked while he worked:

"You know, Sam, I wasn't going to come."

Parker pretended not to hear as he closed the studio door.

"I was just going to leave you flat, go to Phoenix. Big joke. This whole thing," and he took in the studio in a half-wave, "doesn't appeal to me. Then I thought Grandfather, whatever he might think of this, wouldn't like to hear I'd gone back on my word. So, what the hell," he finished lamely.

Bless all grandfathers, prayed Parker silently. He felt like a man who'd just pulled an inside straight while hoping for a simple pair.

"What do you want me to do, Sam?" Whitehorse asked.

"Well, Willie, I want to find out if you four are compatible, soundwise. If you are, I'd like to work you together into a group." Uccelo hit a sour note on his bass and snorted derisively.

"Willie, that's Drivin' Jack Cavanack on skins, Milo Uccelo on bass, and Vincente Rivera on harmonica, organ, Moog, and just about everything else you can imagine. Boys, Willie Whitehorse."

Sam had seen more instant camaraderie among a group of pallbearers.

"All right, Sam, we all know what we play, man," said Cavanack boredly. "Let's get this over with, huh? I got a plane to catch."

"Sure Jack, sure!" smiled Parker hurriedly. Cavanack turned his indifferent gaze on Whitehorse.

"What you want to play, man?"

"I only play my own stuff," Willie replied with equal indifference. "You can follow me if you like."

"Now look here, man . . . !" began Cavanack, rising to his full six-five and glowering over his cylindrical zoo.

"Please, Jack!" Sam pleaded, waving his arms. "It's just for a few minutes. Be the big man for a few minutes, huh?" He smiled desperately.

"Okay, Sam," Cavanack agreed warningly. "But you ask a lot, man." He sat down. Willie set his guitar in his arms with that smooth cradling motion.

"Hey, brother," interrupted Uccelo, "don't you want to tune up?"

Eyes of smoked ice fixed on the bass player, just above tight lips.

"I'm not your brother, Uccelo . . . and I'm *always* in tune."

"Sure, Willie," Sam all but begged. "Go ahead and play something, willya?"

Willie looked over at him quietly. "Sure, Sam. I'll play something."

Willie Whitehorse played.

As a boy my Father told me
When the mountains and the rivers were being
  taken down
Down taken, taken down down down
Down down taken way down
Torn down . . .

He sang and he played and he played and he sang. And Milo Uccelo and Vince Rivera and Drivin' Jack Cavanack, they just listened. Sat and they listened. Any cop who'd gotten a look at their frozen faces would have busted 'em right then, on suspicion. No question, they were high. High and wild, shootin' up on the music of Willie Whitehorse.

Rivera was the first to join in, moving like a dream man, coaxing a sweet quail-wail from his chrome harmonica, finding the blank spots few in Willie's song and filling them in with notes like crystallized honey.

Then a low giant step from the back of the studio, getting louder and louder, moving faster and quicker, the hunger cry of a dragonfly. Drivin' Jack Cavanack, his eyes glazed and distant, put his wheels under

Willie's guitar and Rivera's harmonica and took off down the yellow brick road at a hundred twenty per.

Uccelo fought it, swam in it, gave in to it. His hands seemed to move of their own volition, the deep heavy bell-clear sound coming right out of his fingers, to scatter like black orchid blooms about the room.

Sam felt it too, but he had nothing to bring in. Nothing except the faces at the control-room window, noses and hands of employees and passersby squinched up tight against the cool glass. Bodies beneath moving, heaving, twisting to the irresistible, pounding, relentless power of the music.

This time he saw it twice.

Once it was somewhere in the middle, and once again at the end. Sam saw or thought he saw the steel-silvery outline with the sulfurous sight that burned, burned, bulked in the protective arms of Willie White-horse.

They finished perfectly together, the last note dying a lingering, unwilling death. Sam blinked, looked at his watch.

They'd been playing nonstop for twenty-two minutes.

His shirt was soaked opaque under both arms, and if you'd asked him he'd have insisted he hadn't moved a muscle the whole time. Except maybe in his throat.

Willie calmly unhooked his guitar and walked over to where Sam stood.

"When you want me to play a place, call me, mister agent." He slammed the door behind him.

That seemed to shatter the spell that had settled shroudlike over the studio. The musicians crowded around Sam, but no one shook his hand, no one pounded his back. They were solemn, but it was an excited solemn. That was the way Jack Cavanack looked at Sam.

"I gotta apologize, man. Count me in but excuse me now. I gotta go cancel that Seattle gig."

"Thanks, Jack. I'm glad." Sam had a thought. "Wait, hold up, Jack. This a solo?"

"Yeah. They back me with some locals, I play for awhile. It's a good club, Sam."

"Okay, tell your guy he's getting a whole group for the price of a solo and to dump the college band boys," Sam said rapidly. "Tell him you're bringing your own people."

"Okay, Sam," agreed Cavanack, hand on the studio door. "Anything you say."

Rivera remained on the low stage. He was staring at his harmonica, turning it over and over in his hands as though he didn't recognize it. Sam didn't know much Spanish, but he could identify the musician's mumbled "Madre de Dios, madre de Dios," because he said it over and over. And other things, too. Rivera blew a few simple notes on the instrument. In the now quiet studio they sounded as lost as a paper plane in the Grand Canyon.

Uccelo walked over, looking concerned.

"Hey Sam, my hands are shaking, you know that? How about that?" He held them out. It was barely a flutter to Sam, just a hint of movement in the fingertips, but it obviously meant something strong to the bass player.

"Never had that happen to me, Sam. Ever." He shook his head. "I never played that good before, either. Sam, I swear I never heard a sound like that in my life."

The agent smiled, mopped his balding dome with a dirty handkerchief. "You think he's good too, then?"

Uccelo gave him a funny look. "Good? They haven't invented a word for what that fellow is." He swallowed. "I don't think you'll understand this the way it's meant, Sam, because you're not a musician. But when we were moving up there, really moving, it was better than making it, man." He still looked troubled as he turned away to unhook his bass.

"I'll tell you this, though," he added, working at the wires. "I'll play bass for that man anytime, anywhere. For free, if I have to. But I won't stay in a dark room with him."

V.

Sam smiled sleepily as the 727 dropped through the clouds toward the Tacoma-Seattle airport. In a few hours he'd have a better idea of what he had. That he had something special he'd known since he'd heard that first guitar note back in the Going Higher. But just how special he couldn't tell for sure . . . yet.

Of course, he mused gently as he rolled over in the reclined seat, those people at the studio window had given in to the force of the music as completely as the kids in that club.

Just before he drifted off to sleep, it occurred to him to wonder how anyone had been able to hear the music outside the closed-off, soundproof studio. But he fell asleep then.

SEATTLE 22 JAN (UPI)—The Aquarius, one of downtown Seattle's best-known rock nightspots, was heavily damaged last night when the audience rioted during the performance of the White-horse Band, a new group from Los Angeles. Police, who were called to the scene by Aquarius owner Marshall Patrick, were unable to handle the crowd and were forced to call on the city's special tactical squad for aid. A squad of MPs from nearby Fort Lewis also aided in subduing the crowd, which included a number of young soldiers on leave from the base.

Reports vary on how the disturbance began, but the general impression given was that the crowd was overcome by the fervor of the new group's performance, though conflicting reports raise some doubt on this issue.

The actual disturbance apparently broke out during the final number of the evening, which one young listener out on bail described, somewhat dazedly, as having something to do with "slaughtered babies and howling dogs." Police Sergeant Michael

Washington, a Seattle force veteran, had this to say: "In twenty years on the force I've never seen a crowd behave like this one. It was like a nuthouse. Kids crying, singing, spitting, and squalling like wildcats. Some of my men were scratched up pretty good. Usually it's just the girls, but this time the guys seemed to have gone berserk too. I'll tell you, it scared the —— out of me! I've seen so-called riots at rock concerts before, but nothing like this! Most of 'em don't even seem to know what happened. I don't like using clubs on teenagers, but my men had to do it in self-defense. It was like a madhouse in there."

Damage was heaviest to fixtures and breakables. Owner Patrick commented on the destruction: "This was the worst demonstration I've ever seen, worse even than that last concert in Belgium. But I'll tell you, I'd book that bunch in here steady if I could get 'em! I offered their agent everything short of a blank check and he turned me down. Said if I wanted to hear the group again I'd have to come to the Atheneum in Los Angeles. It didn't affect me the way it did those kids, but there's no doubt about it, that lead of theirs, Whitehorse, really has something special."

(In Los Angeles, John Nat Burns, millionaire owner and builder of the Atheneum, refused to comment on band agent Samuel Parker's statement).

Discussing the band's performance, several members of the audience remarked on the interesting optical effect achieved when lead singer Willie Whitehorse's guitar seemed to take on the outline of a small animal. Some say it was a fox, others insist it was a wolf. All agree the technical device, probably achieved with offstage lights, was quite well done.

VI.

Sam leaned back in the chair in his Wilshire office and contentedly surveyed the list resting on the desk in front of him. It was a list of U.S. cities, and it was now more than three-quarters full. Stops on their first nationwide tour, if tonight's concert came off.

Word-of-mouth is a wonderful thing. No less than six major record companies had waved contracts at him in the two weeks since Seattle. When they heard the minimum terms Sam would accept, they reacted in various ways, from mild amusement to outright disgust. Sam smiled to himself. After tonight's concert they'd beg to sign on his terms.

Yes, word-of-mouth was a wonderful thing. The advertising had been minimal, but the wire-press story had piqued interest and the rock underground had taken care of the rest. All sixteen thousand seats had been sold out the day after the ticket agencies offered them. The Atheneum would be picked for the Whitehorse Band's first major appearance.

The intercom dinged for attention. He pacified it by depressing the proper switch.

"Yes, Janet?"

"Mr. Parker, there's a gentleman here who insists on seeing you. He says his name is Frank Collins."

"Tell Mr. Collins that all business concerning bookings, recordings, or advertising rights is being deferred until after the concert. Give him an appointment— oh, Tuesday, if he wants, and tell him I'm not seeing *anyone* today."

"He knows the concert is tonight, Mr. Parker, but I think you might like to meet him. He's not after money or offering it. At least, I don't think so. He says he has a Ph.D. in psychology. He doesn't look it."

Well, Sam had heard plenty of ploys, but the inventiveness of the human mind is a wonderful thing. For a moment he was tempted to have Janet tell the joker to go peel his bananas. Then he considered that the claim was just weird enough to be legit. Besides, he'd never met a real live scientist. Closest he'd come was Morris, the bookie.

"All right, Janet, send him in. I'll see him." He released the switch.

Janet was one of the few luxuries he'd permitted himself to acquire with the advance from tonight's sellout. She could type 90 words a minute, had a degree from UCLA, an IQ of 130, and a forty-one-inch bust.

Frank Collins wore a dark gray suit and tie, was about Sam's age, had blue eyes, plump cheeks, no chin, a brown briefcase, and much more hair than Sam. For the latter Sam disliked him on sight.

"Sit down, Collins, but don't make yourself at home." The psychologist settled into the chair opposite the desk.

"You're Sam Parker?"

"Unless my mother lied to me. You really a Ph.D?"

Collins had an ingratiating smile. "I like to think of myself as somewhat more than three letters and two periods." He steepled his fingers, grew serious. "I'm very interested in a young man you represent named Willie Whitehorse."

"Who isn't?" Sam acknowledged. He caressed a box. "Cigar?"

"No, thank you. I don't smoke."

"Too bad for you." Sam lit his own, puffed contentedly. From Havana by way of London. Another little luxury. "You're not endearing yourself to me, Collins. What's your angle? Why are you interested in Willie?"

"For the past ten years I have been especially interested in all the parapsychological aspects of rock music, Mr. Parker."

"That's certainly very interesting," nodded Sam. "Suppose you tell me what that is in English, so I can get interested too."

"Perhaps if I explain exactly what it is about rock that has intrigued me—"

"Sure," Sam said, glancing pointedly at the clock on his desk. "Only don't take too long, huh?"

Collins smiled again in a faintly superior way and

began earnestly, "Have you ever noticed the power certain rock performers have over their audiences?"

Sam wasn't impressed. "Naturally. Only the top people have it. Though I don't know exactly as I'd call it 'power.'"

"Oh, but what else could one call it, Mr. Parker? Surely you've had occasion to observe the audience as well as the players. A few musicians, and usually one lead performer, exercising what amounts to total emotional control over thousands and thousands of rapt spectators. Playing with their feelings, juggling their thoughts, all but directing their bodily movements with their music."

Sam chuckled. "You make it sound like witchcraft."

Collins did not chuckle back. Instead, he nodded. "In old times it would be called exactly that. In fact, music sometimes often was called a power of the devil. But it's all far from supernatural. Psychic powers have long been postulated, Mr. Parker. The ability to control others through the power of one mind. Somehow music seems to increase the projection of the performer and the receptivity of his audience. All music does this to a certain extent, but rock music seems to do so to a far greater extent than any believe possible. And my counterparts are still playing with Rhine cards!" The last was uttered almost contemptuously.

"Tell me, what do you suppose a youth at one of these performances is thinking about? Someone who is totally 'with' the music, as they try to be?"

"Beats me. I'm not one of these kids. Whatever the singer is singing about, I suppose."

"Correct, Mr. Parker. And he is thinking that to the exclusion of everything else. Except for the music, his or her mind is a complete blank. 'Becoming one with the music,' it's called. When the music 'moves' them, it *really* moves them.

"Usually this oneness is expressed in actions of joy and happiness. Occasionally, if the music is outrageous or strong enough, it engenders violent, antisocial action on the part of the listener. Emotional telepathy,

Mr. Parker, on a grand scale, and right under our very noses! No wonder their parents don't understand their actions."

Parker didn't completely understand this spiel, but he wasn't buying any of it. "Baloney! All kids don't react that way. Hell, some of 'em don't even like rock music!"

"Perhaps the minds of some are immune to the effect," Collins shrugged. "Others have raised conditioned barriers in their minds to the music. But in those who are receptive, the reactions are universal. A top group will produce the same effects in an audience of young people in Rome, New York, or Rome, Italy; in Moscow, Idaho or Moscow, Russia." His voice got low and excited.

"In some way, Mr. Parker, I believe that today's music releases the blocks against intermind communication that normally exist in the human mind. Today's environment may have something to do with it. So may the use of electronics. Consider! Some of the most popular, idolized figures in rock have what are by professional musical standards no voice at all, and are technically weak instrumentalists to boot. They come from every conceivable cultural background, having nothing in common except this uncanny ability to submerge themselves and their audiences in the music." He relaxed slightly, grew a little less fanatical.

"You see, then, with what interest I would read the report of your concert in Seattle."

"And you think Willie exercises some kind of mind control on his audience when he's performing?" Parker shook his head. "At least you're not a boring nut, Collins."

The psychologist looked grim. "Insults and skepticism do not bother me, Mr. Parker. My statistics prove my contentions. Your Mr. Whitehorse will strengthen that proof. I have seen too many blank, empty, *mindless* faces swaying to the rhythm of today's bands for me to believe otherwise."

"Why'd you come to see me?" Sam asked abruptly. "What do you want?"

The scientist looked sheepish. "I must go to this concert," he explained desperately, "and I . . . I couldn't get a ticket. They were all sold."

Sam hesitated. What he ought to do was throw this idiot out on his ear. This learned idiot. On the other hand, he reflected, there might be some terrific pr copy in this, yes.

"Tell you what, Collins. I'll get you in. But if Willie starts singing about how all nasty mad scientists ought to be strung up, don't blame me for supplying the rope."

It was intended as a joke. Collins did not smile.

VII.

Sam had munched his way through two cigars and was in the process of mutilating a third. Outside, beyond the curtain, was a stamping, screeching mob of what the press euphemistically classified as "young adults." Sometimes their chanting grew typically obscene, sometimes merely impatient. Most often it thundered "WE WANT WILLIE! WE WANT WILLIE, WE WANT WILLIE!"

Well, Sam couldn't argue with them. He wanted Willie too.

Nearby, Vincente Rivera, Milo Uccelo, and Jack Cavanack wore varied expressions of boredom, now shading into disgust. They also wore red leather and fringes. Cavanack was smoking.

Sam broke his thoughts, looked pleadingly at the drummer. "Look, Jack, can't you get rid of that stuff? All I need now is for some overzealous security guard to come sniffing back here and bust you."

Cavanack glanced up and smiled broadly. "Just killin' some time, Sam. Till your buddy-boy Willie gets here. *If* he gets here."

The agent grimaced, looked absently at Rivera.

"If I were you, Sam, I'd have me a fast set of

wheels standing by. Because if we sit here much longer, that crowd's going to get ugly. And I sure as hell am not going to be the one who has to go out there and explain things to 'em."

"Right on," Uccelo concurred. "This ain't no recording-studio jam session."

"Don't you think I know that?" Sam cried. "If that son-of-a-bitch forces me to have the gate refunded . . . !"

"Hey, isn't that him?" broke in Rivera suddenly, standing up and pointing. Sam whirled.

Sure enough, a familiar gangling figure was loping toward them, escorted by a pair of security fuzz. Cavanack had enough presence of mind to pitch his smoke under a hunk of scenery from some long-dead play. Sam halted the singer with a hand on each shoulder.

"Don't do things like this to an old man, Willie. I can't take it anymore. Listen to them out there! They're ready for you. Ready and primed. Now go out there and—"

"I'm not going out, Sam."

Parker stared blankly at him, then grinned sickly.

"Aw c'mon, Willie! Don't joke with me. Like I told you, I'm too old for this stuff."

Willie looked half dead and dead serious.

"I mean it, Sam. I'm not going to play."

Parker stepped away, somehow managed to keep the agonizingly painful smile on his face. It was as real as margarine, but he kept his voice under control.

"All right, Willie. Why don't you want to go out there?"

"Because of this." He fumbled with his shirt, tossed a crumpled ball of paper onto a chair. Sam looked over at it, then back to the singer.

"It's a letter from my grandfather," Willie explained. "He'll never win the Nobel Prize, my grandfather, but he's a great man. You see, he saw the story about the Seattle concert, too. Told me my kind of singing isn't meant for a big group of people. Said that I was embarrassing my ancestors."

Sam tried to understand this, but he couldn't. There was no reference point for him in this cultural desert, and he admitted it.

"I don't follow you, Willie. I'd like to, but I don't. How the hell can playing music disgrace your ancestors?"

Willie stared at him with eyes of limpid oil. "Sam, where do you think my songs come from?"

"I thought you made 'em up, Willie."

The singer shook his head.

"No, Sam. Only the words. Most of the music is based on chants. Old medicine chants, Sam. Passed down in my family for hundreds of years. It's all the inheritance I got. Grandfather thinks I'm misusing them. I don't know that I go along with him—I don't feel so good—but I respect him. So I'm not going to play, dammit! Can't you just believe that and leave me alone?" He stumbled, looked around wildly. "I need a drink."

Sam leaned close to him, sniffed. "On top of what you've had already?"

A silly grin spread across Willie's face. "Does it surprise you?"

"No, of course it doesn't, Willie. Now you just go out there with the boys and give those good people a song or two, and I'll go and get you a nice fresh fifth of good stuff, whatever you want. Not the crud you've been gargling. How's that? Look at it this way; you won't be playing for a crowd, just for yourself. That's okay, isn't it?"

"I don't know, Sam, I—" He blinked.

"I respect your grandfather's opinions, too," pressed Sam, "but you've also got a responsibility to those people out there. Most of 'em stood in line for hours for the chance to hear you, Willie. Listen to them!"

"WILLIE, WILLIE, WE WANT WILLIE!"

"You can't disappoint all those thousands. Be like going back on your own generation!"

Willie stood quietly and for a moment seemed almost sober.

"They're not *my* generation."

"Okay, okay, however you want to look at it." Sam was beginning to lose his patience. "But you go out there and play for them. You've got an obligation to them. And you've also got one to the boys here—" he indicated the three waiting musicians, "—a legal one to me, and to the folks who put up the money for this concert."

Willie tried to draw himself erect but couldn't quite hold it. "I see. That's how it is, huh?"

Sam looked back at him without wavering. "I'm afraid it is, Willie. For tonight, anyway. You'll feel better tomorrow and we can talk then and—"

"No, no, that's all right, Sam, I follow you. I follow you real good." Onyx eyes blinking, the dark side of the moon. He swayed, caught himself. "Bet you think I've been playing for you, huh?

"You—Jack, Milo, Vince—you think I've been playing too, don't you?" He turned back to Sam and smiled that sick, humorless smile. "Well, I got something for you. I haven't been. Not really. Not back in that filthy backwater club where you found me, not in the studio that time, not in Seattle. You want me to go out there and play—all right."

Sam tried to calm the singer but Willie wouldn't give him a chance.

"What's the matter, Sam? It's okay. That's what you want, that's what you get. Get yourself a good seat, Sam. A real good seat. One where you can hear well and see, too. Because I'm going to play, yes." He subsided, mumbled to himself. "Tonight I'm going to play."

He spun and walked toward the stage. The others had to hurry to make the entrance with him.

A tremendous ovation met them, a roar of expectancy as the four musicians appeared on stage. After the long wait the audience was keyed to fever pitch. Some of them had been in the Aquarius that night in

Seattle and had come all the way down to L.A. for this night. They didn't cheer or yell. They just waited.

Uccelo had gone first, running past Willie. He snatched up his bass and hurriedly hummed out the opening warm-up theme he'd composed. The crowd dropped its frenetic greeting and relaxed into a steady, familiar cheering and clapping, maybe a bit louder than that accorded the average new group.

Sam levitated a sigh from the vicinity of his ulcer and patted his face. Tomorrow Willie probably wouldn't even remember what he'd said tonight. Sam picked up the balled letter and shoved it into a pocket. Then he walked into the wings and settled down to enjoy the show.

Willie ignored the crowd and picked up his waiting guitar. He turned it over and over in his hands, ran them sensuously up and down the shiny, spotless instrument. He was smiling at something.

"Play, dammit," Sam hissed, fearful for a moment the singer might do something stupid like chuck it into the audience.

But it was okay. Willie put the strap over his head. He snuggled the guitar firm to his slim body and started to play.

Hush-dead silence greeted the first note.

It was all wrong, that first note. It was too deep, too strong, too *bad*. It woke dark shapes that hid in the back of the mind, woke insect legs that creepy-crawl at night under bedsheets. It made the hair rise on the back of Sam's neck. Willie held it, choked it, wouldn't let it die. It wavered, floated, and finally drifted away crying from its mother the amplifier.

Willie's fingers began to move. A tune emerged from the guitar, a low, ponderous, mephitic melody the like of which Sam had never heard before. It had granite weight and the patience of blowing sand in it, and it came straight from Hell.

Blank-eyed, Milo joined in, his perfectly picked bass a black brother to Willie's guitar. Drivin' Jack grunted and kissed his drums; thunder walked the stage. Rivera took the harmonica from his lips and sat down at the organ. And Willie began to sing.

A first clap, forlorn and naked, peeped from the thousands. Then another, and another. Then the whole sixteen thousand were clapping and moving in unison.

Willie played and he sang and he sang and he played. He played for ten minutes, twenty, thirty. Before you could think to breathe they swung into their second hour, never pausing, never resting, the same Hephaestean beat, the same haunted rhythm, with Willie piling variation on top of variation, weaving a spider web of blood-pulsing harmonics. Somehow Drivin' Jack and Milo and Vince hung on, stayed with him.

Willie sang about the good earth and about rape, sang about young trees and sang about hate. He sang about the things man does to animals and about the animal man. He sang about man poisoning himself with envy, about dead-eyed children and too-young killers. Mostly, he sang about his people and their life and the writhing, insane alienness that was the white man's. He cursed and he prayed and he damned and he praised.

He took that audience up to Heaven and banged their heads against the gates. He dragged them kicking and screaming down to the fiery pit.

And then, the sweat streaming off his face and his clothes hanging limp from his body, pulling him toward the ground in collusion with an evil gravity, he began to sing about the Things That Made no Sense, that were less and more than all that had gone before, and in that was Madness.

The crowd screamed and howled at the constricting concrete sky and steel beams, wanting the stars. They broke and beat at themselves and one another in a frenzy.

Sam sat in the wings and shivered on the lip of his own private delirium as Willie sang hate and burning, sang anger and the final fire that burns in every man's heart. And he saw the wolf.

But it wasn't gray this time. It was a twisting, spinning ball of four-legged yellow flame that shifted in his arms. Willie's right hand was stroking its flank and the crowd shrieked. His left hand scratched an ear and they moaned. Then Willie played a note that shouldn't have been. The wolf-thing opened its jaws and howled an unearthly sound poor Sam Parker could never have imagined. It didn't come from Willie's throat, was sure.

Hunching in his arms, the wolf-thing spun and clamped its fire-teeth over Willie's mouth, and seemed to swallow. Willie Whitehorse became a pillar of flame.

Sam whimpered and fell to the floor, covering his eyes.

Eventually, lots and lots of sirens came.

VIII.

Estes Park, Colorado, is a tourist town, an attractive tourist town, at the eastern entrance to Rocky Mountain National Park. Once upon a time, the park and the rest of Colorado belonged to the Shoshoni and Wind River Shoshoni, the Ute and the Arapahoe. Today most of the state belongs to the Colorado River Land and Development Company and innumerable bastard cousins.

But it was beautiful country and as tourist towns go, Estes Park wasn't bad. Neither were the neat little homes that nestled in the hills behind the town.

A late-model Chevy pulled up in front of one of them and a man got out. He looked at the numbers on the mailbox and then at a piece of paper he held. The paper was wrinkled badly, as if it might have once been crumpled in a fist. The man walked up to the hand-hewn wooden door and rapped on it. There was no bell.

The man who opened the door was very old. But he was straight as his long white hair and had a merry grin to go with the strings of bright beads around his neck, the faded dungarees, shirt, and a big turquoise ring on one hand.

"May I help you?" The voice was wise, patient.

"I'm Sam Parker," the figure said. He glanced at the paper, back at the guardian of the door. "Are you John Whitehorse?"

The oldster nodded. Sam said, "I knew your grandson."

Eyes widened slightly, their owner stepping back from the door. "Come in, please."

They walked into a small but nicely appointed living room. A baby played quietly in a playpen in the far corner.

"Sit down," invited John Whitehorse. Sam did. He looked at the child.

"That is Bill Whitehorse," the old man informed him. "My grandson's son."

"I didn't know," Sam confessed apologetically. "Willie never mentioned him. Is Mrs. Whitehorse . . .?"

"Died in birthing. The boy came in winter, in the middle of a terrible storm. He was very early. The doctor tried but could not get here in time. The woman—" and he gestured at the strong figure standing in the hallway, watching "—and I did what we could. Willie never recovered."

"Then he had no other family?"

The old man shook his head slowly.

"His father, my son, was killed in the last world war. There is a picture of him on the table to your right."

Sam peered over the side of the couch. There was a faded black-and-white photograph of a man in uniform in a small flat glass case. It centered a circle of shiny medals and two oak leaf clusters. Sam noticed the medical insignia.

"His father was a doctor, then?"

John Whitehorse smiled. "All the Whitehorses have been men of medicine. As I am, and my father was, and my grandfather. Beyond that I do not know for certain, but it is so said in Council.

"We wished it for Willie, too, but . . ." He stopped. "Why are you here, Mr. Parker?"

"I took charge of the body. I wanted to make sure there was someone who could aff—would want to bury him." Whitehorse nodded. "Do you know how he died?"

"There was some news in the paper that comes from Denver," said the old man, "but not much." He seemed sad. "It was a very small item. I had to look hard for it."

"There was a riot," Sam began. "Fourteen people were killed. A great many were injured. An important building, the Atheneum, was nearly torn down by the audience during Willie's performance. Many of them don't remember what happened. This sort of thing has happened before at similar concerts, but never anything approaching the scale and violence of this one.

"Two of the musicians who were playing with Willie suffered severe shock. One of them is still being treated by doctors. He may not be able to play again, I'm told."

John Whitehorse nodded. "They were close to Willie and they followed him too far. I am glad they did not die."

"As for Willie," continued Sam, watching the old man with eyes that had lately seen too much, "the story being passed around is that he'd doused his guitar with gasoline. Then he set it afire—as a gimmick, an audience-pleaser—but it spread to his clothes before he could get rid of it. I believe he would burn hot—he had enough alcohol in him—but that's not what happened. There was no gas on that guitar, was there?"

John Whitehorse looked tired. "Nadonema, the wolf."

Sam's mouth tightened, but he looked satisfied. "Yeah, the wolf. Everybody thought it was done with trick lights, with mirrors. How was it done, old man?"

"From birth every Whitehorse is made brother to a creature of the forest. I am kin to the bear. To help make big medicine, he will make a picture of it in his mind and try to partake of its strength. It is a great power that takes much time and experience to learn well. Willie was very young and made his medicine too strong. Or perhaps, for some reason, he did not care."

"And his music?" Sam asked quickly.

"No Whitehorse can make medicine without music, Sam Parker, nor music without some medicine."

Then Collins was right, Sam thought. Music opens the blocks between minds. Pity the psychologist couldn't be here. He was number eleven on the coroner's list. But Sam was still skeptical.

"C'mon, old man. Next you'll be telling me you can make it rain and cure warts."

"Not I, Sam Parker. I am a modern man and have thrown off the superstitions of the ignorant past." And he smiled softly.

"Go ahead and laugh at me, then," invited Sam. "There was a guy named Collins, though, who thought there might be some connection between today's music and a crazy sort of mind contact I don't really understand. At first I thought he was nutty as a loon. Now . . ."

"Do you know, Sam Parker, an interesting thing has come about." John Whitehorse leaned close. "For the first time in this land a generation of whites is growing up that is concerned about the earth and the plants and animals that are their brothers. Is it so surprising that they should be more responsive to their music? Music is the key to so many things. That they should feel deeper and believe stronger and think purer thoughts than you and yours?

"Perhaps it may take one more generation. But as always happens things will come full round one day, and the Indian will have a way to reclaim what is his."

"Yeah, well, I appreciate that, Mr. Whitehorse." The old man's sudden earnestness made Sam nervous. After all, the guy'd lost his son, and now his grandson. He could be pardoned an occasional private madness. Sam stood.

"If you'll excuse me now, I've got to make a connecting flight to New York.

"Willie had a great gift for lyrics and music, that's ll. Maybe unique. It won't happen again, but it was reat while he had it. You'll forgive me if I find your icture of adolescent medicine men taking over the ountry just a little amusing."

"I suppose it does seem rather humorous, Mr. arker. No doubt you are right. You are kind to an ld man who wishes for too much. Still," and he looked : Sam with diamond eyes, "it would be fun to think n what I have said the next time listeners at a concert o not behave in a manner understandable to their ders."

"Sure, sure. Thanks for your hospitality, Mr. White- orse." He glanced over at the cradle. The baby had a al smudge of black hair with oddly familiar dark- ool eyes. He looked back at Sam innocently.

"Your father was quite a phenomenon, Bill White- orse. I hope your great-grandfather raises you well." The baby had a little Hopi-like doll rattle in one and. He gurgled and shook it, rattling the seeds side against the tissue-thin wood.

Parker shivered from head to foot.

Ye Who Would Sing

I love classical music. I love the mountains and
the forest. The forest plays its own songs with
wind and rain and the musings of small crea
tures, but what if it could do even more? . .

Caitland didn't hate the storm any more than he had
the man he'd just killed, but he was less indifferent to
it. It wouldn't have mattered, except that his victim
had been armed. Not well enough to save himself
but sufficiently to make things awkward for Caitland

Even so, the damaged fanship could easily have
made it back to the Vaanland outpost, had not the
freakish thunderstorm abruptly congealed from a clear
blue sky. It was driving him relentlessly northward
away from one of the few chicken scratches of civili
zation man had made on this world.

If adrenalin and muscle power could have turned
the craft, Caitland would have done better than any
one. But every time it seemed he'd succeeded in
wrenching the fan around to a proper course, a fresh
gust would leap from the nearest thunderhead and toss
the tiny vehicle ass over rotor.

He glanced upward through the rain-smeared plex
idome. Only different shades of blackness differen
tiated the sky above. If the Styx was overhead, wha

y below?—granite talons and claws of gneiss, the
npty-wild peaks of the Silver Spar Range. He'd been
own further north than he'd thought.

Time and again the winds sought to hammer the fan
to the ground. Time and again he somehow man-
ged to coax enough from the weakening engine to
void the next ledge, the next crag, the next cliff.

He could not get above the ice-scoured spires; soon
e was fighting just to stay in the air, the fanship
ancing through the glacier valleys like a leaf running
pids. The weather was playing a waiting game with
s life, but he was almost too tired to care. The fuel
uge hovered near empty. He'd stalled the inevitable,
ping for even a slight break in the storm, hoping for
minute's chance at a controlled landing. It seemed
ven that was to be denied him.

The elements had grown progressively more inimi-
l. Lightning lit the surrounding mountains in rapid-
e surreal flashes, sounded in the thin-shelled ship
bin like a million kilos of frying bacon. Adhesive
in defeated the best efforts of the wipers to keep the
ont port clear. Navigation instrumentation told him
at he was surrounded by sheer rock walls on all
des. As the canyon he'd worked his way into nar-
wed still further, updrafts became downdrafts,
wndrafts became sidedrafts, and sidedrafts became
olian aberrations without names. Möbiusdrafts.

If he didn't set the fan down soon, the storm would
t it down for him. Better to retain a modicum of
ntrol. He pushed the control wheel. If he could get
wn in one piece, he ought to be home free. There
as a high-power homing device built into the radio-
m. It would transmit an automatic SOS on a private
annel, to be received by an illegal station near Vaan-
nd.

Caitland was a loyal, trusted, and highly valued
nployee of that station's owners. There was no doubt
his mind that once it was received by them, they
ould act on the emergency signal. Just now his job

was to ensure they would find something worth takin
back.

The fanship dipped lower. Caitland fought the win
with words and skillful piloting. It insisted on pushin
him sideways when he wanted to go up or down.

There . . . a place where the dense green-black ma
of forest thinned briefly and the ground looked almo:
level. Low, over, a little lower. Now hard on the sticl
slipping the fan sideways, so that the jets could cour
teract the force of the scudding wind. Then cut powe:
cut more, and prepare to settle down.

A tremendous howl reverberated through the littl
cabin as a wall of rain-laden wind shoved like a gi
ant's hand straight down on the fanship. Jets still roar
ing parallel to the ground, the fan slid earthward at
45-degree angle.

First one blade, then a second of the double rotor
hit a tree. There were a metallic snap, several second
of blurred vision—a montage of tree trunks, lightnin
and moss-covered earth—followed by stillness.

He waited, but the fan had definitely come to
stop. Rain pierced the shattered dome and pelted fore
head and face, a wetness to match the saltier taste i
his mouth. The fan had come to rest on its side. Onl
a single strap of the safety harness had stayed intact
It held him in the ruinèd cabin by his waist.

He moved to release it—slowly, because of th
sharp, hot pain the movements caused in the cente
of his chest. He coughed, spat weakly. Bits of broke:
tooth joined the rest of the wreckage.

His intention was to let himself down gently to
standing position. His body refused to cooperate. A
the waist buckle uncoupled he fell the short distanc
from his seat to the shattered side of the fan. *Brok*
inside, he thought hazily. Rain seeped into his eyes
blurred his vision.

Painfully he rolled over, looked down the length o
the fan. The flying machine was ruined forever. Righ
now, the walking machine had to get away from i:
There was always the chance of an explosion.

It was then he discovered he couldn't move his left leg. Lying exhausted, he tried to study the forest around him in the darkness and driving rain.

Driving rain. The fan had broken a circle in the branches overhead. It would be drier under the untouched trees—and he had to get away from the explosive residue in the fan's tanks.

It appeared to be the lower part of the leg. All right, if he couldn't walk, he could crawl. He started to get to his knees—and couldn't finish. Hurt worse than he'd first thought.

Never mind the chance of explosion, rest was what he had to have. Rest. He lay quietly in the water-soaked ruins of the fan, rain tinkling noisily off the broken plexidome and twisted metal, and listened to the wind moan and cry around him.

Moan? Cry? His head came up dizzily. There was something more than wind out there. A sharp, yes definitely musical quaver that came from all about him. He stared into the trees, saw no one. The effort cost him another dizzy spell and he had to rest his eyes before trying again.

Nothing in the trees, no. But, something about the nearest trunk . . . and the one to its left . . . and possibly the two near by on the other side. Something he should recognize. Too weak to raise a shielding hand, he blinked moisture away and studied the closest bole through slitted eyes.

Yes. The trunk appeared to be expanding and contracting ever so slightly, steadily. His attention shifted to its neighbors. Hints of movement were visible throughout the forest, movement unprompted by wind or rain.

Chimer trees. *Chee chimer* trees. They had to be.

But there weren't supposed to be any wild chimers left on *Chee* world, nor as many as four together anywhere outside of the big agricultural research station.

Maybe there were even more than four. He found himself developing a feeling of excitement that almost

matched the pain. If he had stumbled on a chime
forest . . .

Neither imagination nor intellectual prowess wer(
Caitland's forte, but he was not an idiot. And even a(
idiot knew about the chimers. The finding of one tre(
anymore was extraordinary, to locate four together
incredible. That there might be more was overwhelming.

So, finally, was the pain. He passed out.

The face that formed before Caitland's eyes was (
woman's, but not the one he'd been soundlessl\
dreaming of. The hair was gray, not blond; the fac(
lined, not smooth; skin wrinkled and coarse in the hol-
lows instead of tear-polished; and the blouse was o(
red-plaid flannel instead of silk. Only the eyes bor(
any resemblance to the dream, eyes even bluer thar
those of the teasing sleep-wraith.

An aroma redolent of fresh bread and steaming
meats impinged on his smelling apparatus. It made hi(
mouth water so bad it hurt. At the same time a stom(
of memories came flooding back. He tried to sit up.

Something started playing a staccato tune on his rib(
with a ball-peen hammer. Falling back, he clutched a(
a point on his left side. Gentle but firm hands exerte(
pressure there. He allowed them to remove his own(
set them back at his sides.

The voice was strong but not deep. It shared mor(
with those blue blue eyes than the parchment skin
"I'm glad you're finally awake, young man. Thoug(
heaven knows you've no right to be. I'm afraid you(
machine is a total loss."

She stood. A straight shape of average height, slin(
figure, eyes, and flowing gray hair down to her wais(
the things anyone would notice first.

He couldn't guess at her age. Well past sixty
though.

"Can you talk? Do you have a name? Or should (
go ahead and splint your tongue along with your leg?
Caitland raised his head, moved the blankets aside(

nd stared down at himself. His left leg was neatly
splinted. It was complemented by numerous other
igns of repair, most notably the acre of bandage that
encircled his chest.

"Ribs," she continued. "I wasn't sure if you'd broke
all of them or just most, so I didn't take any chances.
The whole mess can heal together.

"I had the devil's own time trying to get you here,
young man. You're quite the biggest thing in the human line I've ever encountered. For a while I didn't
think I was going to get you on the wagon." She shook
her head. "Pity that when we domesticated the horse
we didn't work on giving him hands."

She paused as though expecting a reply. When Caitland remained silent she continued as though nothing
had happened.

"Well, no need to strain your brain now. My name
s Naley, Katherine Naley. You can call me Katie, or
Grandma." She grinned wryly. "Call me Grandma and
I'll put rocks in your stew." She moved to a small
metal cabinet with a ceramic top on which a large
closed pot sat perspiring.

"Should be ready soon."

Her attention diverted to the stove, Caitland let his
gaze rove, taking stock of his surroundings. He was on
a bed much too small for him, in a small house. Instead of the expected colonial spray-plastic construc-
tion, the place looked to be made of hewn stone and
wood. Some observers would probably find it charming
and rustic, but to Caitland it only smacked of primi-
tiveness and lack of money.

She called back to him. "I'll answer at least one of
your questions for you. You've been out for two days
on that bed."

"How did I get here? Where's my fan? Where is
this place?" She looked gratified.

"So you *can* talk. You got here in the wagon. Freia
pulled you. Your ship is several kilometers down the
canyon, and you're in a valley in the Silver Spars. The
second person ever to set foot in it, matter of fact."

Caitland tried to sit up again, found it was still all he could do to turn his head toward her.

"You went out in that storm by yourself?" She nodded, watching him. "You live here along?" Again the nod. "And you hauled me all the way—several kilometers—up here, and have been watching me for two days?"

"Yes."

Caitland's mind was calibrated according to a certain scale of values. Within that scale decisions on any matter came easy. None of this fit anywhere, however.

"Why?" he finally asked.

She smiled a patronizing smile that he ordinarily wouldn't have taken from anyone.

"Because you were dying, stupid, and that struck me as a waste. I don't know anything about your mind yet except that it doesn't include much on bad weather navigation, but you're fairly young and you've got an excellent body, still. And mine, mine's about shot. So I saw some possibilities. Not that I wouldn't have done the same for you if you'd been smaller than me and twenty kilos lighter. I'm just being honest with you, whoever you are."

"So where's the catch?" he wondered suspiciously. She'd been ladling something into a large bowl from the big kettle. Now she brought it over.

"In your pants, most probably, idiot. I might have expected a thank-you. No, not now. Drink this."

Caitland's temper dissolved at the first whiff of the bowl's contents. It was hot, and the first swallow of the soup-stew seared his insides like molten lead. But he finished it and asked for more.

By the fourth bowl he felt transformed, was even able to sit up slightly, carefully. He considered the situation.

This old woman was no threat. She obviously knew nothing about him and wouldn't have been much of a threat if she had. His friends might not find him for some time, if ever, depending on the condition of the radiocom broadcaster. And just now there was the distinct possibility that representatives from the other side of the law would be desirous of his company. He could just as soon do without that. Lawyers and cops had a way of tangling your explanations about things like self-defense.

So in many respects this looked like a fine place to stay and relax. No one would find him in the Silver Spars and there was nowhere to walk to. He leaned back into the pillow.

Then he heard the singing.

The melody was incredibly complex, the rhythm haunting. It was made of organ pipes and flutes and maudlin bassoons, mournful oboes and a steadying backbeat, all interwoven to produce an alien serenity of sound no human orchestra could duplicate. Scattered through and around was a counterpoint of oddly metallic yet not metal bells, a quicksilver tinkling like little girl-boy laughter.

Caitland knew that sound. Everyone knew that sound. The chimer tree produced it. The chimer tree, a mature specimen of which would fetch perhaps a hundred thousand credits.

But the music that sounded around the house was wilder, stronger, far more beautiful than anything Caitland in his prosaic, uncomplicated existence had ever imagined. He'd heard recordings taken from the famed chimer quartet in Geneva Garden. And he knew that only one thing could produce such an overpowering wealth of sound—a chimer tree forest.

But there were no more chimer forests. Those scattered about the Chee world had long since been located, transplanted tree by tree, bartered and sold in the first heady months of discovery by the initial load of colonists. And why not, considering the prices that were offered for them?

Chimer forests hadn't existed for nearly a hundred years, as best he could remember. And yet the sound could be of nothing else.

"That music," he murmured, entranced.

215

She was sitting in a chair nearby, ignoring him in favor of the thick book in her lap. He tried to get out of bed, failed. "The music," he repeated.

"The forest, yes," she finally replied, confirming his guess. "I know what you're thinking: that it's impossible, that such a thing doesn't exist anymore. But it's both possible and true. The mountains have protected this forest, you see—the Silver Spars' inaccessibility, and also the fact that all the great concentrations of chimers were found far, far to the south of Holdamere. Never this far east, never this far north.

"This forest is a freak, but it has survived, survived and developed in its isolation. This is a virgin forest, never cut, Mr. . . ."

"Caitland, John Caitland."

"An untouched forest, Mr. Caitland. Unsoiled by the excavators or the predators, unknown to the music lovers." Her smile disappeared. ". . . To the music eaters, those whose desire for a musical toy in their homes destroyed the chimers."

"It's not their fault," Caitland objected, "that the chimers don't reproduce when transplanted. People will have what they want, and if there's enough money to pay for what they want, no mere law is going to prevent . . ." He stopped. That was too much already. "It's a damned shame they can't reproduce in captivity, but that's—"

"Oh but they can," the old woman broke in. "I can make them."

Caitland started to object, managed to stifle his natural reaction. He forced himself to think more slowly, more patiently than was his wont. This was a big thing. If this old bat wasn't looney from living alone out in the back of nowhere, and if she *had* found a way to make the chimers reproduce in captivity, then she could make a lot of people very very wealthy. Or a few people even wealthier. Caitland knew of at least one deserving candidate.

"I hadn't heard," he said warily, "that anyone had

found a way to make the trees even grow after re-planting."

"That's because I haven't told anyone yet," she replied crisply. "I'm not ready yet. There are some other things that need to be perfected for the telling first.

"Because if I announce my results and then demonstrate them, I'll have to use this forest. And if the eaters find this place, they'll transplant it, rip it up, take it apart, and sell it in pieces to the highest bidders. And then I won't be able to make anything reproduce, show anybody anything.

"And that *will* be the end of the chimer tree, because this is the last forest. When the oldest trees die a couple of thousand years from now there'll be nothing left but recordings, ghosts of shadows of the real thing. That's why I've got to finish my work here before I let the secret—and this location—out."

It made things much simpler for the relieved Caitland. She was crazy after all. Poor old bitch. He could understand it, the loneliness and constant alien singing of the trees and all. But she'd also saved his life. Caitland was not ungrateful. He would wait.

He wondered, in view of her long diatribe, if she'd try to stop him from leaving.

"Listen," he began experimentally, "when I'm well enough I'd like to leave here. I have a life to get back to, myself. I'll keep your secret, of course . . . I understand and sympathize with you completely. How about a—?"

"I don't have a power flitter," she said.

"Well then, your fanship."

She shook her head, slowly.

"Ground buggy?" Another negative shake. Caitland's brows drew together. Maybe she didn't *have* to worry about keeping him here. "Are you trying to tell me you have no form of transportation up here whatsoever?"

"Not exactly. I have Freia, my horse, and the wagon she pulls. That's all the transportation I need—

that and what's left of my legs. Once a year an old friend airdrops me necessary supplies. He doesn't land and he's no botanist, so he's unaware of the nature of this forest. A miner, simple man, good man.

"My electronic parts and such, which I code-flash to his fan on his yearly pass over, constitute most of what he brings back to me. Otherwise," and she made an expansive gesture, "the forest supplies all my needs."

He tensed. "You have tridee or radio communication, for emergencies, with the—"

"No, young man, I'm completely isolated here. I like it that way."

He was wondering just *how* far off course the storm had carried him. "The nearest settlement—Vaanland?"

She nodded. That was encouraging, at least. "How far by wagon?"

"The wagon would never make it. Terrain's too tough. Freia brought me in—and out one time, and back again, but she's too old now, I'd say."

"On foot, then."

She looked thoughtful. "A man your size, in good condition, if he were familiar with the country . . . I'd say three to four months, barring mountain predators, avalanche, bad water, and other possibilities."

So he would have to be found. He wasn't going to find his way out of here without her help, and she didn't seem inclined to go anywhere. Nor did threats of physical violence ever mean much to people who weren't right in the head.

Anyhow, it was silly to think about such things now. First, his leg and ribs had to mend. Better to get her back on a subject she was more enamored of. Something related to her delusions.

"How can you be so sure these trees can be made to reproduce after transplanting?"

"Because I found out why they weren't and the answer's simple. Any puzzle's easy to put together, provided none of the pieces fall off the table. If you're well enough to walk in a few days, I'll show you. The crutches I've got are short for you, but you'll manage."

The forest valley was narrow, the peaks cupping it between their flanks high and precipitous. Ages ago a glacier had cut this gorge. Now it was gone, leaving gray walls, green floor, and a roof of seemingly perpetual clouds, low-hanging clouds which shielded it from discovery by air.

The old woman, despite her disclaimers, seemed capable of getting around quite well. Caitland felt she could have matched his pace even if she weren't burdened with the crutches, though she insisted any strenuous climbing was past her.

Despite the narrowness of the valley, the forest was substantial in extent. More important, the major trees were an astonishing fifty-percent chimer. The highest density in the records was thirty-seven percent. That had been in the great Savanna forest on the south continent, just below the capital city of Danover. It had been stripped several hundred years ago.

Katie expounded on the forest at length, though resisting the obvious urge to talk nonstop to her first visitor in—another question Caitland had meant to ask.

Chimer trees of every age were here, mature trees at least fifteen hundred years old; old trees, monarchs of the forest that had sung their songs through twice that span; and youngsters, from narrow boles only a few hundred years old down to sprouting shoots no bigger than a blade of grass.

Everything pointed to a forest that was healthy and alive, a going biological concern of a kind only dreamed about in botanical texts. And he was limping along in the middle of it, one of only two people in the universe aware of its existence.

It wasn't the constant alien music, or the scientific value that awed him. It was the estimated number of chimer trees multiplied by some abstract figures. The lowest estimate Caitland could produce ran into the hundreds of millions.

He could struggle into Vaanland, register claim to this parcel of backland, and—and nothing. One of the things that made Caitland an exceptional man among his type was that he respected his own limitations. This was too big for him. He was not a developer, not a front man, not a Big Operator.

Very well, he would simply take his cut as discoverer and leave the lion's share for those who knew how to exploit it. His percentage would be gratefully paid. There was enough here for everyone.

He listened to the music, at once disturbing and infectious, and wished he could understand the scientific terms the old woman was throwing at him.

The sun had started down when they headed back toward the house—cabin, Caitland had discovered, with an adjoining warehouse. Nearly there, Katie stopped, panting slightly. More lines showed in her face now, lines and strain from more than age.

"Can't walk as far as I used to. That's why I need Freia, and she's getting on, too." She put a hand out, ran a palm up and down one booming young sapling. "Magnificent, isn't it?" She looked back at him.

"You're very privileged, John. Few people now alive have heard the sound of a chimer forest except on old recordings. Very privileged." She was watching him closely. "Sometimes I wonder . . ."

"Yeah," he muttered uncomfortably.

She left the tree, moved to him and felt his chest under the makeshift shirt she'd sewn him. "I mended this clothing as best I could, and I tried to do the same with you. I'm no doctor. How do your ribs feel?"

"I once saw a pet wolfhound work on an old steak bone for a couple of weeks before he'd entirely finished with it. That's what they feel like."

She removed her hand. "They're healing. They'll continue to do so, provided you don't go falling out of storms in the next couple of months." She started on again.

He followed, keeping pace with ease, taking up great spaces with long sweeps of the crutches. His bulk dwarfed her. Towering above, he studied the wasted frame, saw the basic lines of the face and body. She'd been a great beauty once, he finally decided. Now she was like a pressed flower to a living one.

What, he wondered, had compelled her to bury herself in this wilderness? The forest kept her, but what had brought her in the first place?

"Look," he began, "it looks like I'm going to be here for a while." She was watching him, and laughed at that. She was always watching him, not staring, but not looking away, either. Did she suspect something? How could she? That was nonsense. And if she did, he could dispose of her easily, quickly. The ribs and leg would scarcely interfere. He could . . .

"I'd like to earn my keep." The words shocked him even as he mouthed the request.

"With those ribs? Are you crazy, young man? I admit I might have thought of much the same thing, but—"

"I don't sponge off anyone, lady—Katie. Habit."

She appeared to consider, replied, "All right. I think I know an equally stubborn soul when I see one. Heaven knows there are a lot of things I'd like to have done that this body can't manage. I'll show them to you and when you feel up to it, you can start in on them."

He did, too, without really knowing why. He told himself it was to keep his mind occupied and lull any suspicions she might develop—and believed not a word of his thoughts.

He hauled equipment, rode with her in the rickety wagon to check unrecognizable components scattered the length and breadth of the valley, cut wood, repaired a rotting section of wall in the warehouse, repaired the cabin roof, tended to Freia and the colt— and tried to ignore those piercing eyes, those young-old blue eyes that never left him.

And because he wouldn't talk about himself much, they spent spare moments and evenings talking about her, and her isolation, and the how and why of it.

She found the forest nearly thirty years ago and had been here constantly, excepting one trip, ever since. In that time she'd confirmed much that was suspected, all that was known, and made many new discoveries about the singing trees.

They began to make music when barely half-meter high shoots, and retained that ability till the last vein of sap dried in the aged trunk. They could grow to a height of eight meters and a base diameter of ten.

Chimers had been uprooted and transplanted since their music-making abilities had been first discovered. At one time it seemed there was hardly a city, a town, a village, or wealthy individual that didn't own one or two of of the great trees.

Seemingly, they thrived in their new environments, thrived and sang. But they would not reproduce—from seeds, from cuttings, nothing. Not even in the most controlled greenhouse ecology, in which other plants from Chee survived and multiplied. Only the chimer died out.

But few of those wealthy music lovers had ever heard a whole forest sing, Caitland reflected.

The song of the forest, he noticed, varied constantly. The weather would affect it, the cry of animals, the time of day. It never stopped, even at night.

She explained to him how the trees sang, how the semiflexible hollow trunk and the rippling protrusions inside controlled the flow of air through the reverberating bole to produce an infinite range of sound. How the trunk sound was complemented by the tinkling bells—chimes—on the branches. Chimes which were hard, shiny nuts filled with loose seeds.

With the vibration of the main trunk, the branches would quiver, and the nuts shake, producing a light, faintly bell-like clanging.

"And that's why," she finally explained to him, "the chimers won't reproduce in captivity. I've calculated that reproduction requires the presence of a minimum of two hundred and six healthy, active trees.

"Can you think of any one city, any one corporation, any one system that could afford two hundred and six chimers of a proper spread of maturity?"

Of course he couldn't. No system, not even Terra-Sol, could manage that kind of money for artistic purposes.

"You see," she continued, "it takes that number of trees, singing in unison, to stimulate the bola beetle to lay its eggs. Any less and it's like an orchestra playing a symphony by Mahler. You can take out, say, the man with the cowbell and it will still sound like a symphony, but it won't be the *right* symphony. The bola beetle is a fastidious listener."

She dug around in the earth, came up with a pair of black, stocky bugs about the size of a thumbnail. They scrambled for freedom.

"When the nuts are exactly ripe, the forest changes to a specific highly intricate melody with dozens of variations. The beetles recognize it immediately. They climb the trees and lay their eggs, several hundred per female, within the hollow space of the nuts. The loose seeds inside, at the peak of ripeness, provide food for the larvae while the hard shell protects them from predators. And it all works out fine from the bola's point of view—except for the tumbuck.

"That small six-legger that looks like an oversized guinea pig?"

"That's the one. The tumbuck, John, knows what that certain song means, too. It can't climb, but it's about the only critter with strong enough teeth to crack a chimer nut. When the ripe nuts drop to the ground, it cracks them open and uses its long, thin tongue to hunt around inside the nut, not to scoop out the seeds, which it ignores, but the insect eggs.

"It's the saliva of the tumbuck, deposited as it seeks out the bola eggs, which initiates the germinating process. The tumbuck leaves the nut alone and goes off in search of other egg-filled ones. Meanwhile the seed is still protected by most of its shell.

"Stimulated by the chemicals and dampness of the

223

tumbuck saliva, the first roots are sent out through the crack in the shell and into the ground. The young plant lives briefly inside the shell and finally grows out through the same crack toward the light.

"It's the song of the massed trees that's the key. That's what took me twenty years to figure out. No wonder bola beetles and tumbucks ignored the nuts of the transplanted chimers. The music wasn't right. You need at least two hundred and six trees—the full orchestra."

Caitland sat on the wooden bench cut from a section of log and thought about this. Some of it he didn't understand. What he could understand added up to something strange and remarkable and utterly magnificent, and it made him feel terrible.

"But that's not all, John Caitland. My biggest discovery started as a joke on myself, became a hobby, then an obsession." There was a twinkle in her eyes that matched the repressed excitement in her voice. "Come to the back of the warehouse."

A metal cabinet was set out there, one Caitland had never seen her open before. Leads from it were connected, he knew, to a number of complex antennae mounted on the warehouse roof. They had nothing to do with long-range communications, he knew, so he'd ignored them.

The instrumentation within the cabinet was equally unfamiliar. Katie ran her hand up and down the bole of a young chimer that grew almost into the cabinet, then moved her hands over the dials and switches within. She leaned back against the tree and closed her eyes, one hand resting on a last switch, the other stroking the trunk, like a cat, almost.

"Now look, John, and tell me what you feel." She threw the switch.

For long seconds there was nothing different, only the humming of the bat-winged mammals that held the place of birds here. And that familiar song of the forest.

But even as he strained all his senses for he knew

not what, the song changed. It changed unabashedly and abruptly, astoundingly, fantastically.

Gloriously.

Something grand thundered out of the forest around him, something too achingly lovely to be heard. It was vaguely familiar, but utterly transformed by the instrument of the forest, like a tarnished angel suddenly made clean and holy again.

To Caitland, whose tastes had never advanced beyond the basal popular music of the time, this sudden outpouring of human rhythm couched in alien terms was at once a revelation and a mystery. Blue eyes opened and she stared at him as the music settled into a softer mode, rippling, pulsing about and through them.

"Do you like it?"

"What?" he mumbled lamely, overpowered, awed.

"Do you like it?"

"Yeah. Yeah, I like it." He leaned back against the wall of the cabin and listened, let the new thing shudder and work its way into him, felt the vibrations in the wood wall itself. "I like it a lot. It's . . ." and he finished with a feeling of horrible inadequacy, ". . . nice."

"Nice?" she murmured, the one hand still caressing the tree. "It's glorious, it's godlike—it's Bach. The 'Toccato and Fugue in D Minor,' of course."

They listened to the rest of it in silence. After the last thundering chord had died away and the last echo had rumbled off the mountainsides, and the forest had resumed its normal chant, he looked at her and asked, "How?"

"Twelve years of experimentation, of developing proper stimulus procedures and designing the hardware and then installing it. The entire forest is weird. You've helped me fix some of the older linkages yourself. Stimulus–response, stimulus–response. Try and try and try again, and give up in disgust, and go back for another try.

"My first successful effort was 'row, row, row your

boat.' It took me nine years to get one tree to do that. But from then on response has been phenomenal. I've reduced programming time to three months for an hour's worth of the most complex Terran music. Once a pattern is learned, the forest always responds to the proper stimulus signal. The instrumental equivalents are not the same, of course."

"They're better," Caitland interrupted. She smiled.

"Perhaps. I like to think so. Would you like to hear something special? The repertoire of the forest is still limited, but there's the chance that—"

"I don't know," he answered. "I don't know much about music. But I'd like to learn, I think."

"All right then, John Caitland. You sit yourself down and relax."

She adjusted some switches in the console cabinet, then leaned back against her tree. "It was observing the way the slight movements caused by the vibrations seemed to complement each other that first gave me the clue to their reproductive system, John. We have a few hours left before supper." She touched the last switch.

"Now this was by another old Terran composer." Olympian strains rolled from the trees around them as the forest started the song of another world's singer.

"His name was Beethoven," she began.

Caitland listened to the forest and to her for many days. Exactly how many he never knew because he didn't keep track. He forgot a lot of things while he was listening to the music and didn't miss them.

He would have been happy to forget them forever, only they refused to be forgotten. They were waiting for him in—the form of three men—one day. He recognized them all, shut the cabin door slowly behind him.

"Hello, John," said Morris softly. Wise, easygoing, ice-hard Morris.

Three of them, his employer and two associates. Associates of his, too.

"We'd given you up for lost," Morris continued. "I was more than just pleased when the old lady here told us you were all right. That was a fine job you did, John, a fine job. We know because the gentleman in question never made his intended appointment."

"John." He looked over at Katherine. She was sitting quietly in her rocking chair, watching them. "These gentlemen came down in a skimmer, after lunch. They said they were friends of yours. How did you do on the broadcast unit?"

"Fixed some wiring, put in a new power booster," he said automatically. "They're business associates, Katie."

"Rich business associates," added Ari, the tall man standing by the stove. He was examining the remains of a skinned *ascholite*—dinner. He was almost as big as Caitland. Their similarities went further than size.

"It's not like you to keep something like this to yourself, John," Morris continued, in a reserved tone that said Caitland had one chance to explain things and it had better be good.

Caitland moved into the main room, put his backpack and other equipment carefully onto the floor. If his body was moving casually his mind was not. He's already noticed that neither Ari nor Hashin had any weapons out; but that they were readily available went without saying. Caitland knew Morris's operating methodology too well for that—he'd been a cog in it himself for three years now. A respected, well-paid cog.

He spoke easily, and why not, it was the truth.

"There's no fan or flitter here, not even a motorbike, Mr. Morris. You can find that out for yourself, if you want to check. Also no telecast equipment, no way of communicating with the outside world at all."

"I've seen enough electronic equipment to cannibalize a simple broadcast set," the leader of the little group countered.

"I guess maybe there is, if you're a com engineer,"

Caitland retorted. Morris appeared to find that satisfactory, even smiled slightly.

"True enough. Brains aren't your department, after all, John." Caitland said nothing.

"Even so, John, considering a find like this," he shook his head, "I'm surprised you didn't try to hike out."

"Hike out how, Mr. Morris? The storm blew me to hell and gone. I had no idea where I was, a busted leg, a bunch of broken ribs, plus assorted bruises, contusions, and strains. I wasn't in any shape to walk anyplace, even if I'd known where I was in relation to Vaanland. How did you find me, anyway? Not by the automatic com caster, or you'd have been here weeks ago."

"No, not by that, John." Morris helped himself to the remaining chair. "You're a good man. The best. Too good to let rot up here. We knew where you were to go to cancel the appointment. I had a spiral charted from there and a lot of autofliers out hunting for you.

"They spotted the wreckage of your fan three days ago. I got here as fast as I could. Dropped the business, everything." He rose, walked to a window and looked outside, both hands resting on the sill.

"Now I see it was all worth waiting for. Any idea how many trees there must be in this valley, Caitland?"

He ought to be overjoyed at this surprise arrival. He tried to look overjoyed.

"Thousands," Morris finished for him, turning from the window. "Thousands. We'll file a formal claim first thing back in Vaanland. You're going to be rich, John. Rich beyond dream. I hope you don't retire on it—I need you. But maybe we'll all retire, because we're all going to be rich.

"I've waited for something like this, hoped for it all my life, but never expected anything of this magnitude. Only one thing bothers me." He turned sharply to stare at the watching Katherine.

"Has *she* filed a claim on it?"

"No," Caitland told him. "It should still be open land." Morris relaxed visibly.

"No problem, then. Who is she, anyway?"

"A research botanist," Caitland informed him, and then the words tumbled out in a rapid stream. "She's found a way to make the trees reproduce after transplanting, but you need a full forest group, at least two hundred and six trees for it. If you leave at least that many, out of the thousands, we'll be able to mine it like a garden, so there'll always be some trees available."

"That's a good idea, John, except that two hundred and six trees works out to about twenty million credits. What are you worrying about saving them for? They live two, sometimes three thousand years. I don't plan to be around then. I'd rather have my cash now, wouldn't you?"

"Ari?" Caitland's counterpart looked alert. "Go to the skimmer and call Nohana back at the lodge. Give him the details, but just enough so that he'll know what piece of land to register. Tell him to hop down to Vaanland and buy it up on the sly. No one should ask questions about a piece of territory this remote, anyway."

The other nodded, started for the door but found a small, gray-haired woman blocking his way.

"I'm sorry, young man," she said tightly, looking up at him, "I can't let you do that." She glanced frantically at Caitland, then at Morris and Hashin. "You can't do this, gentlemen. I won't permit it. Future generations—"

"Future generations will survive no matter what happens today," Morris said easily.

"That's not the point. It's what they'll survive *in* that—"

"Lady, I work hard for my money. I do a lot of things I'd rather not do for it, if I had my druthers. Now, it seems, I do. Don't lecture me. I'm not in the mood."

"You mustn't do this."

"Get out of my way, old woman," rumbled Ari warningly.

"Katie, get out of his way," Caitland said quietly. "It'll be all right, you'll see."

She glared at him, azure eyes wild, tears starting. "These are subhumans, John. You can't talk to them, you can't reason with them. Don't you understand? They don't think like normal human beings, they haven't the same emotions. Their needs spring from vile depths that—"

"Warned you," Ari husked. A massive hand hit her on the side of the head. The thin body slammed into the doorsill, head meeting wood loudly, and crumpled soundlessly to the floor. Ari stepped over one bent withered leg and reached for the handle.

Caitland broke his neck.

There was no screaming, no yells, no sounds except for the barely articulate inhuman growl that might have come from Caitland's throat. Hashin's gun turned a section of the wall where Caitland had just stood into smoking charcoal. As he spun, he threw the huge corpse of the dead Ari at the gunman.

It hit with terrible force, broke his jaw and nose. Splinters from the shattered nose bone pierced the brain. Morris had a high-powered projectile weapon. He put four of the tiny missiles into Caitland's body before the giant beat him into permanent silence.

It was still in the room for several minutes. Eventually, one form stirred, rose slowly to its feet. A bruise mark the size of a small plate forming on her temple, Katherine staggered over to where Caitland lay draped across the bulging-eyed, barely human form of Morris.

She rolled the big man off the distorted corpse. None of the projectiles had struck anything vital. She stopped the bleeding, removed the two metal cylinders still in the body, wrestled the enormous limp form into bed.

It was time to wait for him again.

Caitland stayed with her in the mountains for another sixteen years. It was only during the last two that she grew old with a speed that appalled and stunned him. When the final disease took hold, it was nothing exotic or alien, just oldness. The overworked body was worn out.

She'd been on the bed for days now, the silvered hair spread out like steel powder behind her head, the wrinkles uncamouflaged by smiles anymore, the energy in the glacier-blue eyes fading slowly.

"I think I'm going to die, John."

He didn't reply. What could one say?

"I'm scared." He took the flimsy hand in his own. "I want it to be outside. I want to hear the forest again, John."

He scooped up the frighteningly thin form, blankets and all, and took her outside. There was a lounge chair he'd built for her a year ago, next to the young tree by the control cabinet.

". . . hear the forest again, John . . ."

He nodded and went to the console (which he'd long since become as expert at operating as she), thought a moment, then set the instrumentation. They'd added a lot of programming these past years, from her endless crates of tapes.

The alien chant faded, to be replaced by a familiar melody, one of his and her favorites.

"I can't reach the tree, John," came the whispery, paper-thin voice. He moved the lounge a little nearer to the tree, took her arm, and pressed her hand against the expanding, contracting trunk. She had to touch the tree, of course. Not only because she loved the forest and its music, but for the reason he'd discovered fifteen years ago.

The reason why she always followed him with her eyes—so she could see his face, his throat . . . his lips.

She'd been completely deaf since the age of twelve. No wonder she'd been so sensitive to the vibrations of the trees. No wonder she'd been so willing to isolate herself, to leave the rest of a forever incomprehensible mankind behind. No wonder.

There was a cough after an hour or so. Gradually cold crept into the other hand, the one he held. He folded it over the shallow chest, brought the other one across, too. Crying he'd have none of. He was too familiar with death to cry in its presence.

Instead he watched as the music played out its end and the sun went down and the stars appeared, foam-like winking friends of evening looking down at them.

Someday soon he would go down and tell the rest of mankind what lived and thrived and sang up here in a deep notch of the Silver Spars. Someday when he thought they were hungry and deserving enough. But for a little while longer he would stay. He and the shell of this remarkable woman, and Freia's daughter, and listen to the music.

He sat down, his back against the comforting massage of the pulsing bark, and stared up into the out-flung branches where loose seeds rang like bells inside hard-shelled nuts and the towering trunk exhaled magnificence into the sky.

This part coming up now, this part he knew well. The tree expanded suddenly, shuddered and moaned, and the thunder of the rising crescendo echoed down the valley as thrice a thousand chimers piled variation and chorus and life into it.

Beethoven, it was.

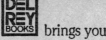

brings you
Exciting and Hair-Raising SF Adventure from

ALAN DEAN
FOSTER